Ralph Ridley in the Hunt for Time

Hayden Perno

HAWKEYE
PUBLISHING

First published in Australia in 2025 by Hawkeye Publishing.

Cover Design by Isabella Lynch

A catalogue record of this book is available from the National Library of Australia.

ISBN 9781923105423

Proudly printed in Australia.

www.hawkeyebooks.com.au

Part I: Solving Space

'What we observe is not nature itself, but
nature exposed to our method of questioning.'

Werner Heisenberg

1

The Arrows of Time

TIME ticked differently for Ralph Ridley.

His curse defied the laws of the universe. To explain it, he often pointed people to his book, *Frozen in Time*. But with every passing year, the more it became clear, everything he thought, everything he solved, continued to turn out to be nothing more than mere stepping stones upon the murky, churning river of reality.

'We're on in five…'

From atop the pile of pillows, Ralph squinted under the studio lights blaring into his sensitive, undeveloped eyes.

'… four …'

On one side of the airconditioned room, staff with clipboards, camera operators, and his sister, Stephanie, stood in the shadows. On the other, sat Ralph, the news anchor, and a cheap plastic table he was sure looked great on TV.

'… three …'

The makeup artist fussing over the news anchor performed one last teeth check, one last shoulder dust, then hurried away.

'… two …'

The room fell silent. The teleprompter scrolled to the next line of dialogue. The cameras blinked red. A finger pointed to the anchor as the news jingle played.

'Welcome back,' the anchor said, offering one of those perfect television smiles. 'From Earth's evacuation and the looming ice age, we now turn our attention to Ralph Ridley, the Boy Who Never Grows.'

Ralph waved a pudgy, uncoordinated hand, realising any movement could result in him falling from his pillow perch.

'Thank you for joining us,' the anchor said.

'My pleasure,' he said, his babbling, high-pitched voice struggling to mesh with the mature authority of hers.

As she studied him in his oversized shirt and trousers, her eyes contained warmth and curiosity. It was as though she could think of nothing more than tucking him in for a nap-nap.

Breaking from her gaze, she gestured to his book upright on the table.

'The equation you speak about in Chapter 8, could you tell us more about it, Mister – uh – Ridley?'

Ralph suppressed a sigh. He hated talking about unfinished equations. There was a reason he'd only mentioned it once in his book. Adding in the hesitation with her use of *mister*, and he felt like calling for his sister.

'Well,' he said, clearing his throat, 'for every year I'm alive, my body ages according to a formula consisting of my Earth years, the golden ratio cubed, and the number 21.6.'

He finished the rehearsed line with an internal grimace, hating how his R's and L's always sounded like W's.

A nearby screen transitioned to display the formula in large, bold text.

$$\text{BIOLOGICAL AGE} = \frac{\text{EARTH AGE} \times 1.618^3}{21.6}$$

'How in the world did you come to this conclusion?' the anchor asked.

He thought back to the hundreds of frustrating nights he'd spent solving each component. He thought back to all the guessing, all the research, all the books he'd read on maths, science, war, art, the lost civilisations of Earth. He thought back to all the nights he went to bed crying…

'Simple,' he said. 'Played around with some geometric series and algebra. Did some calculations in reverse. Before I knew it, Bob's your uncle.'

The anchor nodded, eyes narrowing in journalistic mode. 'So, what do you say to those who associate 21.6 with Revelation 21:6, where it is written, "I am the Alpha and the Omega, the Beginning and the End"?'

Ralph smiled, unsurprised by the same question he was always asked. 'I say the same thing to those who think 21.6 is related to the sacred number of nine: If that means you have an answer to my curse, I'm all ears.'

She chuckled, eyes relaxing, shining with something similar to how his mum used to look at him. 'Could you give us an example of your equation in action?'

He tried sitting up straighter, but the movement, combined with the squishy pillows, sent him toppling. Cheeks warm, gasps coming from the shadows, Stephanie hurried to help him.

'I'm fine,' he muttered.

'I know, Ralphie,' she said, tilting him upright, fixing his collar. 'I know.'

Once his sister had tiptoed out of shot, ignoring the empathetic gazes, he continued.

'Since I've been alive for eleven years,' he said, 'I put eleven into the equation—'

The formula on the screen transitioned to the example they'd preloaded.

$$\frac{11 \times 1.618^3}{21.6} = 2.157$$

'—and receive 2.157.'

The anchor furrowed her brow. 'You're telling us you've been alive for over a decade, yet here you sit as a tiny two-year-old toddler?'

He resented her abruptness. But what could he say? It was the truth.

'Thankfully,' he said, 'my brain doesn't follow the same pattern as the equation.'

'Clearly,' she said, still studying him like the enigma he was. 'Let's talk about the golden ratio. You have an entire chapter dedicated to its controversies and uses in architecture and nature.'

'That's right.'

'A lot of people think you don't know what you're talking about.'

'Well, a lot of people have never been able to solve what's happening to me.'

'What makes you think you can?'

He paused to collect his thoughts. He didn't care if millions were tuning in to the live broadcast. He only wanted to be succinct and intelligent with the explanation.

'I'm a scientist and mathematician at heart,' he said, reciting the line he'd spun for years. 'Which means I can't ignore the impossible. It also means I can't ignore universal ratios and numbers, no matter how controversial they may be.'

The anchor smiled. 'Okay, let's get this straight for our viewers. When you've been alive for fifty years, we'll be able to use that formula to determine how old your body will be?'

He couldn't guarantee it'd be the formula forever. He couldn't even guarantee it'd be important to his time dilemma. But for now, it was good enough.

'Precisely,' he said, glad the interview neared its end.

She held a finger to her earpiece, eyes widening as the screen transitioned.

$$\frac{50 \times 1.618^3}{21.6} = 9.805$$

'Ten years old?'

'Correct.'

'Hold on a second,' she said. 'When you've been alive for fifty years, you'll have the body of a ten-year-old?'

He nodded.

She stared, dumbfounded, smiling like she understood the severity of his circumstance. But she had no idea. No one did. Not even the scientists, mathematicians, doctors, philosophers, priests, and psychics he'd spent most of his life with did. Not even him.

'You really are a wizard at maths,' she said.

'I do have all the time in the universe.'

Whirring helicopter blades filled the void between Ralph and Stephanie on the flight home to Rockhampton. An intermittent rattle in the cabin kept the trip from plunging into awkwardness. The vibrant Brisbane metropolitan below kept him distracted.

As he observed it all, pangs of rejection thrummed through him. From the cars filling the streets to the people filling the paths, the colourful neon signs piercing through the smog, all of it acted as a grim reminder that a life lost in normality was a fantasy far from reality.

'Why won't you talk to me?' Stephanie asked. 'I'm not mum.'

Ralph occupied himself with the frayed stitching on the baby seat.

She touched his hand. 'Please don't. Those seats are expensive.'

He frowned. The monthly commission his curse brought had quelled all money concerns years ago.

'Here,' she said, holding out a banana milk and peanut butter sandwich cut into squares.

'I'm not hungry.'

She threw the items into the lunchbox and slammed the lid shut. 'I don't know what you want me to do then. I have a life too, you know.'

'Then go live it,' he said, exasperated. 'I'm not asking you to waste your teenage years feeding, bathing, and caring for me.'

She leant back, arms folded. 'You know I'd never leave you.'

'But I don't need your help, Steph. I don't need anyone's help.'

An amber light from the streets below flashed inside the cabin for a quarter of a second, illuminating the tears streaking down her gaunt cheeks.

'You can barely open a can of baked beans,' she said.

He turned back to the window. 'Maybe you need to open more of them.'

'And what's that supposed to mean?'

He kept his eyes on the scenery below, allowing silence to fill the cabin once again.

'It's just… never mind,' she said. 'My stomach's been killing me lately. That's all. So, I haven't been eating much.'

He imagined what it'd be like to stand, sit next to her, console her. A normal brother could've done such a thing. But with a body no bigger than her leg, he was useless.

'Will you be okay?' he asked, meeting her eyes.

She scoffed. 'Will you?'

The helicopter banked towards his penthouse. He was fiddling with the buckle before they touched down. Stephanie saw him struggling and leaned forward to unclip it with one hand, before unfolding his wooden wheely walker.

Lifting him from his baby seat, she placed him on the helipad. He leant against the walker, trying to look the age he wished he was.

'You did well today, Ralphie,' she said, running a hand through his few tufts of blonde.

He pulled his head back. 'Thanks.'

'You sure you don't want me to stay? I could make us a snack or something.'

He shook his head. 'I've got a lot to do tonight.'

'I'll come see you tomorrow then.'

'You don't have to.'

She sighed. 'You know I don't like thinking about you being up here by yourself.'

He shrugged. 'It's how it's gotta be. How else can I figure out what's going on before you all…'

He let his sentence trail. But they both knew what he could've said. Everyone dying around him was a fate they'd accepted long ago.

'Have you heard from Mum?' he asked.

'Once or twice. When she hasn't been drinking. They're still in New Zealand. But they haven't been exploring much. Oscar's back keeps playing up.' She winced. 'Sorry.'

'Aging sucks. I understand the concept.'

'I didn't mean that. I was just saying—'

'Tell them I said *hi*.'

She watched him with an intensity, as though resisting the urge to hug or kiss him.

It might've been silly being hasty to Stephanie, the only family member still around. He couldn't blame her for his life. Just like he couldn't blame her for her care or concern. It was easy to appreciate the absurdity of a toddler explaining their experience with time, while also delving into topics like particle physics and time dilation. He just found it easier avoiding putting energy into relationships he knew would deteriorate before he could walk in a straight line.

'Have a good night, Steph,' he said.

He signalled to the pilot. The blades whirred to life. Stephanie turned, a fresh stream of tears falling.

Ralph stayed on the rooftop until the helicopter faded into the distance. He then headed inside for another evening of wheeling back and forth on the balcony, puzzling over the Seven Arrows of Time.

Other than time machines, the Arrows consumed his life. He thought about them every day, writing them down, turning their equations inside out and upside down. But no matter how much he thought about them, he still had no idea how he defied them. It was the riddle that was his life.

The first arrow was the Cosmological Arrow. Dating back to the Big Bang, 13.8 billion years ago, it ticked in accordance with the expansion of the universe.

The second arrow was the Thermodynamics Arrow, relating to the inevitable breakdown of everything in existence, from trees to uranium, planets to particles.

The third and fourth Arrows were the Empirical and Psychological ones. They provided the experience of time ticking, and what humans referred to as the past, present, and future.

The fifth arrow was the Eternal Arrow, representing the cyclic nature of all things – the seasons, the weather, life, death.

The sixth was the Opportunistic Arrow, representing moments in time when action should be taken, like when to plant certain crops or make decisions for careers, hobbies, and relationships.

And then there was the seventh Arrow, the one made famous by Albert Einstein: Relativity. This one provided the perception of time, based on one's location in the universe.

Ralph didn't know how, but one way or another, he would realign himself with the Seven Arrows. He would attain the life he deserved, the life everyone else was blessed with.

But if harnessing time turned out to be impossible, if his destiny entailed walking the Earth alone until the universe stretched to resemble a frozen wasteland, he wouldn't just solve time, he would destroy it.

2
God is Bored

PAPERWORK, textas, and teething biscuit wrappers covered Ralph's living room floor. The early morning rumbling of cars and buses filled the air, providing white noise and a constant reminder he'd never use such vehicles independently.

With a plate of Vegemite soldiers loaded in his wooden wheely walker, he headed back to the chaos, eyes on the golden sun peeking between the Rockhampton skyscrapers.

Before dropping to the carpet, he quadruple-checked the kitchen. Its customised stove, fridge, and bench put all kids' kitchen setups to shame. But from a cleaning and maintenance perspective, along with concerns of being the stupid baby who set an apartment complex on fire, it was also one requiring a lot more work than its plastic rivals.

Satisfied with it in order, he dropped to his butt. He took a Vegemite soldier with coordination his eleven-year-old brain struggled to be patient with and munched it down, enjoying the soothing sensation the crispy toast provided his tender gums.

He scanned the paperwork dispersed on the floor, eyes bleary from another night of research. Studies on particle physics and time dilation made up the bulk of it. The rest consisted of time machine diagrams and phrases he revised for interviews and happenstance encounters.

In his quest to solve his time curse, he'd tried everything. He'd been tested, scanned, experimented on, taken to high altitude, taken to the bottom of the Mariana Trench. He'd meditated. He'd drunk strange broths in South America. He'd covered himself in essential oils, tried lucid dreaming, tried leaving his body while listening to binaural beats.

But the more he'd tinkered with himself and his experience of reality, the faster he'd realised one simple fact: The curse the universe had delivered came with no obvious cure.

And so, he'd dabbled. He'd looked to ancient myths and theories born from the cosmos. He'd read recovered scrolls from the bedrock vaults below Petra, Göbekli Tepe, and the Great Sphinx of Giza. He'd listened to Dreamtime stories told by Aboriginal Australians. He'd crammed his brain with every physics, chemistry, and biology concept he could handle.

A lot of what he learned proved to be a waste of time. But pursuing an answer to his time dilemma meant everything was up for dissection and implementation, from myths to stories, science to life.

Lifting a stack of time machine diagrams, he flicked through them, eyeing their intricate designs, their golden bases and magnetic coils. Some dated back to the Anatolians, the Mesopotamians, and the ancient Egyptians. Some came from popular science fiction. Others he'd sketched with shameful sloppiness.

To replicate such craftsmanship, technology, and finesse in a toddler's body would be difficult. Sourcing the items necessary for the construction of a possible time machine wasn't something easily achieved. Avoiding unwanted attention from the parasites who only ever wanted his time and money would be a feat in itself. But right now, did he have a better plan?

His intercom pinged, breaking his reverie. He crawled over to it, using the fingerprint-stained wall to stand.

The colourless screen displayed Stephanie, arms folded, eyes sunken. Wearing her school hoodie, messy, wet hair draping across her small frame, he was reminded of a wraith from one of his mythology books.

She pressed the button again. The ping echoed through the apartment.

He opened the channel. 'Everything okay?'

'Ralphie,' she said with desperation. 'Please let me up. I really need to talk to you. I haven't seen you for over a month and—'

He cut the channel, cursing under his breath. Unless she had something to say to help with his dilemma, inviting her up would be a waste of time. Like always.

He reopened the line. 'Sorry, I've been busy. I'm getting close to some new breakthroughs.'

He wasn't. He hadn't had a breakthrough with any line of thinking or research in over a year.

'That's great news,' she said. 'I'd love to hear more about it.'

'Sorry, I just had a bath. And I'm about to make breakfast.'

She was silent for a moment. 'What if I make something for you? Please.'

He imagined an alternate reality where he invited her up, made scrambled eggs with cheese, squeezed fresh orange juice, enjoyed a breakfast on the balcony with her before heading to school.

But what an impossible reality that was. His arms, too puny, couldn't do much more than microwave pre-packaged food. As for school, it was off-limits to a toddler, a toddler who'd only ever been told, *try again when you're bigger* and *sorry, the liability is too great.*

'The symposium is in a fortnight,' he said. 'I have to prepare.'

Stephanie stared into the lens, eyes piercing through the screen like she stood in the room with him.

'But I'll call you soon,' he said, and cut the audio.

Her mouth moved through sentences that would forever be lost to the Arrow of Thermodynamics, sentences no doubt entailing an apology for interrupting, an *I'll talk to you soon*, and a *have a good day*.

As she moved out of range, the screen disconnected, leaving Ralph staring at a reflection of a toddler's face he had no affiliation with, as though the real him was being held captive inside a vessel.

He crawled back to his paperwork.

Keeping Stephanie at a distance was complicated but necessary. On the one hand, it gave him maximal time to chip away at his curse. On the other, it protected them.

She might've found it difficult having a vacant, distant brother. But it was only temporary. Once he solved time travel, once he walked between all eras, aging and de-aging according to what he wished and needed to do and see, he'd make it up to her. He'd go back and enjoy life with her. He'd celebrate birthdays. He'd visit their mum.

He couldn't imagine how excited they'd be to know he was a normal boy.

✦

The Sydney Aquarium was the venue for the Quantum Geometry Symposium 2088. Three hundred of the brightest physicists, mechanists, and geometrists gathered to talk about everything from plasma teleportation to the electric universe.

Ralph's talk was held in the main hall under the orca tank. With a flickering blue hue from the sunlight breaking in above, he spoke to a sea of silent, shadowed faces for forty-five minutes.

'In summary,' he said, pointing the laser at the jumbotron, 'by cracking the time travel code, I'll gain the ability to walk between timestamps. Secondly, if my formula remains true, I'll have plenty of time to solve my curse. And finally, if I'm here to watch the sun engulf Earth in a few billion years, I'll make sure to send pictures.'

The crowd laughed and applauded as he exited the stage. Climbing into his electric wheelchair, he headed back to his spot beside Max Bonaparte, the famous Swiss astrophysicist.

'Good talk,' Max said, patting his arm.

Ralph thanked him. 'The crowd seemed distracted.'

Max shrugged. 'They were the same for me. I assume the evacuation has garnered everyone's attention this year.'

Ralph turned back to the stage. True or not, it was clear the novelty of a toddler discussing particle physics had waned. And he was fine with that. He just hoped his improved ability to articulate words hid the fact he'd repeated everything he'd said last year.

The next speaker took the stage.

'That's Dr. Angela Geronimo,' Max said, competing with the thunder of applause. 'She's responsible for the tech on the Ships and in the ground.'

Angela strode for the stage's centre with purpose, white coat flowing. The lights dimmed as the applause faded. The jumbotron transitioned from her title card and photo to an Earth-like planet riddled with shades of blues and browns.

'Proxima Centauri b,' she said. 'Or, what we refer to as Proxim, the planet the Seven Ships will be travelling to in the Alpha Centauri system, 4.2 lightyears away.'

Excited murmurs spread through the hall. The CGI footage zoomed away from the planet, moving past moons, gases, debris, until it displayed a triple star system hovering in the void.

'To make the forty trillion-kilometre journey,' Angela said, 'the Ships will depart from the Moon Docks and head for the wormhole on the outskirts of the Oort Cloud.'

The screen transitioned to show a bubble of ice and rock surrounding the Solar System. An arrow pointed to the bottom right-hand corner, where a sparkling vortex swirled away.

'Once the Ships come out the other side…'

Seven rectangular prisms entered the vortex. After a quick fade to black, the animation showed them heading for the triple star system.

'…they will then use a variety of techniques to complete the journey. Some are tried and tested, like oscillation acceleration, a technique involving periods of speed, inertia, and gravity slingshotting. Others are more innovative, like dark energy reverberation, a technique made possible from the recent solving of a portion of the dark energy equation.'

Ralph settled in for Angela's talk, ready to extract whatever skerrick of data or information he could.

For the next hour, she spoke about how they'd confirmed the wormhole's exit with radiation imaging, how Proxim existed in the Goldilocks zone, and how the journey would open countless opportunities for nearby system colonisation. While she said nothing useful for the formulation of new theories, learning what activities, luxuries, and delicacies would be available onboard the Ships tore Ralph in two.

'God is bored,' Max said. 'That's the best way I look at your situation.'

They were heading down an aquarium tunnel following Dr. Geronimo's talk. Surrounded by fish and beady-eyed sharks, the violet lights lining the floor illuminated the other symposium attendees ominously.

From his wheelchair, Ralph studied Max in envy. It wasn't just his height, gait, wrinkles, or receding hairline that stirred such an emotion. It was how professional Max looked in a suit, while all he resembled was a Gremlin attempting to disguise itself as human.

'In other words,' Ralph said, 'fate's got a different idea for me.'

They stopped to watch a stingray pass overhead, its ivory, leathery underside on full display.

'Eternal youth isn't the worst curse you could be dealt,' Max said. 'Although, on second thought, I suppose the Lost Boys were called lost for a reason.'

Ralph clenched his jaw. His two molar teeth breaking through delighted in the sensation. Only the naïve, those who'd never experienced abnormality, believed eternal youth was a blessing.

'I'm not lost,' he said, pushing the wheelchair's joystick forward.

Max came after him. 'I never said you were. I merely use the reference to imply youth must be cherished, used as a means for preparation. After all, the next phase of life awaits all of us, including you. And you, my dear Ridley, have been given a chance to do more with youth than any of us were ever gifted to do.'

Max offered a smile laced with something Ralph interpreted as sorrow. He took it as an apology for the wisecrack Max had delivered about him being stuck in Neverland.

'The only catch,' Ralph said, 'I lose everyone and everything along the way.'

'Again, I must insist you rethink the offer of coming on the Ships. You'd be a cherished addition, my friend. A celebrity. Someone who may outlive us all before we…'

Max's sentence faded as though he'd realised he'd hit on the very reason Ralph attended symposiums in the first place.

'My place isn't in space,' Ralph said, pretending Max's words hadn't affected him. 'It's here. On Earth. Solving my time dilemma.'

Max watched him for a moment. 'And to that, Mr. Ridley, I wish you all the luck in the universe. Although, I do still pray you solve more than you desire, and one day venture out to meet us in the new system.'

Full of ideas and information, Ralph's subconscious amused itself inside dreamworld on the trip back to the hotel. From the comfort of his car seat, his mind dove through space, breaking quantum mechanics boundaries, traversing wormholes, equipped with a quiver full of Arrows of Time.

Dancing across nebulae, he shot the Arrows without aim. Some struck stars. Others continued on into the far reaches of nothingness. When a moon came out of nowhere, cratered, desolate, he shot the Cosmological

Arrow with precision, striking its centre, and exploding wisps of spiralling colours.

'Ghapiho shighia likofra,' a shade of fuchsia told him.

The phrase made no sense, but his mind unpacked its meaning: We are liars.

'You're a lying colour?' he asked. 'That doesn't make sense.'

'Siluum aoiryry shijanog pali-raf,' a shade of zaffre told him next, morphing between weapons like staves, katanas, whips, and scimitars.

The zaffre's phrase was harder to decipher. But Ralph sensed beauty within it, like a hint leading to an epiphany.

He opened his mouth to demand it tell him more, but a soft shaking dragged him back to reality.

Blinking his eyes open, fending off a yawn, he looked up at his driver's sombre face.

'Mr. Ridley, I'm sorry for waking you. But I have some bad news.'

Ralph's eyes widened. He tried sitting up, but the seatbelt of the baby seat kept him firmly in place.

'What is it?'

The driver swallowed, eyes averted. 'I'm sorry, sir, but your sister passed away this evening.'

3
A Reunion

RALPH arrived at the funeral home an hour early on a blue-sky afternoon. A few puffs of cloud floated in the east. A weak wind swept through the street, swaying the paperbarks. The sun beamed onto the road with a new heat, a reminder summer neared.

'I'll see you in there,' the driver said, placing Ralph in his wheelchair.

Thanking him with a nod, Ralph headed up the path to the entrance.

The funeral home was a repurposed church of the past. Painted beige and outfitted with all the modern metal trimmings, windows, and lights, it nested between a 24/7 supermarket and Stephanie's high school.

The funeral director waited by the door, the same curious eyes he dealt with on a daily basis watching him. When he was close enough, she came forward and enveloped his small, pudgy hands with her large, soft ones.

'Mr. Ridley,' she said. 'I'm sorry for your loss.'

Ralph scanned the building to the bell at its peak, cursing the perfect weather for its insidious ways on a day of mourning.

'Good idea scheduling the service for four o'clock,' she said. 'That should allow plenty of time for Stephanie's friends, fellow students, and teachers to arrive.'

Ralph kept his eyes averted, already dreading the plethora of eyes, comments, and questions from the others as they filed in.

'Please,' the director said, 'this way.'

Ralph followed her into the lobby, where chairs lined the walls and a reception desk sat in the centre. The carpet, a dull maroon, complemented the polished pieces of mahogany furniture. An aroma of cleaning products, masked by cedarwood incense, tainted the air.

'You're welcome to wait here,' she said. 'Or I can take you to the room now.'

The receptionist poked her head above the desk. After spotting the Boy Who Never Grew, she returned to her murmuring phone conversation.

'The room, please,' Ralph said.

The director led him down a corridor to a wooden double door. Before opening it, she turned to him.

'Are you ready?' she asked. 'I mean, I'm sure you are. I figure with your condition you would be.'

Ralph swallowed. He hadn't thought too much about what it'd be like to see his sister lying cold and rigid in a casket.

He took a moment to compose himself, focusing on the bigger picture, envisioning the day he'd no longer be shackled by time.

'I'm ready.'

The director opened the doors to a high-ceilinged, silent room filled with rows of velvet chairs. The open casket sat at the far end, white, trimmed with gold, and padded with a cream, silk cushioning. To its left, a lectern and microphone atop a small stage with a ramp. By the emergency exit, a table strewn with candles, trinkets, and photos of Stephanie.

'I'll leave you to prepare,' the director said. 'If you need anything, there's a service button by the lectern.'

She closed the doors with uncomfortable gentleness. Ralph waited until her clomping heels had faded before heading to the front of the room and up the ramp.

From his vantage point, he peered into the casket where Stephanie lay, angelic, serene, hands folded on her sternum. Her mousy brown hair had been braided. The soft smile they'd given her was one of satisfaction, as though all her worries had finally been quelled. The dress she wore was the same she'd worn to the last interview she'd accompanied him to, where she'd embarrassed him after he'd fallen from the pile of pillows.

He cursed the memory, the moment. Why hadn't the news station prepared suitable seating arrangements? Hadn't they known he was coming? Hadn't they read the stories about the toddler forced to endure what everyone else referred to as "life"?

16

'Sorry, Steph,' he said. 'I should've talked to you more. I should've listened. But I guess this was inevitable.'

His mind ran through the most recent times he'd avoided her. He thought back to a fortnight ago, when she'd landed on the helipad and he'd hidden inside the laundry basket until she'd left. He remembered a month prior, when she'd pinged the intercom, carrying containers of homemade spaghetti bolognese. He thought about the last fight they'd had, where she'd begged to come to the symposium so she could explore Sydney for the first time.

'How was I supposed to know you had bowel cancer?' he said. 'The stomach cramps. The lack of appetite. I've been dealing with my own problems, you know.'

He pounded the wheelchair's armrest with a fist. He was sick of the universe tormenting him. Why had he been the kid cursed with what Max termed eternal youth? Why was he immune to the kiss of death? Couldn't Stephanie have had such a luxury? She'd barely hit sixteen and had already been pulled from reality to do nothing more than remind him of his lonely fate.

'They said it took her without warning,' a woman's voice came from behind.

He turned his head. His wheelchair's black leather backing blocked his view. He shoved the joystick forward in haste, causing the right wheels to slide off the ramp. Before he could rectify his mistake, the chair tipped, and he tumbled to the wooden floor as the metal hulk crashed beside him.

He lay there for a moment, stunned he hadn't been squashed.

'Ralphie,' the woman said, dashing forward to scoop him up like the baby he no longer was.

'Put me down,' he said, hating how whiny he sounded. 'Put me down.'

Her arms were firm, gentle. She cradled him, rocking him back and forth, stroking his head, speaking soft words like a lullaby. He found it shamefully soothing.

'Shh, it's okay, Ralphie,' she said. 'It's okay.'

'Stop it,' he said, squirming. 'Put me down!'

She looked at him with the warmth many looked at him with. But something different glistened in her eyes. Something familiar.

'The service isn't for another forty minutes,' he said.

'Oh, Ralphie,' she said, placing him down. 'I'm so sorry.'

Goosebumps spread down his spine at the way she'd said his name.

It couldn't be, he thought. But his intuition told him otherwise.

'Mum?'

She knelt, grasped his shoulders, tears flowing.

Her blemished face had aged since he'd last seen it. Her hair too. No longer long and straight, but short and streaked with grey. The only familiar thing was her breath, laced with fermented grapes and disguised by peppermint.

Ralph tried to stabilise, to centre. He took a deep breath in, fists clenched in the hopes of suppressing the concoction of emotions bubbling away.

'It's all your fault!' he shouted. 'If you were here, she would've had the care.' He dropped to his butt, bending forward to bury his head between his legs. 'You left us. You left me. You took your little boyfriend to New Zealand and—'

'Stop,' she said, snatching his arm.

He ripped free from her grip. 'Don't.'

Her sobs came. He could feel his own on their way. But he wouldn't let them surface.

'Please stop, Ralphie,' she said.

'No. Only Steph called me that.'

His mum bit her bottom lip. Her body shook as though releasing a thousand emotions that'd culminated over a decade.

'I didn't know,' she said, glassy eyes darting left and right. 'Steph only told me last week. I had no idea she'd been living with the cancer for over a year.'

'And why's that? Why do you think she didn't tell you?'

His mum's face grew severe. 'I could ask you the same thing.'

If he'd been taller, more capable, he would've run away in that moment. He would've headed west for the mountains, established a new life and waited for the ice to consume the planet. Instead, he stared at her, knowing the reality of a toddler staring at anyone was hardly confronting nor terrifying.

'I'm sorry,' she said, shaking her head. 'We're both grieving. We're not ourselves.'

But he *was* himself. He'd had plenty of time to come to terms with her abandoning them.

'No,' he said. 'You left us.'

She swore. 'Well, what would've you done if you'd given birth to a boy like you? You were unlike anything they'd ever seen. A boy who defied logic, someone destined to outlive everyone who ever loved you.'

Ralph climbed to his feet, using the tipped wheelchair for assistance.

Her words were his thoughts. But he wouldn't let empathy dictate where this led. He'd waited too long for this moment.

'Of course, I know how hard it would've been,' he said. 'Don't you think I'd know after living like the outcast I have for the last eleven years? But how does that give you the right to leave? And showing up on the day of your daughter's funeral—'

She threw her hands in the air. 'What about your father? Where's he? Has *he* even contacted you?'

The attempt to deflect was unsurprising when cowardly actions were all she'd ever known.

'Yeah,' she said. 'Of course he hasn't. You probably don't even know his name.'

Ralph stared at her, mouth agape. To bring up the man Steph nor he had ever met at a time like this…

'Well,' she continued, 'his name was Barrie. And he was a drunken carnie who gave me Steph, disappeared, returned promising the world, then left again after giving me you.'

Her nails clawed the wooden floor with a raucous screech. Her shoulders hunched as the shudders took hold.

'And for all I know,' she said, 'he's in a ditch—'

'Mr. Ridley?'

The funeral director stood in the doorway.

'Dearie me,' she said, hurrying over. 'I thought I'd heard a noise.' She flipped his wheelchair upright. 'You should've called for help. Is everything okay?'

Ralph bowed his head.

'I… I'm sorry for interrupting,' she said. 'I only came past to let you know there are three girls waiting in the lobby. They say they knew your sister.'

'Thanks,' Ralph said. 'I'll be right out.'

'I should also let you know, they said they were the only ones coming today.'

Ralph met the director's eyes. 'What?'

'I'm sorry, Mr. Ridley. They told me not too many people knew Stephanie.'

After a curt nod, the director strode for the doors, leaving his mum's sniffles and whimpers filling the ambience. Once the doors had closed, again with uncomfortable gentleness, his mum straightened, wiping her nose with the back of her hand.

'I'm sorry, Ralph,' she said. 'For everything. But I'm home now and I want to make things right. I want to be here for you for as long as I can.'

Ralph stepped forward, placing a hand on her shoulder. Her cheeks were drenched in tears and saliva. Her bloodshot eyes radiated hope, sincere regret, expectation.

'I don't want your help,' he said, softly. 'I don't want to ever see you again.'

Her bottom lip trembled. His stomach constricted.

'I used to imagine you back in my life,' he said. 'I used to think about visiting you when I'd solved my time dilemma. I imagined telling you everything would be okay. But now that you're here, I can see it was all a fantasy, just a way to cope with you abandoning us.'

His words came unplanned, undrafted, unrevised. They were harsh, decapitating, brutal. But they were honest, originating from a place deep within, a place he had no control over.

She sobered, sniffed, ran both hands over her face a few times. 'You know what, Mr. Boy Who Never Grows? The real fantasy is your belief you'll even solve time travel.'

Once again, her words were his thoughts.

'And remember this,' she said, getting to her feet. 'You'll waste away before you even get close to figuring out what no human has ever been able to solve.'

With those words, without him even being able to process them, she stormed for the doors.

'I'll be in the lobby,' she said, slamming them closed.

Ralph stayed staring at nothing for quite some time, insides burning like a furnace. Mulling over everything she'd said, everything he'd said, painted a picture of what he had to do next.

He climbed into his wheelchair and rolled over to Stephanie.

'You were right,' he said, peering over the edge of the casket. 'All the alcohol has fried her brain cells. I'm sorry you had to witness that. And I'm sorry for not being the younger brother you wanted me to be. But I promise I did the right thing. If we'd spent more time together, we probably would've turned out just like her.'

He squeezed the casket until his hands gave way.

He wanted to scream. He wanted to cry. He wanted to curl up inside a seashell where he'd never have to worry about anything ever again.

'But one day,' he said, 'I'll make it up to you. I'll show you all of this was meant to happen, that losing you was just another incentive, just another brick on the road to solving my curse.'

He reached over the side and touched her cold, smooth skin. A sequence of memories, of feelings, passed through him. Some contained the warmth of her hugs. Some contained the love laced in her forehead kisses. Others contained her kind words and patience.

'Buh-bye, Stephie.'

He steered for the emergency exit, passing the table laden with her memories.

4

From College to a Cave

MARCH marked the end of summer and Ralph's fifteenth birthday. It also marked his first day of school. He celebrated the milestones with a glass of Milo, watching Rockhampton awaken.

'Cheers, Steph,' he said, lifting the glass to the sunrise. 'Wish you were here.'

He finished the Milo with a lick across his upper lip, removing the chocolate moustache, and concluded the sentiment with a resolve, a wish, a prayer: 'But one day, you will be.'

Slipping from the chair to the tiles, he headed inside to get ready.

After schools denying him for years, he was finally being allowed to step into the world of structured learning. He knew their change of heart wasn't just because he was tall enough now. But he didn't care. Sealing up gaps in his knowledge was his only priority.

Dear Mr. Ralph Ridley, a Brisbane school had written last month. *We would like to cordially invite you to attend orientation.*

It would be a pleasure to have you, one in Sydney had written.

Please consider us! a Melbourne school had said.

In a perfect world, gestures like these would've come down to people caring about his education, hoping to do everything they could to help solve his time dilemma. But he knew the truth was darker: they only wanted to siphon the last bit of publicity from him before the planet evacuated.

Did it faze him though? Of course not. He chose a school two blocks away, and after he'd bathed, dressed, and packed, his driver dropped him out the front ten minutes before nine.

22

He stood at the front gates, backpack on, wide-brimmed hat strapped to his head. The road and paths leading into the school were a congested mess. Cars and kids and parents crowded the place. Playful horns and loud goodbyes made him miss Stephanie.

'Would you like me to come with you, sir?' his driver asked.

'No. And you should probably go. This whole bonanza with you and me and the car is attracting enough attention.'

The driver followed Ralph's gaze to a group of staring parents ten metres away. After a curt nod, he said, 'I'll pick you up around the corner at three-thirty.'

Setting his hat right, Ralph strolled for the entrance, past the buses, where one unloaded a group of children. He waited for them to file out and hopped in amongst them.

Although all were at least half his age chronologically, most were as small, awkward, and full of energy as him. Best of all though, their distracted, spontaneous conversations implied they couldn't have cared less who he was.

If only the same could be said for the parents pointing, whispering, sighing, and giggling.

There he is. It's little Ralph Ridley. The Boy Who Never Grows. Oh my, he's so cute. Don't ya just wanna squeeze his lil cheeks?

From talk shows and symposiums to being thrust inside a hierarchy of grades and popularity was almost too much juxtaposition to handle. He'd accepted he was a freak. But did it mean he had to be the centre of attention in every social setting? School was going to be hard enough navigating the bullies, boogers, homework, and social interactions.

In his first year, while everyone learned about dinosaurs and how to write their names neatly, he studied superstring theory and quantum mechanics. By grade three, with knowledge surpassing everyone's, including the teachers, they saw no other option than to speed up his schooling, offering an exam to pass each grade.

High school came next. In the halls, he kept his head down, ignoring the cliché comments and questions from the students towering over him. At recesses and lunches, he hid in the library, reading textbooks and listening to MIT lectures, both of which offering far more than his classes. But again, with knowledge surpassing everyone's, by grade nine, they offered him a handful of exams to complete the curriculum.

And then it was time for college.

Being on campus gave him a new appreciation for humans and for learning. From the get-go, he became just like the other students, free to enrol in whatever subject he liked. And enrol he did, in as many as he could, ensuring he hadn't skipped over anything during the years he'd self-taught.

Before college, he'd thought he was well-versed in maths and science. But his professors were quick to expose his weaknesses. They opened his eyes to things he'd never thought about, like the forces governing reality, how particles were always popping in and out of existence, and the intricacies of Maxwell's electric field equations. They also taught him more about atomic theory, quantum theory, dimensions, hidden forces, eventually helping him synthesise an entirely new theory about his time dilemma.

'You really gotta bring this crap up every day?'

Ralph paused mid-sentence to look at his classmate, Bucky. The *crap* he referred to potentially contained the answer to his curse.

'Until I solve what's happening to me,' Ralph said, 'yeah.'

Bucky rolled his eyes. 'We already do eight hours of it every week. Be nice to just chill before class for once.'

Ralph glanced at Violette. Her attention was on a duck and her younglings weaving between lily pads on the pond. Other students surrounded them under the shade of the campus's willow trees. Some sipped coffees, reading notes. Some napped. Others argued about nothing.

'All I'm saying is,' Ralph continued, lowering his voice, 'if a 3D person, like us, showed up in a 2D world, we'd be like a god. We'd be able to do anything. We'd be able to lift a 2D person off the paper, their plane of existence, and teleport them to a new location.'

To Ralph, this stuff was interesting. To his classmates, he was just a four-year-old kid rambling about stick figures.

'In other words,' he said, 'a being from a higher dimension could disturb a being in a lower dimension. So, a 4D one could mess with a 3D one. A 3D one could mess with a 2D one. And so on.'

Violette turned to him. 'You mean like a multiverse kinda thing?'

He shook his head. 'Same universe, different dimension.'

She furrowed her brow. 'Is that really what you think happened to you?'

Bucky hurled a stone at the ducks, scattering them. 'Seems a little farfetched.'

'But think about it,' Ralph said. 'Imagine what it'd be like for a stick figure to see a human.'

'Kinda reminds me of Plato's Allegory of the Cave,' Violette said.

'Exactly!' Ralph said, perhaps with too much excitement. 'The stick figures would have no idea what they're looking at. And the same could be true about me. Maybe someone or something my brain can't even articulate has done this.'

'But how?' she asked, popping a piece of gum into her mouth.

Ralph removed an organic chemistry textbook from his backpack and placed it upright on the ground. 'The universe is filled with 3D objects. Each object – books, ducks, trees, me – has a length, a width, and a height.'

Their blank faces told him to shut up, but he couldn't stop now.

'The spine of this book depicts its height, right?' he asked.

Chewing away, Violette nodded.

'And the base depicts its length,' he said, running a finger along it. 'While its cover and pages depict its width. Right?'

Again, Violette nodded. Meanwhile, Bucky cracked a soda, chugged half of it, and finished with a loud burp.

'But here's the trick,' Ralph said, putting the book on its spine. 'By rotating the book ninety degrees, the spine becomes its length, the base becomes its height. And if we add the fourth dimension of time into the equation, everything changes.'

'So…' Violette said, brows furrowed.

'In other words, it doesn't take much for something from a higher dimension to tamper with reality.'

'You really think someone targeted you?'

Ralph sighed, sat. 'I don't know. But none of this seems right. Or fair.'

They were silent for a moment. He didn't know if they were thinking about what he'd said, or if they'd listened, or if he'd even made sense. In any case, he decided to keep his thoughts to himself from then on.

'C'mon,' Bucky said, checking his watch. 'We're gonna be late.'

For the rest of the day, Ralph remained enveloped in his thoughts about higher dimensions. The possibility of being tampered with by something he couldn't see, accidental or otherwise, artificially or naturally, seemed too plausible of a theory to let go of.

If he'd been rotated out of time's regular flow, could he blame someone from a higher dimension? Could he blame a hidden force, a cosmic event?

Quantum mechanics had an answer for such questions: Where there is quantum theory, there is hope. But was that enough to hold on to?

Graduate degree over, he walked into a theoretical physics doctorate. When that was complete, he left college as Doctor Ralph Ridley, full of knowledge, yet still stuck in a five-year-old's body, and still no closer to solving his time dilemma.

Nearing the biological age of six, he moved into an apartment overlooking Moreton Bay and landed a job at the University of Queensland. By day, standing atop his desk, he taught the smirking students about astrophysics and Super Relativity. By night, he studied and meddled with every particle physics theory known to man.

For hours, each and every day, he scribbled in large A3 sketchpads, shuffling equations, inverting them, adding in hyperspace principles.

His fellow professors called him obsessed. His students called him crazy. All loved reminding him no matter how elegant a theory appeared, it was doomed if it didn't agree with reality.

But he was always quick to remind them an answer didn't always have to be found, and instead, he could find comfort in locating its shadow.

✦

Years passed. The seasons changed. Summer brought less heat. Winter came frostier. Bucky and Violette married, moved away. Ralph's students graduated, moved on. His fellow professors retired, passed away. The population dwindled as Earth began dispatching humans to the Alpha Centauri system.

At the biological age of seven, with over thirty Earth years under his belt, Ralph quit his job in the city. He'd grown tired of the hustle and bustle. With the last two Ships set to depart from the Moon Docks in the final months of 2112, he wanted to be away from everything – the distractions, the people, the loss and emotions.

So, he packed his apartment, bought a 4WD, and modified it for his physique. He filled it with camping gear, canned goods, and his most treasured textbooks, sketchpads, and science equipment. He attached a trailer and loaded one male and one female of every animal he could get his hands on – chickens, lambs, pigs, dairy cows. And after some final interviews and book signings, he headed west for the Simpson Desert.

The drive out to the red sandy wasteland took him a week. It could've been faster, but stopping to check on the livestock every so often slowed him down.

On the fourth day, he suffered his first mishap: a burst tire. It took him the rest of the day to learn how to seal and repump it.

On the fifth day, he stopped by a river to let the animals roam.

On the sixth, he helped a kid his height remove a brown snake from a cubbyhouse.

And on the seventh, he arrived in the desert.

It was vast, desolate, hot, just like he'd expected. But it was flat, and he hadn't expected that. Wanting to set up a permanent home, he needed somewhere high, safe, temperature regulated, and with enough land to keep the animals.

He continued on.

Nine days after leaving Brisbane, he made it to Uluru. He stayed by the sacred rock for three days, gazing at its beauty, letting the animals graze, dealing with the insects.

His breakfasts consisted of dried apricots and green tea. His lunches, salami sticks. His dinners, kidney beans and fresh milk.

Although plenty of potential residences were hidden amongst the caves in the area, none were large enough for his needs.

So, again, he continued on, heading south-west for the city of Adelaide. Along the way, he came across Coober Pedy, the conservation park where people once lived underground. Now deserted, empty dwellings, piles of belongings, and homemade signs riddled the place.

GOODBYE, AUSTRALIA! GOODBYE, EARTH!

CHEERS FOR THE MEMORIES!

ONWARDS TO ALPHA CENTAURI!

AND OUR NEW LIFE!

During the quiet nights under the stars, Ralph had listened to the transport vessels leaving the atmosphere. But he'd always done his best to not look at or think about them. To him, it seemed stupid they thought the answers to their problems would be found in space when they had everything here – families, friends, jobs, lives.

Everything he wished he had.

On the fourteenth day travelling through the desert, he found his new home. It was an untouched mountain a few kilometres north of Coober Pedy, at the coordinates of -28.85 latitude and 134.71 longitude. A winding track led to its mesa. A river flowed to its east. Five acres of flat land surrounded it.

Over the next two days, Ralph unpacked his 4WD and trailer. Using bricks, mud, and wood, he built a bed inside the highest cave on the mountain. He strung cord for his clothes. He built electromagnetic coils to power the basics. He sectioned off pens for each species with barbed wire. He planted the first seeds of cucumbers, spinach, tomatoes, and potatoes.

It took him a fortnight to be content with his dwelling. Another fortnight before the livestock were happy. And another week before he was clearheaded enough to return to his studies.

In the city, he'd taken the creature comforts for granted. Now, with the bare necessities to keep himself fuelled, hydrated, rested, and dry, he was free to innovate and experiment. And without the distractions of responsibilities and people he always said goodbye to, he began solving things he never thought possible.

5
Dust Extraction

Day 88

NEARLY three months after Ralph arrived in the desert, the final transport vessel left for the Moon Docks. He watched it go from his perch on the mountain, sipping on a loose-leaf mint tea.

As the blue flames ignited, enlarged, faded, a cold sadness crept in. The silence that followed was sickening, made worse by the dark of the night, and broken only by the treading hooves and munching jaws in the farm below.

'Adios,' he said.

The vessel breached the atmosphere with a faint sizzle. The flames then dampened, swallowed by the vacuum of space.

He'd always wondered what it'd feel like to be alone on Earth. Now the moment had arrived, he didn't know how to feel. Or what to think. While not everyone had been selected or chosen to leave, those staying behind would be thinly dispersed across the planet, some in locations he couldn't reach, others he had no idea about.

He stroked the fur of the dingo beside him. 'At least I've got you, eh, Cyclops?'

The gentle creature lifted her head. Scar tissue had already formed in the empty eye socket, a result of the rooster attack in the farm a week ago.

He held a piece of chicken towards her. She took it delicately.

'Until I outlive you as well, that is.'

Day 91

Ralph had forgotten to bring a lot of things to the desert.

His basic needs were covered. He had food and a pillow. He had a river to bathe in. He had textbooks and sketchpads and enough equipment to experiment with.

But breaking free from the shackles of time had never been done before. To discover if any hidden forces were messing with his life, he needed access to all kinds of items and devices, from those that could be melted and exploded, to those that could be altered and electrified.

He just needed somewhere to store them all. But with ports aplenty along the South Australian coast, he knew exactly where to go.

After readying his 4WD, he drove five hours south to Port Germein. Other than the odd, vandalised vehicle abandoned on the side of the road, the highway was smooth sailing.

He passed a small settlement along the way. But he didn't bother stopping to interact with the people there. He couldn't. Such an action brought too many complications.

What if they recognised him? What if they attacked him? What if they followed him home and destroyed his setup?

Besides, he didn't want or need the distractions that came with humans. The less interaction, the less relationships, the better.

That was the whole reason he'd moved to the desert. That was the whole reason he'd said no to climbing aboard the Ships.

Pulling up outside Port Germein's compound, he ditched the 4WD by the looted office. Recently recommissioned and refurbished to aid evacuation preparation, the place was reminiscent of a ghost town. Ships, tugboats, forklifts, cranes, and trucks were parked haphazardly all about. Yellow, salt-stained shipping containers covered portions of the long jetty, many still stacked and stocked.

After finding a semitrailer with a full tank, he climbed in. Cobwebs covered its side mirrors. A tattered trucker hat sat on its dusty dashboard. A faded, pine tree air freshener dangled from its rearview mirror.

Using folded-up pieces of cardboard for height and a hatchet to press the accelerator, he acquainted himself with the controls. When he was confident enough, he emptied five of the shipping containers, then hauled them home to the mountain, one by one.

Day 94–101

Equipped with sufficient storage, he spent a week raiding the surrounding vacant towns, bringing home a variety of objects: glass, metals, woods, gems, rocks, jewellery, chemicals, electronics, wires, generators, graphics cards, memory cards, quantum chips, satellites, Tupperware, saucepans, cutlery, crockery, bedding, yarn, silks, fabrics.

To him, everything had a purpose.

Day 117

He'd fallen into a groove.

By day, he studied and theorised under the shade of the gumtrees by the river. By night, he put his plans into action in the lab he'd built in the mountain.

From sundown to sunup, he tinkered, melted, mixed, and magnetised items. He exploded things. He heated objects until they produced dangerous levels of radiation, warped, burst, disintegrated. He blew molten glass into useable instruments. He melted gold, silver, copper, brass, forged the sludge into devices, fitted them with electronics.

He'd become a mad scientist, doing whatever he wanted inside his lair made of sandstone.

And he loved every bit of it.

He didn't always have clarity on what he wanted to achieve, but it was fun, and his intuition told him there was merit in fiddling with everything he could get his hands on.

Day 128

Following an evening breakfast of boiled eggs on the mountain's mesa, Ralph headed down to his lab.

The size of two caravans, it resembled a chemistry lab from college combined with a workshop. At the far end, he kept a steel workbench, his science equipment, and two shelves lined with textbooks and sketchpads. On the northern side, he kept containers and boxes of hoarded items. On the southern, a bed for Cyclops, and a bowl filled with snacks from the garden.

After putting his lead apron, taaffeite glasses, rubber boots, and titanium gloves on, he headed over to his workbench, where a sketchpad lay open. The equation used for dark energy reverberation, a technique Dr. Geronimo had spoken about at the symposium, covered its pages.

Although the equation was almost four thousand years old, only within the last few decades had it been associated with dark matter, the mysterious phenomena said to bind the universe.

Over the years, Ralph had dabbled with the ancient equation. He'd scribbled it countless different ways, shuffled it, inverted it, added random powers. He'd condensed it with higher dimension principles. But no matter what he'd tried, nothing ever led to a solution he could make sense of.

He knew something hid inside it. Dark matter and dark energy couldn't comprise more than ninety percent of the universe and not have something to do with any potential forces messing with him. But every angle he took, everywhere he looked, every path, every rabbit hole, all of it, did nothing but continue to mislead and deceive him. Just like his curse.

Leaning back, pen in hand, he tapped away on the steel workbench. The mollifying sound of the flowing river outside intertwined with Cyclops's rhythmic breathing. The calmness of the moment called to him, telling him to stop worrying, to stop seeking, to stop wasting any more time.

But he pushed the offer away. Submitting to such a seduction would be idiotic, like telling his mum to put him down at Stephanie's funeral, like exiling himself to a desert, like refusing to go with everyone to Proxim.

He looked at the equation again, squeezing the pen until the plastic cracked.

It was bad enough being cursed and alone. Being confused about what to do next made everything worse.

Yes, all the experiments he'd done since arriving in the desert had been new and exciting. Yes, the dark energy equation might've been his best lead right now. But how many more dead ends would he face? How much longer would he suffer? How many more harrowing heaps of nothingness would greet him?

He missed the simplicity of reading books, listening to lectures, going to school. Now all he seemed to contend with were decoys.

He looked up from the sketchpad, eyes widening in sudden realisation.

He spun around to face Cyclops.

'What if this equation is just that, a decoy?' he said. 'What if it's like the time machines and isn't worthy of all this consideration? What if…'

Cyclops's left ear twitched, but she didn't budge. He knew she didn't care, just like his classmates, colleagues, and the fame-seeking journalists had never cared. But voicing his thoughts sometimes helped silence feelings of solitude.

He spun back to the bench, mind in overdrive.

Turning to a fresh page, he jotted down his train of thought: *What if science is flawed?*

It was a big question to ask. But could he ignore the possibility he'd been fundamentally wrong in his pursuit? Could he ignore that a blind attachment to science's rules and protocols, something he'd never questioned, hadn't been derailing his success?

'Science isn't magic,' he said, voicing his cascading thoughts to his dingo sidekick. 'It's only a system for detecting anomalies, creating theories, testing and concluding theories. And with each conclusion comes the possibility for the next theory to be upended. And that's the whole point of science, Cy. No guarantees, no certainties, no sacred facts, only temporary conclusions that allow for progression.'

Cyclops yawned. Ralph scoffed, writing notes as he continued explaining everything aloud.

'Once upon a time,' he said, 'black swans were considered an impossibility, Pluto was a planet, and people drilled into brains to solve mental health conditions. If I've been seduced by science's spell, maybe I've overlooked something.'

He knew thinking like this would put him back to the start of everything he'd ever worked on. But if science had been used as a weapon, a political talking point, and a scapegoat for centuries, what if someone had missed or warped something along the way? What if *he'd* missed or warped something along the way?

'And if that's the case, Cy, maybe I, Ralph Ridley, the walking anomaly, the one no modern scientist ever predicted or solved, owe it to myself to consider all possibilities. And if that means going back to the start, so be it.'

Day 129

The scientists of the past had done well to discover the fundamental particles responsible for reality. But Ralph wanted to go deeper than them, further. He wanted to check they hadn't missed smaller ones, elusive ones, ones that might've ruined his life.

Which meant it was time to build some new equipment.

The first device he needed was an atom smasher. Normally found in major labs across the globe, this device accelerated particles close to lightspeed, before colliding and fragmenting them to see what was inside.

Using his copy of *101 Quantum Devices and Their Quirky Uses*, he got to work.

Melting two kilograms of gold and silver, two highly conductive metals, he poured the sludge into six placemat-sized moulds. When the sludge had solidified, he joined the rectangles into a box resembling a microwave. Once cooled, he fitted all the regular atom smasher components: magnets, coils, lasers, lights, and a monitor.

The second piece of equipment he needed was a particle extractor, also known as a Planck Gun. This proved harder than the textbook made it seem. The precise threading of the vacuum tube was one thing. Moulding and fitting the crystal magazine was another. But calibrating the electronics gave him a total of three headaches in the process.

Thankfully, the final device – a quantumscope – only required the basic recoding of a regular microscope.

Day 133

As the desert heat waned on another day, he started his next phase of experiments.

Heating a handful of copper shards to 1084°C, just shy of their melting point, he placed them into the atom smasher, closed the door, and switched it on.

He stayed by the device for two hours, reading the columnizing text on the monitor. Every time something happened, a new line of text formed, detailing events like the copper atoms fragmenting, their nucleuses rupturing, and their elementary particles being released.

In particle physics, there were two main elementary particles fundamental to reality: fermions and bosons. Fermions formed physical objects and consisted of quarks (and their six states: up, down, top, bottom, strange, charmed) and leptons. With varying charges, masses, and spins, fermions had opposing particles with opposing charges (quarks had antiquarks, leptons had antileptons).

Bosons, on the other hand, formed forces, consisting of gauge and scalar particles. With an overall neutral charge, bosons were known as both particles and antiparticles.

Once the elementary particles had clashed and annihilated one another inside the atom smasher, Ralph powered it off. Taking the Planck Gun, he loaded the crystal magazine and extracted whatever was left inside.

Although he'd tried doing better than the scientists of the past, he came away with the same particles they'd always attained.

Day 147

'It isn't fair.'

He'd just spent a fortnight smashing atoms.

'I've tried every metal, wood, rock, and crystal I own. There has to be more than quarks, leptons, and bosons at the bottom of everything.'

Cyclops got to her feet and moved closer to the fire. He slid across the dirt to join her, one hand resting on her fur.

'Maybe I need rarer items,' he said. 'Maybe some nobelium, carnelian, or chrysolite would help me find the secret particles that ruined my life.'

Cyclops buried her cold, wet nose into the crook of his knee. He leant forward and took two strips of lamb from the ceramic dish by the fire. Feeding one to Cyclops, he tossed the other into his mouth.

'What am I missing?' he said, chewing the meat, scanning the obsidian sky.

The Milky Way and its silver stars blinked and flashed. To the west, the golden thumbnail of the new moon hung. Above it, Venus flickered away.

'How can I have studied for so long and still be so stuck?' he said. 'Time machines. The dark energy equation. Elementary particles… Every crevice I dig, I remain frozen in time.'

Where there is quantum theory, there is hope.

He spat. That phrase was like an itch that couldn't be scratched.

'Maybe I've reached my limits, Cy. Maybe I've hit peak intelligence.'

He offered Cyclops the lamb chop bone.

'Or maybe my fellow professors were right. Maybe I am obsessed. And maybe it's time to stop caring.'

Day 150

As the sun breached the horizon on a new day, Ralph was back in the lab.

After spending a few days revising notes, he'd returned with a new mentality, birthed by rereading a famous quantum mechanics experiment from long ago: the double-slit experiment.

In this experiment, scientists had demonstrated atoms behaving differently, depending on whether or not they were observed. Curious to know if a similar quantum phenomenon rang true for his own experiment, he placed a fresh batch of heated copper shards into the smasher, powered it up, then headed down to the farm.

For the rest of the day, he worked on his neglected property. He combed the animals for ticks, lice, and leeches. He topped up water troughs, tightened barbed wire fences. He trimmed and harvested fruits and vegetables.

For lunch, he enjoyed a chilli, potato, and egg stir-fry, followed by a river swim. For dinner, he indulged in a smoked chicken and spinach sandwich, followed by a mint tea on the mesa.

When he returned to the lab well into the evening, he slammed a fist against the steel workbench when he read the monitor.

In his absence, the elementary particles had gone to war.

The fermions had proven too powerful, eliminating every boson. But that wasn't all. The quarks had then taken over, annihilating every last lepton. And with the quarks and antiquarks reigning supreme, they'd gone on to produce a new state, a seventh state, one Ralph named mercenary.

Sweat beading his forehead, he read and reread the monitor.

'Have I just beaten the Thermodynamics Arrow?' he asked himself. 'Have I moved past the entropy boundary, where the universe's end has always been prophesised?'

He left the atom smasher whirring and wobbling away for another hour, just to be sure. On his return, the device sat completely still. It was as though the mercenary quarks had been aggressively negotiating and had finally come to an agreement.

He read the monitor. The letters and numbers were scrambled. The software had no idea what'd happened. Just like him.

He powered the smasher off and extracted the leftovers with the Planck Gun. Placing the crystal magazine under the quantumscope, he peered into the lens. His mouth dropped open.

Swirling away inside the tube was a multicoloured mass of glowing plasma. Surrounding it, a distortive haze, similar to heat rising from a hot road.

Questions bombarded him. Had he just extracted an energy more powerful than the hydrogen bomb? What was the distortive haze? Heat? Radiation? Why had no one ever discovered this seventh quark before? What role did it have in the overall energy balance of an atom?

Another thought came to him, hearkening back to organic chemistry: What if he distilled it?

He got to work.

To test the plasma's volatility first, he performed reflux on it, attaining its boiling point of 2539°C. Next, he poured the broiling, colourful solution into a rotary evaporator to remove any impurities. He then collected the solvent, dried it with a laser, and performed vacuum filtration.

By the end of the three-hour experiment, he collected 0.032 milligrams of a rainbow powder, similar to sherbet. Studying it under the quantumscope, he was pleased to find the distortion field still emanating from it.

Pessimistic Ralph would've said it was a side effect that would wane. Optimistic Ralph would've said it was a powerful energy fluctuation he could use to escape his curse.

But it didn't matter what his intuition told him. His new, open-minded system of science demanded feelings play no part in intentions or outcomes.

6
Nodes of Silver

Day 152

A light afternoon wind swept through the valley. By the river's edge, a herd of camels had gathered to chew cud and replenish their water. From the shade of the gumtrees, with an assortment of paperwork and sketchpads scattered across the ground, Ralph watched on, scratching mindlessly at Cyclops's neck.

His dingo sidekick raised her head. Their eyes met. His stomach sank. A premonition came to him of the day she, like everyone else in his life, would be gone.

He shook his head, banishing the thought, the emotion. It wasn't warranted. He'd just discovered something existed beyond the Thermodynamics Arrow. No one else had done that.

He focused back on the paperwork…

But his mind danced to the past, to the times he once studied the same way on his living room floor, when Stephanie would check on him, when he wasn't so isolated in the middle of a desert.

'Stop it!'

Cyclops shot to her feet. Two camels started, hopping backwards on their spindly legs.

'Sorry, Cy,' he said, patting her. 'I can't concentrate today.'

He glanced at the sun. More than five hours of light remained before he normally headed up to the lab. But how could he keep a regular schedule when the mercenary quark dust occupied his mind?

He gathered his things.

'C'mon. We're starting early today.'

38

They headed up the winding track to the cave-lab. As Cyclops got comfortable in her bed by the entrance, he kitted up.

Tonight's first project was simple: build something to protect the rainbow dust from the elements. He'd spent the morning planning designs and materials, sketching various bags, boxes, and cylinders, before settling on a small sack design.

Using tungsten steel microfilaments as the material, and with an image of a coin sack in his mind's eye, he put the thing together in a few hours, sealing it with a thin strand of flexible titanium.

With the dust safe, it was time to collect more.

Then he would figure out what it could do.

Day 156

After running the smasher for three days straight, he'd collected close to a kilogram of rainbow dust. Storing most of it in tungsten sacks, he kept the rest in glass beakers, its distortion field exposed to the world.

'Okay,' he said to Cyclops, who lay cosy in her bed. 'Let's find out how powerful this stuff is.'

Taking a steel beaker filled with distilled water, he sprinkled a few grains in.

An outside observer might've expected an elaborate contraption or a hundred pages of scribbled equations to test the dust's potency. But Ralph didn't need to change the game. He just needed to know what he was dealing with.

As the dust struck the water's surface, the liquid churned, bubbled, settled.

He added more.

Again, the water churned, bubbled, returned to normal.

Since water was a powerful solvent with an overall neutral charge, dissolving everything from sugar to salt to Milo, the reaction told him the rainbow dust possessed a naturally positive or negative charge.

This was good news.

If positive, it could unlock more power to use in his experiments. If negative, it could possess the power to disrupt reality.

He peered into the beaker. Clumped at the bottom was a blob of what looked like rainbow toothpaste. He took a chemical spoon and scraped it out, placing it under the quantumscope.

Unlike the dust, the paste lacked a distortion field.

This was bad news.

He grabbed a pen and jotted down his findings: *Mercenary quark dust converts to paste when placed in water + distortion field is swallowed. Implication: energy goes into a protective "hibernation" to stop H_2O molecules bonding and dissolving it.*

He finished writing with a curse under his breath.

If the implication was correct, he might've been barking up the wrong tree his entire life. From writing *Frozen in Time* to solving the golden ratio equation, all the research he'd done on science, maths, time machines, all of it could've been one big waste of time.

He took a stone from the ground and covered it with the rainbow paste. The distortion field reawakened, encircling the colourful stone. He grabbed his pen.

Distortion returns when paste touches another object. Implication: mercenary quark possesses powerful energy that can be provoked out of hibernation.

He inspected the stone closer. The sound of sucking air now accompanied the distortion field.

He retested.

Sprinkling more dust into the water, he retrieved another blob of rainbow paste. This time, he smeared it on an unripened kiwifruit.

The distortion field returned.

Distortion caused by mercenary quark's energy reacts to charges in the environment (air, water, objects). Theory: powerful energy can be found at the quantum level of all 3D objects.

He dropped the kiwifruit to the bench. It struck the steel with a clang. Its distortion field then amplified, reaching for the stone's.

'What the—?'

He leaned closer.

The ripples from both objects spread in rhythmic patterns, as though allowing one another space to trade paths.

The display continued for a few minutes before reaching some sort of equilibrium. A calming thrum of vibrative energy then surrounded the objects.

Ralph frowned. He might've wasted his life with stupid pursuits, but this phenomenon was interesting. Its potential unsettled him, but the mad scientist within begged him to find out what would happen if he pushed it further.

And who was he to deny such a request?

Grabbing a spool of copper wire, he cut a metre portion. Connecting one end to an electromagnetic coil, he lay the rest across the rainbow-pasted stone and kiwifruit.

In an instant, the distortion field swelled, expanded. Spreading from the bench through the lab, it brought a painful hissing sound.

He backed away, ears covered, as dirt kicked up from the ground. A whirlwind swirled into existence next, whipping items around the room. Equations and images pinned to the sandstone walls fluttered. The row of test tubes and beakers, made from glass he'd blown himself, rattled and chattered.

He lunged forward and ripped the copper wire from the electromagnetic coil.

The whirlwind and vibrations remained, as though the process had taken on a mind of its own.

Eyes frantic, he scanned the room, looking for a way to stabilise the out-of-control reaction. He spotted a container of miscellaneous wires and dashed over to it. Emptying them to the ground, he carried the container back to the bench, where he shoved the stone and kiwifruit in, before dousing them in water.

Although the dose of neutrally charged water should've swallowed what he believed to be the quark paste's negative energy field, it grew. A high-pitched ringing also replaced the hissing.

He grabbed two spools of gold from the mess of wires and dropped them into the water. A burst of bubbles rippled across the surface. A sharp snapping sound followed, and the hungry energy field vanished.

He sighed in relief, turning to Cyclops whimpering in her bed.

'Sorry, Cy. I didn't—'

A dull, menacing vibration arose, shaking the cave-lab, sending him to the ground with twitching, itchy skin. Ignoring the sensation, he scrambled to his feet, finding Cyclops on all fours, growling low, teeth bared, eye darting everywhere.

'What is it?' he asked.

She barked, back arched, prepared to launch.

'What is it?'

But he didn't need to ask. He could feel it too.

Something had arrived. Something was watching him.

'Keep going, Ridley.'

The voice came from nowhere, everywhere, inserting itself inside him.

'You near answers.'

Ralph's heart pounded. His skin leaked a cold sweat.

'There is more to this than you can imagine,' the voice said.

'Who are you?' Ralph asked, turning on the spot.

'There is much more to solve, much more to do, much more to see.'

A silence fell. The vibrations waned.

Ralph scanned the lab. But whatever had arrived had vacated, leaving nothing but fallen paper and three shattered beakers. Cyclops was even curled up in her bed again, as though nothing had happened, as though she'd never barked at the *thing* that'd invaded.

He turned from her to the lab, scanning everything. His eyes caught the rainbow-pasted stone and kiwifruit flickering in the container, like a glitch in a video game. In the time it took him to grasp what he was witnessing, they sat there like normal. In the next, they'd traded appearance.

He rubbed his eyes. He pinched his forearm. He looked around for the cameras like he was on some sort of reality TV show.

He stepped closer to the bench.

'Impossible.'

But it wasn't. What he'd seen was true.

No longer was the stone rough and blemished, but covered in a thin, brown fur. As for the kiwifruit, while its egg shape remained, it'd become smooth and sandstone in colour.

Day 166

Ralph named his primitive form of alchemy particle transference. Wanting to learn as much as he could about it, he abandoned his routine, studying the technique every day, filling sketchpads with information, rarely sleeping, rarely eating.

After repeating the experiment a dozen times, he branched out. He tried trading stone particles with gold ones, potato particles with silver, aluminium foil particles with butter.

The more he experimented, the faster he learned it wasn't as simple as he'd initially thought. Instead, a handful of rules applied, rules he referred to as kinship rules.

Once these rules became apparent, the periodic table helped determine what objects worked best. And with practice, he was transferring iron with copper, brass with silver, and mercury with gold in a matter of weeks.

The kinship rules seemed restrictive at first. But they were simple enough.

Iron traded with copper because the two metals were only three protons different. Brass, a combination of copper and zinc, traded with silver because they differed by one electron. And mercury traded with gold because their atomic masses were less than four Daltons different.

Day 211

Comfortable with particle transference's kinship rules for metals, Ralph moved on to common household items.

He tried kettles with stone, silver, and sand. He tried hedge trimmers with mushrooms, mahogany, and marble. He tried wooden spoons and brooms with pearls, silks, and gold.

At the end of most experiments, he obtained failed messes of melted, cheap plastic and flimsy, flaking wood. But sometimes, when things worked in his favour, he synthesised new, interesting objects like mahogany hedge trimmers and shiny golden rods.

Day 226

Tampering with reality was a big deal. While solving such a thing should've been rewarded with a Nobel Prize and not just lambs bleating in the distance, he didn't have too much to complain about.

He now wielded a technique that altered 3D objects. This opened a door for him like never before. If he learned how to use it at a larger scale, it was possible he could warp reality enough to pull, break, or rotate himself free from the shackles of time.

Maybe.

But to disturb enough particles, he'd need more than coils and wires. He'd need to embody the technique. He'd need to become it.

Day 229

Centuries ago, Nikola Tesla had done the impossible with his Wardenclyffe Tower. After capturing electrons from the air, he'd sent them into the ground, before retrieving them at a different location wirelessly.

Ralph wanted to attempt a similar energy transfer with his own technique.

He'd already dabbled with the idea of coiling wires around his body. He'd sketched electromagnetic coil backpacks, hats, and shirts. But every plan had dissatisfied him.

He didn't want to rely on cumbersome equipment or be burdened by materials. He wanted a one-to-one connection, a clean way to control particle transference, a way to use the power of the mercenary quark's negative energy to its fullest extent.

And so, after three days of musing, pondering, and designing, he reached a conclusion he couldn't deny: What if he used his own body?

The thought was extreme. But if the human body consisted of electrolyte-rich water, laced with thousands of kilometres of nerves, where else would he find something so capable?

Keep going, Ridley. You near answers.

'What answers?' he asked the memory of the lab invader's words. 'Where and when? How? And why didn't you show up when I'd lived in the city, when my life had made more sense?'

Day 232

After a sunset breakfast of eggs and tomatoes, Ralph headed to the lab and kitted up.

Taking the *Atlas of Human Anatomy* textbook down from the shelf at the back of the room, he flicked to the nervous system section.

For the next few hours, he revised the upper limb nerve junctions and branches, drawing them on his skin in permanent marker, from the brachial plexus at his shoulders to the nerve endings in his fingertips.

With all the months slaughtering and dissecting livestock, he had enough confidence to go ahead with his plan. But before committing, he took a moment.

'Am I really about to slice into my flesh to access my own electricity?' he asked Cyclops, scratching her neck.

She watched him with one eye, licking his knee.

He sighed, burying his head in his hands.

'If only Max Bonaparte was here,' he said. 'If only Steph was. If only someone – anyone – was here.'

The mad scientist in him was peaking. He'd been alone so long, he didn't know if he was even thinking clearly anymore.

'Maybe I don't need to be so invasive,' he said. 'Maybe there's another way to control and channel the paste's energy.'

He headed over to the items he'd synthesised with particle transference. Sorting through the assortment of brass kettles, wildflower earmuffs, and spinach garden gnomes, he took one of the shiny, golden rods and coiled a length of silver wire around it, boosting its conduction.

Back at the bench, he covered an iron shard and fragment of coal with rainbow paste.

The distortion fields arose, combined, disturbing the pages of the sketchpad on the bench. He pointed the coiled rod into the distortion. Placing a free hand on the piece of coal, he closed his eyes. Focusing on delivering his energy into the two items, he waited. And waited. And waited some more. And when nothing happened, he rolled his eyes.

'What do I think I am,' he muttered, 'some kind of sorcerer?'

The initial plan resurfaced in his mind. Before logic latched on to deter him again, he dragged a box of silver bars over to the workbench. Melting two of them, he shaped the sludge into thirty buttons. While waiting for them to solidify, he pierced tiny incisions in his arms with a scalpel, following the permanent marker, and spacing them an inch apart.

With the open wounds still stinging, he inserted the warm, silver buttons.

Day 234

It took two days for the scar tissue to take hold of the silver nodes. By then, his electrical current had synchronised with them.

It was odd watching the nodes glow in accordance with his heartbeat.

But it was also pretty cool.

When he was ready to try the transference technique again, he covered the iron shard and coal fragment with a fresh layer of rainbow paste. Placing a hand on each item, he closed his eyes and focused on delivering his energy into them.

Although he felt stupid, although he had no idea what he was doing, he embraced the thrumming that surrounded and swallowed him.

Day 237

He awoke on the ground three days later with Cyclops licking his face.

Neck stiff, mouth dry, a tingling sensation moved up and down his spine.

Getting to his feet, lightheaded, clumsy, he looked at the bench and smiled.

No longer did the iron and coal resemble their original designs. Instead, they'd become hybrids of one another: black, metallic, crumbly.

7

A Trip to the City

Day 354

THE stretched shadows cast on the sandstone walls told Ralph he'd been unconscious for at least a few hours.

He sat up, rubbing the back of his head, cursing under his breath.

No matter how much he practiced particle transference, the energy demand still took its toll.

It made no sense. Humans adapting to stimuli was one of their signature traits. From health to skills to overcoming adversities, practice always led to development, and, in most cases, improvement.

So why was tampering with matter using his own central nervous system so complicated?

He stood, laughing. Did he even have to ask such a question?

Tampering with reality wasn't child's play. People from all walks of life would've killed to know how to perform such a technique.

But maybe that was the problem. Maybe a lack of recognition for solving matter manipulation fuelled an impatience. Maybe he needed to show someone what he'd been working on, prove he hadn't been wasting his life.

After cleaning the lab, he headed down to the farm. The early morning sun hadn't quite rid the dew from the land.

He trudged across the crunching grass to the animal pens. The chickens scurried on his approach, returning when he scattered scraps of food for them to peck at.

He tended to the rest of the animals before harvesting dinner – three spinach leaves, two sweet potatoes, two tomatoes. He then headed up the winding track with Cyclops, stopping at his bedroom on the way to collect some smoked chicken from the icebox.

On the mountain's mesa, he lit the fire. He hung the pot of water above the flames and tossed the potatoes and spinach in, placing the chicken on the ceramic plate to thaw. He then opened his sketchpad.

But when the potato had softened and the spinach had wilted, no ink had been spent.

His mind was too consumed, too wired, too lost. Although he distracted himself with work each day, solving things no human had solved before, he couldn't shake the longing for interaction, for conversation, for play. He missed the small talk of everyday life. He missed the gossip and the banter.

How's the weather today? Catch the game last night? What'd you get up to on the weekend? Shoulda seen ol' Margie and her pug yesterday. I'm tellin' ya, mate, she's lost her marbles.

Conversations like these had been absent from his life for so long, he almost couldn't remember how they went. While many had lacked substance, distracting him from his mission, he missed them.

Cyclops rolled onto her side, exposing her belly.

Normality, he thought, scratching it. That's what she represented.

But what was normal anymore? Sitting on a mountain in a desert with a dingo, silver nodes embedded in his arms, manipulating matter with a rainbow paste made from mercenary quarks in a cave-lab…

Normality? That was a term he no longer understood.

Draining the pot, he served their meals. They then devoured them, watching the animals roam below on another lonely day in the desert.

Day 359

On first light, Ralph packed the truck. With the one-year anniversary since leaving Brisbane fast approaching, he couldn't think of anything worse than sitting around feeling sorry for himself.

Unsure how long he'd be gone, he filled an esky with boiled eggs, fruit, and water. He loaded a steel container with a fresh batch of rainbow paste. He filled the animal troughs with enough food and water for a few days. And after putting Cyclops in the front passenger seat, he set course for Adelaide.

The journey south took a little less than seven hours. He stopped a few times on the way to snack, stretch his legs, and check out abandoned settlements. Some he came across had wheelless caravans stacked on bricks, surrounded by piles of burnt junk. Some had frayed sheets flapping in the wind. Others had rusty, mossy water catchments that told stories about how long the people had been gone.

It wasn't all bleak though. At the hill leading into the city, he came across a small village still thriving and functioning. A group of children played tip by the road. Emaciated goats and dogs roamed. Near the settlement's centre, amongst tents and huts, teenagers and adults chopped wood, tilled the land, and tended to crops.

Ralph stopped the truck and clambered onto the bonnet as the kids playing tip closed in on him. When one tried dodging the others, they stumbled onto the road, spotted Ralph, and came to a standstill. The others came up beside them, gawking, trading words.

Each kid wore dirty, torn clothing. Their skin was tanned, freckled, tarnished.

Jealousy radiated within Ralph at their vibrant demeanours. Each of them showed every characteristic of a life lived, of being out in the sun, of having friends and a family. Of aging.

Ralph raised a hand in greeting. The children shrank back, afraid. Their expressions reminded him of stories about humans invading indigenous tribes, making him wonder what they thought of the seven-year-old kid standing on a truck, silver nodes flashing on his arms, wearing nothing but faded boardshorts and a flannelette shirt with its sleeves rolled up.

'Hello,' he said, feeling strange to communicate with something other than an animal.

A woman's voice came from the settlement's centre, scattering the children.

Ralph hopped off the truck and strode towards the adults. But noticing their body language, which implied they either wanted him gone or were thinking about eating him, he slowed.

He raised his hands in surrender. 'Sorry. I don't mean to disturb you.'

They traded glances, muttering exotic words to one another.

Ralph considered grabbing his rainbow paste and demonstrating the power of particle transference. But their uncertain eyes made him second guess himself. For all he knew, performing the technique would lead to him being burned at the stake by sundown.

'What year is it?' he asked, trying to appear casual, friendly. 'The weather sure is nice today.'

'We no want you,' a woman wearing a faded smock said, looking him up and down in disgust.

'I…' He cleared his throat. 'Do you know how long the Ships have been gone?'

She stepped forward, waving an index finger. 'We no want you!'

'I'm sorry. I've been by myself for a very long time. I was hoping—'

'Leave us,' she said.

And with that, she turned away. The others followed suit, returning to work as though deeming him harmless, and leaving him standing there like an idiot.

As he walked back to the truck, he felt perplexed by his arrogance. He'd never considered this possibility. Just because he wanted the interaction, didn't mean they had to cater to his needs. After all, these people had chosen not to travel to Alpha Centauri. Why would they be interested in talking to him? To them, he was a nobody, someone from a different era, just another passing weirdo.

He scanned the village one last time, hoping, waiting, almost begging someone to ask him in for a cup of tea. But no one did. No one cared. The Boy Who Never Grew had become a spectacle of the past.

Climbing back into the truck, he released the handbrake.

As he rolled into the city, the children gathered on the road to watch him go. He let out a sigh as they dipped out of sight in the rearview.

Adelaide was more post-apocalyptic than he'd expected. The faded roads were cracked with the hands of time. Trees had broken through the unused pavements. Weeds and vines covered decaying cars and lampposts. Kangaroos and emus had taken to the area, grazing like humans had never existed.

He spotted more wheelless caravan settlements as he drove through the city. Although most appeared abandoned, no doubt ditched in favour of the empty apartments, he didn't bother stopping at any of them. And no one bothered coming to see who was rumbling past in the noisy truck either.

Life had moved on.

In the city centre, he parked and climbed out with Cyclops.

From the paved streets to the blend of modern and colonial-era buildings, Adelaide seemed reminiscent of a museum. The broken neon signs and billboards took him back to another life. Spotting litter gave him doses of nostalgia. Coming across bus terminals covered in graffiti transported him back to a time when most humans still called Earth home.

In one of the less damaged bus stops, he stopped to study a map. It felt good reading street names, looking at tourist attractions, thinking back to when buses transported the public around.

In the map's bottom lefthand corner, an inverted pentagram had been drawn over the location of the launch facility. It got him wondering what it was like and why people had become so spiteful towards the evacuation.

'Let's go check it out, Cy.'

An hour later, they arrived at the facility on the outskirts of the city. Positioned on the dry, flat land by Carrickalinga Headland, it overlooked the St. Vincent Gulf. Spanning two square kilometres, a fifteen-metre-high steel fence surrounded it. Windowless jeeps and buses were parked by the boom gates, which, after lining the truck up, Ralph ploughed through, sending them clanging to the ground.

The launch facility was similar to an airport. Large, open, and concrete, a tourist information centre, souvenir store, amenities block, and bar lined its perimeter.

As he roamed around, he tried imagining what it would've been like for the passengers counting down the hours to lift-off. An emptiness stirred inside his stomach at the thought of them sitting at the bar together, laughing, drinking, clashing glasses. The excitement in the air as the vessels departed for the Moon Docks would've been intoxicating, inciting some of Max Bonaparte's final words to come to him: *I must insist you rethink the offer of coming on the Ships.*

'Let's see what we can find,' Ralph said to Cyclops, who was already sniffing her way around.

He scavenged the area. It was clear most of the good stuff had already been taken. But he did manage to find two backpacks made of a lightweight, weatherproof fabric designed for space. Putting one on, he threw the other into the truck's cabin. He then headed up the control tower's stairs, powered the generator on, and found a computer as Cyclops took off in pursuit of rodents.

For the next few hours, he scoured every file on the server. He read emails and articles. He watched videos about the Ships and their marbled floors and white-walled halls. He printed off everything to do with the Alpha Centauri endeavour, including techniques, trajectories, formulas, and research papers, knowing that if he ever solved his dilemma, going after the Ships would be his next priority.

He didn't bother researching anything about Ralph Ridley, the strange boy who'd exiled himself to the desert. Nor did he look into where his mum or dad had ended up during the severance.

Ignorance, irrespective of it providing bliss, was the way forward.

When he was done, as he went to power the computer off, his eyes caught the date in the lower righthand corner: Friday, August 8, 2256.

He stared at the date for a moment, double clicked it, opened the calendar.

If correct, he was around 143 years off with his counting.

He powered on another computer. The same date greeted him.

He flicked through the stack of research papers. The most recent one was from the year 2112, the year the Ships disembarked.

Which was supposed to only be a year ago.

'Malfunctioning pieces of crap,' he said, powering the computers off.

Before leaving, he scavenged the control tower. He found a box of biros and a handheld coordinates device capable of triangulating one's position in the universe. While some simple maths, a telescope, and knowledge of constellation patterns could solve that, it was still a cool toy to attain.

Shoving his findings into his pockets, he shut the generator off and called down the hall.

'Let's go, Cy!'

Cyclops took several minutes to return. When she did, she came limping and panting.

He crouched beside her. 'Something get you?'

He checked her for scratches, ticks, bites, and blood. He found none. But he did notice how specked with grey her golden fur had become.

'When did you get so old?' he asked with a smirk.

She put her chin on the floor with a whimper.

'C'mon,' he said, hoisting her into his arms.

He carried her down to the truck and loaded her into the front seat.

'Hello.'

The voice came from the backseat.

Turning, he found a girl and a boy, no older than thirteen, strapped in. They wore clothes similar to the kids playing tip. They had long, knotted hair finishing in uneven, butchered angles. Their skin was dark and riddled with several scars and scabs.

'We heard you arrive,' the girl said.

Ralph remembered the moment he'd ploughed through the boom gates. 'You're from around here?'

'We came from island,' she said, pointing.

Ralph followed her finger to where a portion of Kangaroo Island could be seen. 'How long ago?'

'Thirty-two moons,' she said. 'We've been living on beach.'

'And your parents?'

She shook her head.

Ralph nodded. 'Me too.'

'We come wiv you?' the boy asked, eyes bright, eager.

Ralph's excitement for interaction told him to say yes. But taking them home to his lair and obsessive quest brought too many ramifications.

'Probably not a good idea,' he said, tucking Cyclops's fragile limbs close to her shivering body.

'I am Piri,' the girl said. 'And this is my brother, Jamaki.'

Ralph suppressed a sigh. Of course they were siblings. It was the perfect right hook reminder delivered by the universe for what he once had.

Jamaki dug something out of his pocket and held it to Ralph. 'We come wiv you?' He opened his hand, revealing a polished, cerulean cicada. 'Blue very rare. Yours now.'

Ralph shook his head. 'I can't take it. And I can't take you. I live in the middle of nowhere and don't have time to look after you.'

The kids traded a few words Ralph had never heard before.

'We will help,' Piri said. 'We will make garden and catch rabbits to eat.'

'Pwease,' Jamaki said.

Ralph eyed them. 'How old are you both?'

'168 moons,' Piri said. She pointed at Jamaki. '122.'

Ralph divided the numbers by twelve. 'But I work a lot. I don't have time to be your friend.'

The pair stared at him with innocence and hope, smiles forming on their friendly faces.

Ralph couldn't help but let his own smile form as well. 'I'm Ralph.'

Their smiles became grins.

'Are you hungry?' he asked, lifting the esky's lid.

They leaned forward and peered inside.

'Take what you want,' he said.

They each snatched a kiwifruit with nervous, twitchy reflexes, as though expecting someone else to take them first.

Ralph watched them bite into the fruit. It'd been so long since he'd seen such a simple sight, it almost seemed surreal. While he'd made the trip to the city in search of interaction, he'd never thought it'd turn out like this.

'You really want to come with me?' he asked.

Green juice leaking down their chins, chomping on the fruit like they hadn't eaten in weeks, they nodded.

'Well,' Ralph said, climbing into the driver's seat, 'let's get going then.'

He fired up the truck and set course for the mountain.

8
Energy Debts

Day 360/51,480

THE following day, Ralph found Cyclops's bed empty in the morning.

Searching the farm, he called her name, hands cupped to his mouth. He checked the animal pens, between the crops, out by the river's edge. But she was nowhere to be seen.

After making the rounds for half an hour, he headed up to the mountain's mesa for a better view.

In the east, the sun breached the horizon with timidity. Clouds trimmed with pinks and reds spread across the pale, blue sky, like floating clumps of fairy floss. The ashes of last night's fire smouldered away under the campfire tripod. And beside them, lay Cyclops, legs rigid, eye vacant.

With a stifled yell and a curse, Ralph slid across the dirt on his knees to her.

He grabbed her. He shook her. He stroked her frosty fur flecked with more greys than she'd had before Adelaide.

Her sole, dark eye had been replaced by a hollow white abyss. The sight of it stirred a vortex awake inside his chest that pulled on him, beckoning for him to succumb to reality's relentless reminders and embrace. And the only way out seemed to be to scream at the sky, clawing the dirt like his mum had clawed the floor at Stephanie's funeral.

What had happened to his dingo sidekick? The way she'd aged… Faster than anyone. Was that normal for dingoes? But she'd been fine before they'd left…

No.

He was to blame. And of course he was.

'What happened?'

He turned his head but didn't – couldn't – make eye contact.

'Just another act of comedy dealt by the hands of the universe,' he said.

Piri approached him. 'What does that mean?'

He knew she probably found it odd talking to a boy who barely looked eight years old, who spoke in such a way, who'd built a life in the desert. But how could he begin to explain what he meant?

He wrapped his arms around Cyclops, burying his face into her fur. 'I never should've taken you to Adelaide.'

Piri placed a hand on his shoulder. It was the first time anyone had touched him since he'd shaken the boy's hand after helping him remove a brown snake from his cubby.

Ralph flinched it off him. 'Don't.'

Piri withdrew her arm.

'Just,' he said, 'leave me alone.'

She stayed, hesitating. 'We have lost as well—'

He wheeled around, tone elevating to a level he hadn't used since facing his mum. 'And you don't think I have? You don't think I've lost people trying to solve the unsolvable, sitting in my lab every day, staring at equations? This is why I didn't want to bring you here. All I do is lose!'

Piri watched him, bottom lip compressed. 'Our shaman always said everyone is taken by time.'

Ralph turned back to Cyclops. 'You don't know the half of it.'

As she headed for the path back down the mountain, Jamaki in tow, he realised the irony in telling her to leave. He'd gone to the city to quell his isolation.

But he didn't feel apologetic or guilty for how he'd reacted. The Adelaideans had no idea what he'd been through.

Carrying Cyclops's frigid body out to the river, he buried her under the shade of the gumtrees.

'Sorry, Cy,' he said, patting the small mound. 'Wish I could've given you some of my time.'

For the rest of the day, he stayed by her grave, chipping away at the stack of research papers he'd printed yesterday. If he didn't have something new to focus on, another road trip would've been the only way to keep his mind busy.

Flicking through the pile, he read their titles: *Symmetries of the Heterotic String and its Application with the Uncertainty Principle, Energy Debts and their Impacts, Primordial Black Holes and Polarising Pulsars, What Riemann Overlooked – 2D vs. 8D.*

He got started.

> *Forces are consequences of geometry. The greater the Riemann's metric tensor value is, the greater the crumpling. Thus, the more crumples, the bumpier the terrain.*

With a grasp of most physics concepts, he didn't take away too much.

> *Primordial black holes were some of the first destructive pockets of energy in the universe. Their electric, polarising effect is fuelled and amplified by nearby pulsar stars.*

It was unfortunate. He didn't want to revise things he already knew.

> *The heterotic string consists of a closed circuit with two types of vibrations – clockwise and counterclockwise. The varying magnitude of these vibrations help synthesise quantum particles.*

He wanted to know more about hidden forces, entropy limitations, what the dust's negative energy distortion field could do.

> *Quantum interferences suppress energy fluctuations. In 2089, Kirby et al. discovered how fluctuations lead to energy inequalities, resulting in his 'energy debt' theory.*

Ralph sat up straighter, reread the paragraph, circled it.

> *Imagine the universe is run by bankers,* the paper continued. *While the universe prefers using dark energy as the currency, the bank prefers using light energy. Anytime someone spends dark energy, the bank charges interest. The longer someone spends it, the more interest they charge. Furthermore, anytime someone spends it, the bank is forced to send light energy into the area to balance the universe's account.*

Too congruent with his experience of the rainbow dust, he circled these paragraphs, scribbling notes on the border: *Dark energy equation.*

Dormant energy. Energy debts. Question: What if there is another form of energy beyond the mercenary quark dust?

The silver nodes on his arms flashed, breaking his concentration. He glanced at them moments before a warm melody floated through the valley.

'I'll come see you later,' he said to Cyclops's grave, gathering his things.

Nearing the mountain, the melody became more distinct. Without a soul for kilometres, he knew its origin had to be the Adelaideans. Not wishing to disturb them, he hiked to the mesa, where he peered into the farm on his hands and knees.

Below, Jamaki raked animal droppings, placing them in the compost. Piri cleaned the chicken pen, tossing rotten food scraps into a bucket. They both sang while they worked, their voices swelling through the otherwise silent desert.

It'd been so long since Ralph had heard music, he welcomed it.

Their wavering, soothing harmony sounded like a conversation without articulation. Their melodies complemented one another's. Her voice told the story. His gave it depth. Ralph wondered if they were helping him mourn.

After indulging for ten minutes, he stood and waved, wanting them to know he'd been listening with gratitude. But their singing stopped abruptly when they spotted him, and they stared back as though determining his predatory nature.

With an awkward, apologetic wave, he moved over to rekindle the fire for some tea, mumbling about his stupidity.

As the water boiled, their singing resumed.

He sighed. If it wasn't for the image of Cyclops's stiff body imprinted in his mind, today would've been a perfect day to abandon his experiments, get to know the new arrivals, show them around. But it was almost like her death had come at just the right time, reminding him how pointless it was to nourish any relationship.

Day 376/51,496

The full Moon's white light illuminated the ghostly fog above the river. From the mountain, laughter and conversation, courtesy of the Adelaideans, spread through the valley.

Ralph started the evening in the western quadrant, where the five shipping containers lived. Rummaging through them, he searched for materials for the next phase of experiments.

Since reading Kirby et al.'s energy debt theory, he'd reached an inescapable conclusion: To disrupt enough particles making up reality, to cause an energy debt he could potentially make use of, he needed to see if anything lay beyond the mercenary quarks and antiquarks he continued to extract.

Which meant it was time for a new atom smasher.

With knowledge of the rainbow solution's reflux occurring at 2539°C, he chose materials that handled more than that. For the shell, he chose osmium, a metal with a melting point of 3000°C. For the moulds, he chose black diamond, a mineral with a melting point of 4000°C.

Backpack filled and sealed, he headed to his lab and kitted up.

After melting the black diamond, he shaped the sludge into six squares the size of drink coasters. Once solidified, he poured melted osmium into the diamond moulds. When that had solidified, he joined the osmium squares into a cube the size of a Rubik's, fitting all the regular electronics along the way.

Next, he ran the original smasher with a fresh batch of heated copper shards. He then extracted the colourful plasma with the Planck Gun. Before distilling it and collecting the dust though, he injected the plasma straight into the osmium cube, placed a hand on top, and channelled his energy until it hummed and thrummed.

One hour into the smashing, steam seeped from the cube's seams. In his impatience, and perhaps arrogance, he ignored it, pushing on, embracing the fatigue setting in.

Two hours in, his numb arm dropped from the cube, severing the connection, and resulting in a fiery explosion that sent thousands of hot osmium shards in all directions. Some embedded into his arms. The rest embedded into the sandstone walls. While his lead apron and titanium gloves saved him for the most part, his eyebrows were lost in the flames.

Day 377/51,497
To prevent another osmium cube explosion, Ralph added a positive feedback loop into the design. This would help him infuse enough energy

to get the process started, before stepping away to let the mechanism take over.

To achieve this, he added smashed magnets into the osmium sludge. He then assembled three more cubes, varying how many magnet walls each had: the second had two magnet walls, the third had four, the fourth had six.

He also equipped each new cube with a Geiger counter and kill switch. If the heat and radiation climbed too high during the smashing, the Geiger would trigger the switch, halting the process, and giving his eyebrows more time to grow back.

Day 379/51,497

With his three new osmium cubes loaded with rainbow plasma, he channelled his energy until each hummed and thrummed. Releasing his hands, he let the feedback loops take over.

One hour into the smashing, the steam seeped from the seams. Two hours in, a vibration arose, reminding him of the time the presence had invaded his cave-lab. But before anything showed up to speak more riddles, the sound of glass shattering halted everything.

He approached the bench cautiously.

This was a critical moment. He'd gone beyond the modern understanding of particle physics before. If he did it again, what would that mean for the tangibility of reality? What would that mean for any hidden forces potentially messing with him?

He found one of the cubes disintegrated. The other two still sat there though, gently humming away.

He touched the two-walled magnet cube. Cold. He touched the four-walled one. Hot. He read their monitors:

> *Cube #2: Aberrant configuration; particles annihilated [4,023,452].*
> *Cube #3: Aberrant, docile configuration; particles annihilated [3,456,543].*
> *Cube #4: Error. Reconnect and try again.*

Mind dancing with possibilities, he took the Planck gun and inserted it into the cold cube. As the extraction began, a flash of black plasma laced out, lapping his silver nodes. He pulled his arms away with a yelp as a gasp came from behind.

He wheeled around. The Adelaideans stood in the entrance, mouths open, holding hands.

Ralph shook his head. 'No. You can't be here. It's not safe.'

They stared.

He made a hurried, shooing gesture. 'Go away.'

Their eyes flicked from the cubes to him.

'Please,' he added.

With a slumping of shoulders, they walked away.

Ralph turned back to the bench, shaking his head. He hadn't considered the danger he posed to them with his experiments. But this was yet another reason why he'd never wanted them to come home with him.

He refocused on the experiment.

Taking the Planck Gun, he inserted it into the cold cube and completed the extraction. He then placed the crystal magazine under the quantumscope.

Inside, glossy, obsidian flakes floated about in some kind of transparent oil.

His heartrate elevated. This seemed promising.

He inserted the Planck Gun into the hot cube. A flash of white plasma laced out and lapped his nodes. But this time, he didn't yelp or jump back. He completed the extraction, placed the magazine under the quantumscope, and peered into the lens.

Inside, glittery, ivory grains, similar to rice, swirled about.

He smiled as questions came to him like rapid-fire: What were the obsidian flakes made of? What were the ivory grains made of? More quarks? A new quantum particle? Another decoy?

It was time for distillation.

Day 385/51,503

Jamaki knelt beside Ralph, studying the glowing, silver nodes on his arms. Standing a foot taller than him, he made Ralph feel childlike. But that feeling was not unfamiliar.

'They help me conduct electricity for particle transference,' Ralph said.

Jamaki ran a finger over each bump.

'Yep,' Ralph said. 'I'm a weirdo.'

Jamaki watched his lips with deep concentration. 'Weirdo? What dat word say?'

Ralph smiled. 'It means strange.'

Jamaki raised an eyebrow.

'Do you like it here?' Ralph asked.

Jamaki snapped his attention to the path down the mountain. He always knew when his sister was coming. Scurrying back to his favourite spot atop a rock, he sat cross-legged in waiting.

A moment later, Piri appeared, cooking pot in hand. She smiled at Ralph as she passed, glancing at his missing eyebrows.

'No work tonight?' she asked, attaching the pot above the flames.

Ralph straightened at the question. Since moving to the desert, he'd never been confronted with one like it. He opened his mouth to respond, but found a response impossible, for his mouth had turned dry.

Piri knelt to the ground. Pulling her thick, braided hair back, she tucked it into her shirt. She then began chopping the shallots, potatoes, and chillis for the soup she was preparing.

'If you not working tonight,' she said, 'maybe tell us a story? Like, where is family and what happened in lab last week when lightning came from cube.'

'Why don't you tell me about yourselves?' Ralph said. 'That'd be more interesting.'

Piri looked at Jamaki, who was now hunting a cricket.

'We already tell you our life on way to mountain,' she said.

Ralph stared into the flames. She was right. They'd filled him in about everything – their village collapsing, how they'd fled to the sea on horseback, how they'd taken a boat to the South Australian coast.

'I'm sorry about last week,' he said, standing, dusting his backside. 'But I can't have you guys interrupting me again. It's too dangerous.'

The girl looked at him blankly. The boy mimicked her.

Under the starry sky with the warmth from the sun still stored in the mountain, he would've loved to invest in the moment. He would've loved to tell them about his life and the world before everyone had moved on. But with three dusts potentially possessing the power to finally fix his life sitting in his lab, how could he?

He gestured at the bubbling broth. 'Thank you for taking the time to prepare this meal.'

He strode off for the path.

'Why you no like us?' Piri asked. 'Why always in cave? We can leave if you want. We used to situation like this.'

Ralph stopped, sighed. 'Maybe once I break free, I can spend time…'

His words trailed as his mind dipped to the past, remembering how hard Stephanie had tried to be part of his life as well.

Piri scraped the chopped food from the wood into the pot. 'You are hot and cold. It is strange.'

'Weirdo,' Jamaki said as he seized the cricket with both hands.

'You don't understand,' Ralph said. 'I don't have time for your food, your hospitality, or your company.'

He wanted to add something about a relationship with him being pointless, about how his parents had been right to abandon him, about how his sister had been lucky…

'But why?' Piri asked.

Ralph threw his arms in the air. 'Because I'm a mutated freak in the midst of a war with time. And if I don't figure out what's happened to me, I'll lose you guys like I lost Cyclops, and again I'll be riding this rotten log on the river of reality all by myself.'

Jamaki's cricket jumped free from his hands as he stared at Ralph.

'Enjoy your dinner,' Ralph said, then turned for his lab.

Piri called after him. 'Maybe we help?'

Ralph stopped, bowed his head, shook it. 'It's not that simple.'

9
Playing with Particles

Day 418/51,536

RALPH, Piri, and Jamaki were on the western side of the mountain. They'd just spent the morning covering the truck's trailer and a shipping container with obsidiary paste, a combination of the obsidian and ivory dusts Ralph had extracted from the osmium cubes. With cicadas dominating the ambience, with frill-necked lizards basking in the mild midday sun prophesising the century-long winter, Ralph surveyed their handiwork.

'Looks good,' he said, nodding, standing akimbo.

Piri joined him. 'They will change like stone and kiwifruit?'

'That's the plan.'

'And if they don't?'

He ignored her question, as though dismissing any possibility of failure. 'Where's your brother?'

Frowning like she still had something to say, she pointed at the shipping container.

Ralph called out. 'How's it looking up there, Jamaki?'

The Adelaidean boy scurried on all fours to the container's edge. Peering over like a cat preparing to pounce on prey, he held two thumbs up, his smile almost as wide as his obsidiary paste-smeared face.

Ralph smirked. 'Alright, let's find out what this paste can do.'

Jamaki leapt from the container, tumbling across the dirt with elegance and ease. He then joined Piri on a nearby rock.

'Remember,' Ralph said, 'if I pass out, make sure a camel doesn't squash me.'

'And eagle?' Jamaki asked, pointing at the sky from a deep squat.

Ralph tracked the boy's finger to a circling eagle. 'Yep, no pecked eyes either.'

He got into position between the trailer and container. Placing one hand on each object, he closed his eyes.

After a fortnight testing the obsidian and ivory dusts, he was eager to witness their potential. While he collected less after each distillation compared to the rainbow dust, less was needed to initiate particle transference. And by combining them, he'd unlocked three significant perks: kinship rules were thrown out the window, a shorter transfer time, a decreased energy demand on his body.

In less than an hour, the shipping container and trailer had traded various aesthetics. Hints of burgundy steel, rubber, and cables now spliced the container, while the trailer had become a shade of vermillion striped with yellow, taking on a weather-beaten quality Ralph doubted would have the same towing capacity as its original formation.

As Jamaki ran off to check his rabbit traps, Piri approached Ralph.

'This is a success?' she asked.

Ralph shrugged. 'It's not as clean as a smaller transfer. But it's a start. I'll get better at it.'

'How do you feel?'

'Like I said, it's a start. I don't know if it'll help me with my curse, but—'

'No, I mean energy. How do you feel?'

'Oh.' He took a moment to assess himself, opening and closing his hands, rotating his shoulders. 'Fine, I think.' His response was laced with thoughts he wasn't used to verbalising.

'It is good you not wake up on ground with sore head like other times.'

Ralph nodded distractedly as a new hypothesis dawned on him, one he couldn't believe he'd never considered: If substituting particles between large objects became simple, what stopped him from substituting them with the air? Out of everything he'd tried, wouldn't that be the best way to disrupt enough reality to potentially escape it?

Day 430/51,548

Sometime near midnight, the kids struck up their singing as they made the rounds on the farm. Cold tea in hand, Ralph headed outside for a brain break and to listen in.

Their melody spread through the air with a calming resonance. Despite its lack of words, it told a story, their story, Earth's story, one of loss and sacrifice. One of change. It was like a medicine to Ralph, an elixir, a reminder of simpler times before he'd discovered particle transference, before he'd learned how to manipulate matter.

He gazed at the constellations in the sky. A brief, solitary meteor tracked across it, dissipated.

He felt close to a breakthrough, but what would it be? Another dead end? Perhaps. But how many more lay ahead before the odds turned in his favour? How many more years would he suffer? How could he possess so much potential with his three dusts, yet still have no idea how to use them to solve his time dilemma?

He took a stone from the ground and hurled it at the Moon. He lost sight of it before it curved downwards.

He tuned back in to the singing, letting it wash over him.

His silver nodes slowed their blinking.

'What?' he said. 'You don't like me thinking about something other than your insatiable need to manipulate the universe?'

After a fade and a faulter, their normal pulsing resumed. With an impatient groan, he headed back inside to his workbench, where sketchpads filled with notes about air composition and designs for harnessing air particles lay open. On one of the pages, the eight words that haunted him were scribbled at the top: *Where there is quantum theory, there is hope.*

He scoffed. That quote was the real enigma, not him. Yes, the possibility for possibilities gave him hope. But reducing everything to possibilities opened too many infinities. And even with so many possibilities, where was the one that fixed his life?

'And where are you now, weird presence?' he asked the ceiling. 'Show up when you want and leave me with nothing but riddles.'

His nodes flared. A moment later, Piri entered the lab, humming and carrying a bowl of something steaming. She placed it beside Ralph, ran a hand across one of the sketchpads, and turned to leave.

'Wait,' he said. 'Please stay.'

'But I thought you say we only help with experiments, not study?'

He gestured around the lab, at the piles of sketchpads, textbooks, and boxes of failed transference items. 'I'm sick of it all, Piri. All this crap haunts and taunts me.'

She examined the page of diagrams in front of her. The way she towered over him thrust him back to high school, where the halls were crammed with pointing, staring teenagers.

'But you will make device for air transference,' she said, nodding. 'You will solve next thing. You will see.'

He shook his head. 'I'm sick of making things. I'm sick of solving things. I want to be like you and Jamaki. You guys have it right. You know what life is about.'

'Then stop,' she said, shrugging. 'You are young. You have plenty of time to learn new experiment.'

Ralph hit the steel bench with a fist. 'I know you might think I'm just a kid, Piri, but I'm a lot more moons older than the both of you.'

She frowned. 'When we lose parents, Ralph, we feel like you. We believe it over. We in village without anyone, only people who did what they want. Shaman our only friend. But even he very distant like you, always study, always meditate. And when village on fire, we run to ocean, lose everyone, everything, even shaman.'

'I know you've been through loss—'

She covered his mouth with a hand. 'I not tell you for sadness. I tell you because we still here.' She released her hand. 'As shaman used to say, when we lose things, if we not dwell too long, we can find lesson. Then we become more than we are. It is a human trait, he say. Soul always likes to learn, to be free.'

'But that's the problem,' Ralph said, gesturing at the sketchpads. 'The more I look, the more I find. When I wanted to look for particles beyond the ones humans had been studying for centuries, I didn't just find the same ones, I found a whole new rabbit hole. And I'm sick of finding rabbit holes. I don't want to keep chasing rabbits and losing my head.'

'Then stop looking,' she said, simply, too simply, almost shocking him. 'Focus on what you know and have.'

He buried his face into his hands. 'You don't understand. None of you ever understand.' He met her eyes. 'One day, you'll be gone, and I'll still be stuck as a stupid kid, aging in accordance with my cursed dance of reality.'

She placed a gentle hand on his back. His instincts wanted to shrug it off.

'You already change item with dusts,' she said, 'you will change with air. You just have to follow kinship rules you tell us. Maybe new dust has new rules.'

'Well,' he said, 'it doesn't. It has the same quark and antiquark tendencies.'

'Then it is another quark? An eighth?'

Ralph opened his mouth to respond, closed it. He'd been so focused on finding out the power of the new dusts, he hadn't even bothered to find out *what* they were.

'Piri,' he said, 'you're a genius.'

She raised an eyebrow.

'You're right,' he said. 'I don't know what these new dusts are. The monitor only registered them as *aberrant configurations*.'

A smile broke out across his face. He'd thought he was on track. Collect dust, use dust, bada bing, bada boom. But no.

'I've done this before,' he said. 'When I relied on science, I never thought to check if I'd missed anything. And I've just done it again. That's why I'm in this rut.'

She raised the other eyebrow. 'So, you will find another dust like you found rainbow?'

He laughed. 'I only found the rainbow dust because I gave up.'

'I understand,' she said, nodding. 'You will give up again and make more osmium cubes.'

He shook his head. 'No more cubes. No more dust. No more rabbit holes. I'm going to do what you said and focus on what I have.'

For the next few hours, Ralph read over old notes and textbooks from college. It'd been so long since he'd revised any of it, he was ashamed to find he'd forgotten even the most basic concepts.

Piri left at some point, returning with mint teas and a yawning Jamaki. They fell asleep on Cyclops's bed a short time later, their soft snoring filling the lab.

Day 431/51,549

When the first rays of light crept into the lab, Ralph, still hunched at the bench, came across a page from fourth-year physics. After reading the sentences he'd highlighted all those years ago, he jotted down some notes to refresh his memory:

- *Quarks are held together by the strong force (gluons).*
- *There are ~~six~~ seven types (flavours): up, down, top, bottom, strange, charmed, mercenary.*
- *There are three quark colours (properties): red, green, blue.*
- *There are three antiquark colours: anti-red, anti-green, anti-blue.*
- *Quarks and gluons entangle inside protons and neutrons near the speed of light, colliding, exchanging energy, forming new quarks/antiquarks.*
- *Quarks make up 1% of a proton/neutron's mass.*

His pen came to a standstill.

The rainbow dust was potent enough to warp objects. The obsidiary dust, even more so. But if quarks only comprised one percent of a proton and neutron's mass, what was the other ninety-nine?

'Energy,' he said.

'What?' Piri's tired voice came.

Ralph spun around, struck with a déjà vu moment from the time he'd turned to Cyclops to explain his scepticism with science.

'Gluons also make up a proton,' he said. 'And gluons are a force. An energy.' He spun back to the bench. 'How did I not see this before?'

Piri approached him, rubbing her eyes. 'What is a proton?'

He flicked to a fresh page. Drawing a vertical rectangle on the lefthand side, he pointed at it.

'This is a copper shard,' he said. He drew an arrow pointing from its right to a small circle. 'And this is an atom, a tiny thing containing energy and particles. Atoms make up the copper shard, you, me, this bench, this mountain.'

Piri looked from Ralph to the shelves of glass apparatus on the sandstone walls. 'Tiny circles make the world?'

'Sort of. Well, maybe. There's something about strings, but we won't get into that.' He drew another arrow beside the circle, followed by three smaller circles stacked atop one another. 'These are the three main particles that make up an atom.' He labelled each circle: Proton, Neutron,

Electron. 'The proton is positively charged. The neutron is neutrally charged. The electron is negatively charged.'

Piri furrowed her eyebrows.

Ralph drew two branching arrows from the proton and the neutron. 'These two particles are made of quarks, antiquarks, and energy. But the electron is a lepton, an elementary particle, which means it appears to be made of nothing else.'

Piri nodded. 'I remember. Elementary particles are quarks, leptons, and bosons.'

'Exactly.'

'So the new dust is—'

'Gluon energy,' he said. 'I think. Or transient quark-antiquark energy.' He pondered his statements. The latter seemed more likely. But voicing it sounded odd, confronting. 'Remember when I first showed you the stone and kiwifruit transference?'

'Of course. We talk about your magic all the time.'

'Remember how I said particles are always popping in and out of existence, too fast for us to see?'

She nodded.

'Well, that includes quarks. And as they pop out of existence, they leave a shadow. Or a stain. A trace. An unmonitorable remnant of erratic, powerful energy. I'm not sure. But it's like—'

He clicked his fingers, searching for the words. Piri's eyes locked onto his hand in amazement, as though she'd never seen such a gesture in her whole life.

He stopped clicking with a determined chop of an index finger. 'It's potential, Piri. It's possibility itself. The ivory and obsidian dusts have come from the briefest moment between the quarks and antiquarks popping out of existence.'

He laughed. He wasn't the only thing frozen in time. The captured energy also shared his fate.

'And this makes so much sense for the colour of the dusts too,' he said.

'Why they are black and white, you mean?'

He nodded. 'What happens when you combine a red, green, and blue light?'

'I have never done.'

'You get the colour of the sun,' he said. 'White. And what happens when you invert that?'

'Black?'

'Bingo. Which means the ivory dust could be the shadow of the quarks, and the obsidian dust the shadow of the antiquarks.'

Her eyes widened. 'So new dusts are not another quark. They are energy from when they leave and come back?'

'Yep. Pure, trapped energy. Exactly what Einstein solved all those years ago.'

'Who?'

Ralph flicked to a new page and scribbled one of the most famous equations known to humanity: $E = mc^2$.

'In the old world,' he said, 'everyone knew this equation. They mightn't have known what it meant, but they were familiar with it.'

'And what does it mean?'

'The E stands for energy. The m for mass. The c for the speed of light, which squaring makes for an astronomical number.'

She stared at the equation.

'Basically,' he continued, 'this equation says a small amount of matter can turn into a lot of energy, or a lot of energy can turn into a small amount of matter. It's this conservation of energy, this balance, that allows for a window to collect this remnant, transient energy.'

Piri smiled. 'You stopped energy and collected it?'

He returned the smile. 'I think so.'

'It is amazing, Ralph. You will fix life now? Bring back family?'

Ralph's mind danced with everything he'd told her.

'If I'm right,' he said, 'yes.'

He went on to explain how particles popping in and out of existence meant it was possible they travelled to another dimension in the interim.

'And if this is true, if I can figure out how to channel the quark energy, teleporting objects will be easy. Then the bigger question will become: Can I disrupt enough of my own particles to pop out of this dimension and into the one that makes sense?'

Day 437/51,555

After a week of theorising and planning in the shade by Cyclops's grave, on an evening when an icy wind whipped through the desert like a flock of silver gulls, a new phase of experimentation began.

Scalpel in hand, Ralph sliced long, thin lines into a wooden broom handle. Lacing the crevices with obsidiary dust, he sealed it with rainbow paste. He coiled a length of silver wire around the rod to boost conduction, then performed particle transference on it to turn the whole thing gold.

With the Adelaideans in Cyclops's bed, quilt pulled to their chins, Ralph began the show.

'Welcome,' he said, with an eccentric bow. 'Since obsidiary dust contains energy without direction and purpose, tonight I'll attempt to guide it, like a symphony conductor you probably have no idea about.'

Piri's eyes were fixed on Ralph. Jamaki was busy playing with the huntsman he'd caught yesterday. But Ralph didn't mind who listened or watched. He'd solved so much by himself, he barely expected any attention.

He raised the golden rod. 'Using this, I will channel my energy to disrupt the air particles around it. If all goes to plan, with one hand on this silver bar covered in obsidiary paste, I'll transfer it into the air, and teleportation will no longer be confined to science fiction.'

Piri clapped with glee. Jamaki realised he was missing out on something and copied her.

Ralph got into position.

What he was about to do made sense on paper. In the best-case, the experiment would work. In the worst-case, the potent energy would destroy him, the kids, the mountain.

'Here goes nothing,' he said.

Pointing the golden rod into the air, he placed a hand on the silver bar, gritted his teeth…

And a shiny shroud fell upon the world. He rubbed his eyes, peering through it.

His lab had changed. His textbooks were gone. The steel workbench was upside down. Pipes and valves made of a cobalt-blue metal laced the stonewalls, spraying steam. The Adelaideans were nowhere to be seen, replaced by swirls of dark mist and a domineering, sinister energy.

Ralph tried to make a break for the exit, but his feet felt like concrete.

'What do you want?' he said.

Three hooded figures morphed from the array of instruments and furniture in the lab. They stood over eight feet tall, wearing elegant, ashen cloaks draping to the ground.

'Who are you?' Ralph asked.

'You near answers, Ridley,' they said in baritone unison, voices reverberating.

A wind picked up from the floor, stirring dirt, paper, litter.

It was his imagination, he told himself. He was overworked, on the edge of a mental breakdown.

The wind grew and grew, engulfing the lab in its torment.

'The ancient dark energy equation is useless,' the hooded three said. 'It was merely a task given to Earth to change, to evolve. The same can be said about most things you've been pursuing, Ridley. But it is all for a purpose.'

Ralph found it difficult to tell if he was hallucinating or dreaming. 'What do you mean? What purpose?'

'Always remember, Ridley, all equations are concepts, like objects, like your mind. Your senses dictate reality.'

'I don't understand.'

'But there is a beyond. And at this beyond, there is no more seeking or doing, no more trying, achieving, or failing.'

'Just tell me what to do,' Ralph said, defeated. 'Tell me why you want me to suffer.'

'You do not need help, Ridley. You have arrived. Today is the beginning of it all. And I am proud.'

With a ripple of hot air, the hooded figures dissipated.

'Don't go,' Ralph said. 'Please.'

The golden rod dropped from his hand as a sparking trail of blue electricity splintered the air. He tracked it, blinked once, twice…

And awoke on the ground beside the shattered remains of the golden rod. Piri knelt beside him, wet cloth pressed to his forehead.

'Where did you go?' she asked.

Ralph took a moment to get his bearings.

'Look!' Jamaki said.

Perched on the steel workbench, the boy pointed at two strands of a thin, shimmering silver string, curling and hovering in defiance of gravity.

Ralph scrambled to his feet. 'Be careful.'

'Look like star,' Jamaki said. 'Shiny.'

Ralph nodded. 'They do.'

Below the strings, the silver bar sat, riddled with cracks like it suffered desert dehydration.

They stayed watching the silver strings until morning. By midday, more had joined them in the air. By afternoon, they'd merged into a silver clump. By evening, they'd slammed to the workbench.

Day 439/51,557

It took the silver bar two days to reform. By then, Ralph had practiced air transference on various items – a pen, a cucumber, an iron, a dead cockroach. Each time, the same chain of events had unfolded.

First, with the golden rod pointed at where he wanted the item to transfer, his energy was sapped.

Second, as the item fractured and flickered, he blacked in and out of consciousness.

Third, he felt the presence return and became aware of the tangible, tradeable energy of the universe.

Fourth, as ripples spread, air transference commenced.

Fifth, reality would stabilise, return.

Sixth, he'd find himself sore, hungry, and cotton-mouthed.

It was nowhere near a perfect technique. But who said teleportation was going to be easy?

10
Conglomeration Catastrophe

Day 536/51,654

THREE months into practicing air transference, Ralph was transferring objects to a few metres away, then a few hundred, all while strengthening his ability to withstand the energy demand.

Objects of all sizes, shapes, and genetic makeup became possible with his new transference. Nothing was too heavy, too light, too large, or too small. He could transfer feathers and gravel, rocks, metal, wood, dirt, drums of oil, hatchets, TVs, even strands of hair.

The Adelaideans watched on as he performed his experiments, laughing and clapping, delighting in the spectacle. Their attention made him feel warm on the inside, interesting, wanted, reminding him of circus shows from long ago.

Day 1304/53,422

Two years into practicing air transference, he'd mastered the technique. He'd reduced transfer times and energy demands, compiling thorough notes in the process:

1. *The denser the object, the longer the transfer.*
2. *The further the transfer, the longer the transfer.*
3. *The paste must cover at least 80% of the object.*
4. *The coiled golden rod is useful to direct/guide the process.*
5. *Practice (and patience) strengthens the nervous system and speeds up transfer rates.*

Day 1313/53,431

After more than a week of contemplation, confident with his capabilities, Ralph prepared to try transference on the most complex object he possessed.

Himself.

Like many famous scientists before him, he went all-in with his experiment.

He didn't bother painting himself with the paste. He didn't bother embedding more silver nodes into his body to boost conductivity. He simply waited for the Adelaideans to go to bed, then sprinkled a pinch of obsidiary dust into a beaker of distilled water, swirled it around, and downed it before it churned and bubbled.

With a golden rod in hand, he pointed at the other side of the lab. He focused his energy, his attention, ignoring the nausea arising.

It took a few minutes before anything happened. But when it did, it happened all at once.

As his senses faltered, strong, surging tingles spread through his body. A strange sensation of particles leaving him came next, followed by a lapsing in and out of consciousness until he no longer existed.

He had no idea how long this portion of air transference lasted. It seemed to stretch forever yet simultaneously exist as a blink, like being anesthetised.

Before he knew it, he was back, coherent, aware, and looking at a multitude of colourful lines hovering above the location he'd left.

Day 1345/53,463

As the day faded, Ralph and the Adelaideans huddled by the fire, snow jackets zipped to their noses. The icy breeze rolling in from the south trembled the mesa's sparse, shrivelled shrubbery.

'I'm not sure how long I'll be gone,' Ralph said, attaching the pot above the flames. 'Maybe a week or two.'

He planned to visit every capital city, rounding up everyone interested and versed in maths and science. If possible, he would bring them back to the mountain to study the dusts with him. While his priority was to solve his time dilemma, he was also open to beginning work on a spaceship to head to Proxim.

'Where will you go first?' Piri asked.

'East to Canberra,' he said. 'Then Sydney, Brisbane, Darwin. The more north I go, I should have better luck finding people where it's warmer. And who knows, maybe I'll come across an entire establishment of scientists studying the best ways to get humanity through the predicted century of frigidity.'

It felt risky leaving the safety of the mountain. For all he knew, the remaining humans had turned savage and would love to devour a boy and harvest his silver nodes.

'Do you have enough food?' Piri asked.

Ralph opened his backpack. Inside, he'd packed a sleeping bag, two bottles of water, a notepad and pen, the coordinates device he'd found at the launch facility, a golden rod, a tungsten microfilament sack filled with rainbow dust, and a black diamond sack filled with obsidiary dust. He also had two steel containers loaded with food the Adelaideans had prepared, one filled with dried fruit, the other with a mixture of lamb and rabbit jerky.

'Plenty,' he said. 'If I run out, I'll forage or come home early.'

Jamaki came forward, cerulean cicada held out in his gloved hand. 'Hurry back.'

Ralph took the cicada, pocketed it, then wrapped his arms around Jamaki.

'I'll try,' Ralph said. 'Australia's a lot bigger than you might think. But my particle transference should make the journey easier.'

Jamaki stepped back. Ralph's stomach twisted as the boy's eyes turned glassy.

'You are like a sailor,' Piri said.

Ralph smiled. She was right. Preparing to set off on a voyage in search of people, gambling his life on the mathematics and science of what he'd solved, was exactly what they'd once done.

'Will you guys be okay?' he asked.

Piri shrugged. 'We are fine by ourselves.'

'I know. Your connection to the land has given you survival skills I've never bothered to hone.'

Jamaki stepped closer to Piri. She put an arm around his shoulders.

Ralph looked between them. Was he really about to leave the only two people he knew on an evacuated, empty planet?

'How about a quick transference while we wait for the water to boil?' Ralph asked.

The Adelaideans traded glances, exchanging words Ralph knew implied excitement.

'To the river and back?' he asked.

Jamaki clapped his hands. 'Yes!'

Placing a pinch of obsidiary dust under his tongue, Ralph pointed the golden rod towards the river. He closed his eyes, focusing on the imprint of it in his mind, channelling his energy.

In one moment, he was thinking. In the next, everything collapsed.

Plasma and radiation replaced reality. Nothingness replaced everythingness. Everythingness replaced nothingness.

The uncomfortable portion of the transfer came next, where he saw things, heard things, smelled, felt, and tasted things. But it all seemed muffled, masked, warped, as though he observed reality from inside a soundproof glass box.

And then, he was back, standing on the other side of the river, watching the kids leap across the rocks to greet him.

Now a foot taller and two years older since climbing into his truck, they knelt in front of him like a captivated audience. Their attention and love for him was unparalleled. Other than his sister, he'd never had anyone treat him like they did, even when he'd been at the height of his fame.

'Another?' Ralph asked.

They nodded eagerly.

With the previous dose of obsidiary dust still tingling his body, he pointed the golden rod at a group of trees to the north. Closing his eyes, maintaining the visual imprint, he thought about their trunks and dying branches, the gentle creaking noise they made after the cold had sucked the life from them.

His awareness collapsed.

And then he was back again, standing amongst the gums.

He turned to the mountain, his home. The faint glow of the fire boiling the water for their tea flickered away on the mesa. The Adelaidean silhouettes beside it told him the transference had taken a little longer than usual. But that didn't matter. Ever since he'd come into the world, time had been elusive.

He took a deep breath in, eyes on the stars overhead, feeling free, content. How his life had changed in the past two years both astounded and unsettled him. Never would he have thought it'd start to make sense.

He had some cool tricks up his sleeve, two kids who enjoyed his company, a farm full of animals, and enough items and lines of thinking to experiment for centuries. He'd never felt more secure. Or happy. It was almost like everything was telling him to stop, to be still, to no longer worry about fixing his curse.

But he wasn't naïve enough to accept such a calling. It was a lie, a trick. The Adelaideans wouldn't be around forever. Much like Stephanie, Max, and Cyclops, they too would move on or pass away.

It was only a matter of time.

He looked to the sky, to the south, locating the Alpha Centauri system. He tried imagining what everyone was doing on the Seven Ships heading there. How far away were they? How many had chosen to roam and enjoy the luxurious, white-walled rooms and halls he'd seen in the videos at the launch facility, rather than existing in hibernation?

Not too many, he decided. Unlike him, the peculiar human who didn't age alongside regular cell deterioration, some humans had always been obsessed with youth. With a choice between staying awake or entering hibernation preservation for the forty trillion-kilometre trip, he doubted many would've actually selected the former.

'One day,' he said, eyes on the Alpha Centauri system, 'I'll come see you all.'

He scanned the rest of the sky. Without light pollution from nearby cities tainting it, blinking dots of every luminosity filled every centimetre. The Milky Way streaked through the centre of it all, its gases, colours, and twinkles unwinding his mind.

Despite being in the desert for so long, it'd been a rarity to stop and reflect, to gaze at the immensity of the cosmos beyond. Its billions upon billions of stars, more than all the grains of sand on all the beaches on Earth, each of them lightyears away, each existing as a window in time, a remnant from a younger universe, offered more possibilities than quantum mechanics itself.

For every star, how many planets surrounded it? What kind of planets? Sand planets? Snow planets? Forest, lava, city planets? Did those planets have life? What kind of life? Did they also create art, read books, study science?

How big was the universe anyway? How far away was its edge? What did that even mean? How could there be an edge if it was forever expanding thanks to the Cosmological Arrow?

He felt the shift before it happened. He saw the blink of a blue aura before it surrounded him. He felt the tingles spread before he'd had enough time to abort.

In one moment, he stood amongst the dying gumtrees. In the next, he hovered hundreds of metres above the ground, surrounded by a glowing, translucent blue sphere, similar to a hamster ball.

His mind ticked, danced, dove. He held his breath, unsure how this had happened, unsure *what* had happened, frightened by the sheer height of his altitude.

'No,' he said. 'No.'

He scanned the landscape for the mountain. He spotted the tiny flicker of the fire on the mesa. He pointed the golden rod, closed his eyes, and…

Nothing happened. Nothing changed. No tingles spread. He remained hovering in the blue bubble, surrounded by the dark of the night.

He cursed himself for not returning after the first river transference. Why had he been so stupid?

He touched the glowing, blue thing surrounding him. It sparked, tracing polygons across its translucent surface.

He inhaled sharply.

What was this blue bubble? How was it suspending him in the air? Had the lab invader done this to him?

He shook his head. He didn't have time to think. He'd think back in his lab, safe, warm, drinking tea with the Adelaideans.

He took out the black diamond sack of obsidiary dust from his backpack. Placing a fresh pinch under his tongue, he squeezed his fists as the nodes brightened.

Fixating on the glow of the fire far below, he pointed the golden rod at it and closed his eyes.

The tingles spread. The vibrations encircled him.

But again, nothing happened.

He opened his eyes, clenched his jaw, thrashed, yelled, swore.

This wasn't fair. This wasn't right. He needed to get back to the kids, the farm, the lab. His life. And he needed to do it before the bubble collapsed and sent him plummeting to his demise.

He turned on the spot, hoping to locate someone or something.

But no one was in the sky. Nothing was. No birds. No planes. No helicopters or hot air balloons. Not anymore.

He looked up and instantly regretted it.

As his body recompiled, he found himself higher than before, high above the clouds, higher than the planes of the past once travelled.

He cursed and squirmed, screamed. He tried swimming to the ground. He tried folding himself into a cannonball as though jumping into a pool.

But nothing worked. Nothing helped him descend or transfer. Nothing helped him feel like things would ever be okay again.

A thought struck him, a revelation: He'd been an idiot to meddle with so much energy.

'Shut up,' he told his brain. 'Shut up, shut up, shut up.'

He yelled at his surroundings, at the lab invader, at the three hooded figures in cloaks.

'Why are you doing this to me?'

No response came. The air around him remained still, silent, stress-inducing.

He tried calming himself, closing his eyes, thinking about the mountain, the river, the gumtree he used to sit under with Cyclops…

The tingling came. His heartrate climbed. He began lapsing in and out of consciousness.

It was working! Things were going to be okay.

He reformed on the edge of the atmosphere, snug between the firmament and the dark void of space.

His mouth fell open. He shivered. His stomach lurched at the scenery, at the stretches of sand and rocky terrains, the greenery, the oceans. The sun peeking to the side reminded him of something he'd seen in movies a hundred times before. But being on the edge of Earth, on the shore of the cosmic ocean, was nothing like a movie, and nothing close to comforting or breathtaking.

It was terrifying.

The blue bubble aura dimmed, vibrated. It was failing. He didn't have long.

He tried getting his bearings, turning on the spot.

Go home, Ralphie, he told himself. Go home.

Please.

He focused on the land below…

But no tingles spread, no consciousness dipped. He tried transferring a few metres forward, but something seemed to deny his movement, his re-entry, like some sort of glass barrier or shield.

He refreshed his dose of obsidiary dust, focusing his energy and intention.

'Please,' he said.

The transference began.

When he returned, he found himself further from his mountain home than ever before, as though the invisible barrier had repelled him, reflecting him into the far reaches of space.

But how? But why?

He swore again, spinning on the spot, stopping as a sphere of dull, grey-white rock riddled with craters came into view. He rubbed his eyes, taking in the enormous, metal docking gantry beside it, the same one he'd seen in the designs for the Seven Ships.

The Moon?

The Moon?

He'd just travelled almost 400,000 kilometres in the blink of an eye?

How?

He wanted to hurl. He wanted to cry. He wanted Stephanie to rescue him. But the more he squirmed, the more he lost grasp of his emotions and reality.

The safety of Earth, gone. His life, falling apart. His mind, on the verge of implosion.

And none of it made sense.

He tried thinking about home. He tried envisioning the mountain. He tried concentrating on decompiling his particles, one by one.

When he reformed, he found himself inside a tornado of hissing, angry dust soaring at him from all directions.

He flung his arms about, swiping at the dust. He covered his face, squeezing his mouth shut to prevent it from entering him.

But it was futile. The angry dust breached the gaps in his defence, striking him until all he could do was curl up like a little baby and whimper.

He cursed his stupidity. He cursed his greed. He cursed his arrogance.

His punishment for tampering with reality was complete. He never should've abused air transference. It wasn't magic. It wasn't a toy. It was science. And now, because of his idiocy, here he was, lost in a sea of particles, alone in the unknown without a clue about how to get home.

Part II: Into Space

'The more I examine the universe and the
details of its architecture, the more evidence I
find that the universe in some sense must have
known we were coming.'

Freeman John Dyson

11

Energy Pockets

LACERATIONS peppered Ralph's body as the buzzing whirlwind of particles continued to strike him. He felt blood leaving his body. He felt death calling.

How had this happened? Why had this happened? He'd had everything on Earth. His mountain. His sketchpads. His equipment. The animals. The Adelaideans.

He should've known he couldn't mess with matter and not face the consequences.

But no. He couldn't see that far. He'd been blinded, hellbent on his pursuit. He'd let greed take over. Arrogance. He'd let his obsession, his distraction, his vice, consume him, like evil consumed the weak.

He'd sacrificed everything to solve something that was supposed to help. But in the end, it didn't, it couldn't, it only led him to another dead end in the labyrinth. As a result, Earth had ejected him, thrown him into the void with nothing but a backpack and a peculiar blue bubble aura surrounding him.

Curled up in a ball, arms shielding his face, he peered through the debris.

Nothing but the cosmos — deep space — sat beyond. Stars of all luminosity and hue filled every portion. The Milky Way scratched the centre of it all like a stroke of faint, white paint, comforting him in this nightmare, telling him he hadn't gone too far from home.

He turned on the spot, hoping for relief from the onslaught of dust and rocks.

He wasn't quite so lucky. But he did glimpse a blip of light breaking

85

through the painful fuzz.

His mind raced. The Sun? A satellite? A spaceship? A supernova? Whatever it was, he wasn't close enough to see or feel its heat properly.

If it was the Sun, he could use it to locate Mercury, Venus, then Earth, and he'd be home before the kids had prepared breakfast. And if it turned out to be something else, maybe it would still be useful.

He took out the black diamond sack from his back pocket. Sprinkling a pinch of obsidiary dust under his tongue, he clenched his fists as the silver nodes in his arms flashed and flickered. His body erupted with tingles, sending a surge of energy outwards, brightening the blue bubble aura, deterring the debris.

As the rocks transitioned to fine grains of sand, softened, concluded, he refocused on the blip of light. Without the particles berating him now, its shape became more apparent, its distance became more coherent.

It was the Sun!

There, in all its glory, it hovered in the otherwise infinite wasteland.

He could barely believe what he was looking at. And how.

In the blink of an eye, his life had become some sort of science fiction horror film. He had no idea where he was, which way was up, or which way was down. He had no idea what the blue bubble aura was, or how it protected him from the vacuum of space, the cold of space, the radiation, or even the Sun's beams.

He had no idea about anything anymore. It felt like being stranded in the middle of the ocean at night, with no land or boats in sight.

If he was on Earth, he would've been able to figure things out. He would've been able to use the Sun to determine his location. And not just because of its light, or knowing how far away it was and how its rays took eight minutes to arrive, due to the speed of light being close to 300,000 kilometres per second.

He would've been able to because Earth's trusty ornament in the sky did more than illuminate. It acted as a perfect marker, a waypoint, governing, guiding, and providing life with a way to orient alongside its eastward rising and westward setting.

But out here, in space, the Sun didn't look or act or feel like it looked or acted or felt on Earth. It seemed smaller, weaker, providing nothing more than a disingenuous, almost conniving, sense of direction.

He shook himself from his reverie, adding these thoughts to the story he would tell Piri and Jamaki later.

Raising his golden rod, he pointed it at the Sun. Closing his eyes, the tingles spread, the transference—

He snapped his eyes open in horror.

What if he transferred too close to the Sun? What if he transferred directly into its core, where nuclear fusion took place at over 15 million °C? Or what if he overshot his mark and ended up in interstellar space?

Goosebumps spread down his spine at the thought. He couldn't let that happen.

He adjusted his aim a little to the left of the bright blip of hope, focusing on a spot, imprinting it.

The bubble aura shifted, sparked. His consciousness collapsed.

When his mind returned, slivers of indigo had bled into the translucent blue bubble.

He looked over his shoulder, locating the blip further than it'd been before the transference.

He swore into the vacuum. Now where was he?

He'd already passed the Moon when he'd first been ejected, so he had to be further than that. Maybe he was closer to Mars and its two moons, Phobos and Deimos. Or maybe he was near the asteroid belt, remnants of a destroyed planet or one Jupiter's gravity had never allowed to form.

Jupiter. The King of the Planets. If anything could work as a reference point to find Earth, it had to be the giant, gaseous red planet with its ninety-plus moons.

He spun on the spot.

But what were Jupiter's coordinates? Where would he wait to watch it soar by?

He sighed.

Despite Jupiter being large enough to fit a thousand Earths inside, despite its dazzling display of swirling, colourful gases, finding it would be equivalent to finding a marble in the Pacific Ocean. If only it'd absorbed more matter when the Solar System had first formed. Then it would've been heavier. Then it would've undergone thermonuclear reactions. Then it would've radiated its own light, and he would've been able to use it and the Sun to navigate home.

A realisation struck him: the coordinates device!

He flung the backpack off his shoulders, dug inside, and pulled out the gadget.

Switching it on, he waited for it to boot up. When it had, an array of letters, numbers, and symbols, scrambled at first, locked into place across the main LCD screen:

$$13.92\text{AU} / 2.201\text{e}^{-4}\text{ly} / 6.748\text{e}^{-5}\text{pc} \mid 22\text{h } 27.24\text{m } 05.35\text{s} + 11° \; 49' \; 0.02'$$

Below, the second screen displayed another confusing readout:

$$\text{SS}8.3(15°\alpha12.6)1\text{b}[3.10(15\pm5°)25.3]25\gamma(9.10^{25})6.18_1\text{MW}$$

He stared at the mumbo jumbo, dumbfounded.

SS? Solar System? MW? Milky Way? Maybe. But what about the numbers? The top row told him his distance from something. But what?

He cursed his Solar System ignorance. At most, he knew the planets and their moons. He could recite each in order, their rough distances from the Sun, their aesthetics. He knew their orbital periods, from Mercury's 88 days to Neptune's 165 years. He even knew Sedna's, the dwarf planet with an orbital period of over 11,000 years. But how would any of that help while floating out in the nothingness, as though suspended by cables in an empty, darkened auditorium?

He let the coordinates device drop from his hand. It floated to his feet, exited the bubble's base, before reappearing above to repeat the cycle. He let it do this a few more times before snatching it and shoving it into his backpack with anxious, frustrated urgency.

Now what?

He took a deep breath in, out. He had to relax. Being unhinged in space wouldn't help him figure out how to get home.

He scanned his surroundings. Without Earth's atmosphere and pollution, the stars shone more vividly, more surreal. Every shade of colour within the constellations and nebulae seemed more distinct upon the black backdrop. The spectacle resembled something like terror laced with an emptiness. But hidden inside it, he sensed freedom, possibility.

If he couldn't get home, what if he headed into the void? What if he chased down the Ships travelling to Alpha Centauri? What if he journeyed to another galaxy and discovered a civilisation with science or technology that helped break him free from his time dilemma?

Where there is quantum theory, there is hope.

The phrase that'd ruined his life came like a shy reminder.

Finding himself in space was the worst thing to ever happen. But could he use this blunder to his advantage?

Turning his back on the blip of light, he faced the infinite.

He was being stupid. He knew this. The mad scientist within was taking things too far this time. But he'd already come this far…

He studied the 360-degree view of the cosmos. His brain barely fathomed what he was looking at. But the longer he gazed at it, the more his eyes adjusted to the wonder and the beauty, the spectacle, and the faster something familiar caught his eyes.

Pleiades, a star cluster more than 400 lightyears away, burning bright and blue.

He didn't know too much about the cluster. He knew it existed in the Taurus constellation. He knew its brighter stars were named after Atlas's daughters. But such facts seemed trivial compared to the possibility and wonder of witnessing it with his own eyes. Even if his blue bubble aura disintegrated the moment it came into view.

He pointed his golden rod at Pleiades.

This was it. No more safety. No more mountain. No more comfortable routine of planning in the shade and experimenting by night.

He focused on the blue stars, imprinting them in his mind.

The tingles spread. The transference began.

He reformed in a different kind of darkness. Other than a few stars blinking in the distance, nothing surrounded him. No blip of hope. No constellations. No Milky Way backdrop.

No Pleiades.

An existential crisis begged to arise. But he denied it.

He may have just blasted through the Oort Cloud, past the wormhole the Ships were heading to, travelling further than anything humankind had ever created, including Voyager 2. But with more than 100 billion galaxies in the universe, he'd eventually come across someone or something. Wouldn't he?

He pointed the rod at the distant stars and transferred again.

He was in self-destruction mode. But he didn't care. He would wait until safe on a planet or moon before indulging in a meltdown.

He reformed and transferred again. And again.

With no reference point of where he was going, with no true consideration of what he was doing, no rising or setting sun, no kids singing in the farm, no Cyclops trotting to bed, he transferred over and over again for an unknown amount of time.

With every decompiling and recompiling, everything he'd worked on became more of a distant memory. It was like he was pushing everything into the past with bitter resentment. He may have felt alone on the mountain before the kids arrived. But out here, his loneliness had reached a whole new level.

After more than thirty transferences, he recompiled a few million kilometres away from two stars, binary stars, each varying in size, colour, and luminosity. The larger one was yellow, vibrant. The smaller, pale blue one churned as it leeched life from its bigger brother.

Although Ralph was close enough for their light to blind him, the bubble aura continued filtering out any damaging rays. As a result, he was free to admire their aesthetics, studying their pulsing glows, their roiling surfaces.

Were there planets surrounding these stars?

He transferred closer.

Was there life?

He transferred closer. And closer. And closer still. With every transference, he felt his energy wane. It was like the hungry, blue star also extracted his own life essence, provoking a sensation that typically came seconds before vomiting.

He ceased transference.

His nodes slowed, faltered. The bubble aura changed again as more indigo devoured the blue, bringing whispers of violet and burgundy into the mix.

He furrowed his brow. He didn't want to think about science at a time like this. But such a drastic change proved difficult to ignore.

Stop thinking, he told himself. Keep moving.

He transferred away from the binary stars four times.

As he reformed, all violet disappeared from the bubble, replaced by a maroon streaked with scarlet.

He shook his head. Whatever the thing keeping him warm and oxygenated was doing, it reminded him too much of the Doppler effect, where blue was associated with things moving closer, and red was associated with things moving away.

Was the bubble aura trying to tell him something? What would it be trying to tell him? That he was moving away from Earth? From Proxim?

Refreshing his obsidiary dust, he transferred back the way he'd come.

When his consciousness returned, the scarlet in the bubble vanished.

He transferred again in the same direction six more times, observing how the maroon shifted through the colour spectrum, from purple to indigo and back to blue.

'Impossible,' he said.

But was a thought like that even allowed anymore?

Out of curiosity, he transferred to his left, again and again. It wasn't long before the blue aura became tinged with violets and reds.

He backtracked until the blue returned, then tried another direction.

He continued chasing the blue and avoiding the red, as though playing a game of Marco Polo.

Twenty-something transfers later, he arrived on the edge of an orange vapour. Like the air before a summer storm, it felt damp, humid. It spread for thousands of kilometres, millions, filling his view in every direction. Clumps of dark and bright white gases specked throughout it. In its centre, a trio of stars spun, uniform in size and colour, reminding him of moon-sized macadamia nuts.

He watched the hypnotic motion of the stars, trying to comprehend what was happening to him. The longer he did, the more he noticed fragments of colours hidden inside the vapour, like one big cloud of rainbow dust.

He knew of the Orion Nebula, a star factory made by a supernova. Could this be another one? Were the pockets of gas new stars? If so, what star died to make this factory? How long ago?

He transferred closer.

Inside the vapour, he gained a better view of the macadamia stars. Grandiose and volatile, they orbited one another with great speed, scattering the colour fragments like puzzle pieces. Each time the trio of stars disturbed a curl of colour, the vapour slowed, opening spots void of any light.

He transferred again.

Reforming, his blood vessels throbbed in his temples, his brain, down to his feet. He gritted his teeth, squeezing his head with both hands.

He'd done it again. His greed had ruined everything!

He closed his eyes, tried transferring away. But something stopped him, pulled on him, spoke to him, bringing an alienlike dose of knowledge he didn't know what to do with.

He snapped his eyes open as a new clarity came over him. The bubble aura glittered a brilliant sapphire, as though prompting and encouraging him.

He located a vacant spot in the vapour and transferred towards it, without the rod, without refreshing the dust, without even closing his eyes.

As he recompiled, he found himself inside a haze of oscillating tones and vibrations.

He transferred again, following the calling.

While he held no imprint in his mind, while he had no idea what lay ahead, what trap, what possibilities, the pockets of energy held an intention, a desire, and he didn't mind complying.

As he decompiled and recompiled through the oscillating, humming haze, he travelled deeper through the universe. He passed patches of blinding light and suffocating darkness. He passed planets, moons, stars, clumps of unexplainable contortions. He spotted barrel and spiral galaxies, nebulae.

Every time he came out close to a celestial body or congregation of energy, time ran slower, his mind and movements were delayed. Every time he came out in the middle of nowhere, time ran faster, and the more enjoyment for this freedom he had.

This was what being a human was all about – exploring, venturing, discovering, living the life of a nomad. It felt great.

But it didn't last long.

When the pockets of energy ran out, he recompiled near a colossal metal structure made of nine discs stacked atop one another. A rod penetrated their centres, blossoming golden lightning from each end, encasing the structure in a sphere, similar to a plasma ball.

Although he wanted nothing to do with the structure, its magnetic pull told him he had no say in the matter.

12

The Stack

RALPH cursed all the movies he'd grown up watching. No matter how many he'd consumed, none had prepared him for such a sight. To find a metal oasis floating in the middle of nowhere, like an abandoned space station following a virus outbreak, was incomprehensible. But it was his reality.

Still a few hundred kilometres from the stack of discs, its magnetism was strong. Its energy was robust, enveloping. It flickered his nodes. It interacted with his blue bubble aura, illuminating the polygons in an erratic fashion.

As he moved closer to the structure against his will, he gained a better view of the nine discs. Each seemed to span the size of six football stadiums. No buildings were present on them. No forestry. No mountains, deserts, snowfields, or oceans.

Two hundred kilometres out, he spotted a black maelstrom, flaring and swirling nearby. Half the size of one of the discs, it glowed with a subtle, amber corona. Dark, gaseous tentacles reached from its outer edges, interacting with the structure's golden lightning and the lilac, luminous nebula acting as its backdrop.

Ralph averted his eyes. Something about the maelstrom unnerved him. It reminded him of the ancient Evil Eye, something that tempted then devoured, while also telling him how much he'd screwed up in life.

He returned his attention to the discs. Drawn closer, they seemed to multiply, stretching and contracting in each direction like an accordion.

Was it an illusion? Was his mind imploding? How delirious, hungry, and overworked was he?

One hundred kilometres out, buildings came into view. Bunched in groups of twelve, twenty, and thirty-two, they were curved in design and varied in shades of copper. None peaked higher than ten floors. Other than a few stragglers, most occupied one quadrant of each disc.

How far away was this place from Earth? Had humans known about these discs? Had humans built them? If so, why had they kept it a secret? If not, who or what owned them?

His peripherals caught movement to his left.

More blue bubbles heading for the structure.

More bubbles?

His heartrate climbed. Other bubbles meant other people. But who? And why? Had they also been ejected from Earth? Had they also used particle transference to get here?

He didn't like thinking about any of that. It seemed to cheapen everything he'd ever thought about, solved, endured.

He went after the bubbles. He didn't even need to try to transfer. As he willed it, the energy of the stack of discs provided enough flux to begin the decompiling.

As he reformed, the intricacies of each disc became visible.

Made of a harmonious combination of bronzes and silvers, they were far more beautiful than what they'd appeared hundreds of kilometres out. Their surfaces were etched with thin, spiralling patterns, which looped towards the central rod like a mandala. Their perimeters were lined with statues of various creatures, including ones with wings and weapons.

A part of him wanted to be hesitant about approaching the discs. But their energy continued to call to him, calming him, telling him exactly where he needed to go.

He looked at the third disc from what he perceived to be the bottom. Focusing on its curved, gleaming surface, he began the transference.

Recompiling, the bubble aura vanished, leaving him floating in the void, a few metres from the edge.

Before he had time to freak out though, the structure drew him forward between two twelve-foot, metal statues. One resembled a reptilian hawk, its beak and talons sharp and authoritative. The other was a mix between an upright echidna and a trilobite, its snarl unreadable, its paws placid.

Ralph touched down on the disc's metal surface. A pulse reverberated through him like a heartbeat – deep, heavy, revitalising. It entered the soles of his feet, travelled up his body, exiting the crown of his head. It brought knowledge he didn't know what to do with, telling him he was in a place projected by his mind, while assuring him he was meant to be here.

Another beat. It spread through him, up, out.

A flash of fluttering gold streaked past. He jerked back to avoid it, but it hit him square in the sternum.

'Get off me,' he said, swiping at it with a reactive hand as it made its way to his right shoulder.

'*Ah, yes,*' a voice came, as cryptic and jumbled as he remembered from his cave-lab. '*The splinter sparrow chose you this time.*'

Ralph wheeled around, looking for the voice. 'Where are you?'

But there was no use in looking or asking.

It was already gone.

Another beat – deep, monotone, invigorating.

The golden thing on his shoulder ignited like a lantern. Sending a sonar wave of shine outwards in four-second intervals, it illuminated the world around him.

Ralph took in the scenery.

The bronze buildings looked ancient, perhaps millions of years old, maybe even billions. Zigzagging metal poles connected them, like a network of spiderwebs. The roads and paths, much like the buildings, were polished to perfection.

For a place of such grandeur, such beauty, clearly built for an entire civilisation, it was strange how empty it was.

Another beat – warm, nourishing, cleansing.

The lantern thing on his shoulder enhanced its sonar shine. Sending it out in shorter, slower intervals, creatures came into view, like phantoms appearing in the night.

There were tall creatures, short creatures, round and spaghetti ones, blobs made of goo. Some floated. Some had big eyes. Some had no eyes. Some didn't even have heads.

As the sonar shine pulsed and spread around Ralph, the creatures flashed in and out of existence like particles. If he concentrated on any of them long enough, they remained in his awareness. But as soon as he looked elsewhere, they were gone.

His instincts screamed out, telling him to be afraid of where he was and what he was witnessing. But the calming energy of the discs counteracted.

'Look at the sparrow.'

A new voice, reassuring, controlled.

Ralph scanned the area, waiting for the pulsing shine to illuminate its owner. But differentiating between the horde of unknown creatures blinking in and out of existence was borderline impossible.

'Which one are you?' he asked.

'Look at the sparrow.'

Ralph stepped out of the way of a barrel-chested, thin-limbed plastic creature sliding past too close for comfort.

'Look,' the voice said.

Ralph looked at his shoulder. Resting there, just as the voice had called it, was a sparrow. It was just like one from Earth, only golden, shiny, and as tiny as a pebble, and unlike anything he'd ever seen before. It chirped in greeting, before narrowing its sonar shine to a few metres away.

Ralph tracked the beam to a six-foot creature with four legs and two arms, standing like a lunar module. Clad in a black and white robe covered in a sprinkling of bronze glitter, their ears were as large as their hands. Their legs were as long as Ralph's body. They had skin like him. They had hair and eyebrows like him. But they weren't human. A hybrid? Maybe. A failed experiment? Possibly. Something from a horror film?

'Who are you?' Ralph asked, stepping backwards.

The creature smiled. 'I am Ca'zehro. Do not worry, I am not going to hurt you.'

Famous last words, Ralph thought. But the stack of discs told him he needn't be afraid.

'Where am I?'

Ca'zehro maintained his polite smile, studying Ralph like a parent who'd caught him stealing from a cookie jar. His eyes moved to the silver nodes embedded in Ralph's arms.

'Curious,' he said. 'You are early in your journey if you are still asking questions.'

A passing creature entered the visual field the splinter sparrow created with its beam. It faded in and out in a flash.

'What do you mean, "early in my journey"?' Ralph asked. 'I'm supposed to know what this place is?'

'Where are you headed?' Ca'zehro asked.

Ralph was stunned by the question. 'I'm… I'm not going anywhere. I was drawn here after Earth discarded me.'

'Then why are you here?'

Ralph shrugged, searching his mind for an adequate answer. 'I was trying to figure out who or what had messed with my life. Then the energy pockets in the star factory… Wait.'

He flung his backpack off and took out the coordinates device. Firing it up, the previous displays scrolled into position, flickered, split, scrolled to new ones.

$$\sim\!1.094e^{12}\text{AU} \ / \ \sim\!17.3\text{Mly} \ / \ \sim\!5.30\text{Mpc} \ | \ 01\text{h } 0\text{m } 0.88\text{s} \pm -01° \ 11' \ 0.08'$$
$$\text{TD-}\Delta0651\text{-}0661\text{-}0387\text{-}0888\varphi\text{-}0690^{b}\text{-}0301\text{-OD}$$

He studied the screens. The top row told him he was further from Earth than before. But the uncertainty in the readings confused him. As for the bottom row, he tried identifying something recognisable or significant. But he came away with nothing, not a clue, not an inkling.

'Why are you here?' Ca'zehro repeated.

Ralph returned the device to his backpack, taking in the enormity of the place. The sparrow shifted its sonar shine, enhancing and dispersing it to provide him with a better view.

'I guess it'd help if I knew where here was.'

'Here has many names,' Ca'zehro said, simply. 'Many creatures speak of it differently. Some call it Sterquilinis. Some call it Nibavu. But most like you refer to it as Exadosa.'

Ralph's hope amplified. 'Most like me? There are other humans here?'

Ca'zehro's expression resembled a teacher instructing a clueless student. 'We have had them before, yes. But you are the last.'

'What? When were they here? Where are they now? Is that who was in the other bubbles?'

Ca'zehro waved a hand through the air, clearly uninterested in so many questions. 'Human is a concept. An idea. Your life energy is the same as most. But it seems by tampering with your body you have attained an early, yet intriguing arrival.'

Ralph's head hurt. 'What do you mean? I'm a human from Earth and my name is Ralph Ridley.'

'Was.'

Ralph didn't know what to say to that. His thoughts spun; his angst rose. 'I don't get it. Why am I here then? Why did that blue bubble aura make me come? There must be a reason.'

Ca'zehro furrowed his brow, pondering. 'Indeed, you are early in your journey. The bubble you refer to is the will of this place. Only those who are ready to come can see it.'

Ralph's emotions, as suppressed as they were, wanted to scream and shout. Standing on a stack of discs, surrounded by strange creatures, showed just how pointless his life had been. Earth, his sister, his job at the university, his cave-lab, Piri, Jamaki, Cyclops, all the research he'd done, all the experimentation, all the worrying about science leading him wrong – everything had been annihilated, like a particle in an osmium cube.

'You don't understand,' Ralph said, shaking his head. 'I'm not supposed to be here. This was never supposed to happen. I was on Earth. I was solving things with science. I never even considered heading into space to solve my time dilemma.'

'You call out here space, Ralph Ridley? That is interesting. Do you not think it is teeming with life and possibility?'

Ralph was frustrated by Ca'zehro's calm tangent. 'I don't know! I don't even understand how we are communicating.'

'That is simple. All energy has the same origin. The energy of this place bypasses and filters any noise accumulated since the beginning, allowing for a seamless trading. With practice, with intention, with focus, one can do such a thing anywhere if one wishes to.'

Every word Ca'zehro spoke made sense. But the meaning behind his sentences escaped Ralph.

'Well,' Ralph said, 'it feels like limbo here.'

Ca'zehro nodded. 'Some say that.'

'Purgatory.'

'You may call it what you want.' Ca'zehro's tone reminded Ralph of an underpaid post office worker. 'You are only here because it is where all must go.'

'Is the thing that ruined my life here?'

The creature seemed indifferent. 'Everything is nothing and nothing is everything.'

'But that doesn't answer my question.'

Ca'zehro stepped closer to Ralph. 'You were always meant to come here, Ralph Ridley. Do not be angry. Do not be spiteful at my words. Simply enjoy, for this place is outside of time.'

Ralph swallowed, unsure if he'd heard him correctly. 'Outside of time?'

For a brief microsecond, the four-legged creature flashed, triplicated.

'Yes,' he said, his body stabilising in Ralph's perception. 'Where time stands still.'

13
Where Time Stands Still

LIVING outside of time proved to be a strange experience.

As the Cosmological Arrow ticked, light spread, worlds were birthed, life was synthesised. But on the Stack, none of this happened. Sleep didn't beckon. Hunger didn't pang. Life was not created nor destroyed.

Time standing still froze everything. It was like standing in the centre of all centres, watching things shift, expand, grow, implode, explode.

'If time stands still here,' Ralph said, 'how do I know I exist?'

Ca'zehro smiled. 'A better question to ask is, why do you believe existence is only predicated by time?'

The gold lightning from the Stack's central rod sparked and laced, encapsulating the structure. Its tendrils reached into the cosmos, trading energy with the lilac fog.

'How long have I been here?' Ralph asked.

'That is not the right question to ask.'

They were heading down the main street for the art gallery. Small, domed homes, like igloos, lined the polished, bronze street. The taller, curved buildings dwarfed them, reaching to the disc above.

The splinter sparrow, still nesting on Ralph's shoulder, maintained its steady sonar, providing light for his surroundings.

'Why do you not have one?'

Ca'zehro looked at the sparrow. 'I do not have to be limited. Not anymore.'

'Limited?'

'The sparrow stops you from being overwhelmed, Ralph Ridley. Too much information at once can destroy a creature like you. By filtering and restricting what you can see, your central nervous system does not burn out.'

A burger was placed in front of Ralph. He jerked his head back.

Ca'zehro smiled. 'Another timelapse?'

Ralph looked around the café. Creatures filled the booths, eating food, sipping beverages. A familiar odour of fried delicacies and coffee laced the air.

'Weren't we going to the gallery?' Ralph asked.

Ca'zehro lifted a piece of meat and tore it in two. 'It takes a while to get used to.'

Ralph's mind faltered as a flood of memories came in. He saw them at the gallery. He remembered the paintings, the crowd, the souvenir store. He remembered the walk to the café, stopping at Ca'zehro's place on the way so he could drop off the book he'd purchased. He remembered watching in amusement as Ca'zehro scaled the walls with his four legs, rather than taking the stairs like him.

'If you like,' Ca'zehro said, 'you can stay in a hotel until you get your own place. Or you can continue staying in my guest room.'

'How long have I stayed with you?'

Ca'zehro placed a strip of meat into his mouth. 'You know that's not the right question, Ralph Ridley.'

Ralph nodded. He'd been told that more than a dozen times now.

'Then why am I even eating?'

'Just because there is no time,' Ca'zehro said, 'does not mean eating is not satisfying nor comforting.'

Ralph looked at the burger's glazed bun. He couldn't remember the last time he'd eaten anything like it. Such a sight would normally provoke salivation, an urge to indulge. But living without appetite, satiation, and digestion, he didn't know what to think.

He lifted the burger and took a bite, delighting in the heat of the meat, the tanginess of the sauce. The cheese melted on his tongue, infusing with the crisp crunch of the pickle.

Ca'zehro was right. The familiar act of chewing and swallowing comforted something deep within, reminding him of meals shared with the Adelaideans, while also filling an inner emptiness he'd accumulated travelling through the cosmos.

'I think I need to leave,' Ralph said. 'I need to keep going.'

Ca'zehro wiped sauce from his cheek. 'Why? Is here not everything you ever wanted? A place where you are not affected by the hands of time. A place where you can learn, create, be.'

'I spent so much time learning maths and physics, tinkering with things to break free from my curse. But I still haven't solved anything.'

Ca'zehro stroked his chin. 'Your concept of time is primitive. Does this place not show you there is more to reality than you believed?'

Ralph didn't want to seem weak or stupid. But living without the regular flow of time mystified his mind more than anything ever before. The only way to track life seemed to be through memory. And even then, that was fickle.

Outside the café, the street was busy. Various creatures passed by, fading in and out of existence alongside the sparrow's shine. Some looked like they were heading to work, hurrying, carrying small bags. Others looked like they were tourists, wandering, staring, pointing.

'How was your burger?'

Ralph blinked. They were outside again, heading to the statue park on the outskirts of the disc. He didn't let Ca'zehro notice his disorientation as the timelapse wrapped up. He maintained, or so he hoped, a perfectly straight walking gait. But just like Jamaki had always known when Piri was returning, Ca'zehro always knew when Ralph had been hit by a timelapse.

'It was good,' Ralph said, remembering the meat's texture, the chilli sauce's tanginess.

Ca'zehro smiled. 'I'm glad. Adjusting to life here is never easy.'

They walked under a bronze, reflective archway into an open area filled with statues. Ralph spotted humanlike figures with impressive frames, wearing robes, hats, and armour. Some had rotted flesh and missing limbs, wielding swords and hammers twice their size. Some had masks and stood akimbo. Others had combinations of various animalistic aesthetics: wings, fangs, furs, feathers.

'What is life without time?' Ralph asked, as they wandered between two rows of seven statues leading to a fountain.

'What is time without life to observe it?'

They stopped beside the fountain. It bordered the edge of the disc.

Decaying, ivory vines wrapped its base and wound to the peak, where a trickle of silver liquid leaked from a spout into the main pool.

'Do you see that?' Ca'zehro asked, gesturing at the dark maelstrom swirling and churning beyond.

Ralph recalled the feeling he'd had when he'd first laid eyes on the thing. He nodded.

'What is it?'

Ca'zehro turned to him. 'Balance.'

✦

Travelling to the Stack had already taken an unknown amount of time. Living on the Stack had proved even more elusive. But the longer Ralph stayed, the more his memories of life on Earth began to fade. He started forgetting who he'd been, what he'd been working on, why he'd left, how he'd made it to the discs, confused why he'd dedicated so much time to equations and experiments.

'But everything you worked on enabled you to get here,' Ca'zehro said. 'If you didn't learn what you did, if you didn't contemplate and experiment, you would not be sitting there.'

They were in Ca'zehro's apartment, sipping fruity teas on the balcony.

'But here feels meaningless,' Ralph said. 'Here makes me feel even more stuck and cursed as I navigate my stupid river of reality.'

Ca'zehro sat forward at Ralph's words, eyes narrowing. It was the first time he'd looked at Ralph with so much intensity.

'What do you know of the Rivers, Ralph Ridley?'

'What?' Ralph asked, confused. 'It's just a saying I have.'

Ca'zehro leant back, studying him. 'As I have said before, you are here because you are meant to be. Just like you met me when you were meant to meet me.'

Ralph started teaching particle transference to the creatures on the Stack. Sometimes, they told him how unique the technique was. Other times, they told him how others had developed something similar. But no one could explain who or what or when or even why.

To the younger creatures, who watched him in awe as he demonstrated the power of particle transference, he was like a magician. To the older creatures, a jester, someone who distracted them. To those who'd given up thinking, he was a revolutionary philosopher, scientist, and psychic all rolled into one.

After seminars, creatures would often invite him to their homes, offering him food and tea and gifts. But no matter how kind, receptive, and accepting the people of the Stack were, Ralph knew he didn't belong.

'My time dilemma still haunts me.'

'You are mistaken,' Ca'zehro said. 'The Arrows of Time lie to you. You might think you still have things to do. But time has ticked, it is ticking, and will forever tick.'

'How you speak will be the death of me.'

Ca'zehro smiled.

'I know, I know,' Ralph said. 'Death can't happen in a place outside of time.'

Ca'zehro laughed. 'Past, present, future — these are concepts your species created, Ralph Ridley. To truly exist, you must delete your understanding of life and its divisions. You must delete your understanding of senses. You must delete your understanding of time.'

Ca'zehro's words reminded Ralph of the cave-lab invader: *Your senses dictate reality.*

Ralph didn't like thinking about everything being an illusion, even if he did live on a stack of discs in the middle of nowhere.

'Thank you for coming,' he said to the creatures leaving a seminar.

A hovering, emu-like creature paused, gave him a slow nod. The other attendees vanished alongside the beat of the Stack.

Ralph frowned. What he'd just taught them would've garnered far more attention if they'd been human. But he couldn't take their disinterest to heart. To him, particle transference had been everything on Earth. On the Stack, it was akin to a spectacle of the past, like a remnant of an old life, like the Boy Who Never Grew, just another component of the never-ending story of the cosmos.

'It feels like no one cares,' Ralph said, alighting the monorail with Ca'zehro.

'And why should they? Everyone here is also dealing with their own lives, thoughts, and memories, Ralph Ridley.'

Ca'zehro was right. Ralph couldn't warrant any emotion directed towards any of the creatures. They weren't here to chat or make friends. They were here for themselves. And they'd only come because it'd been unavoidable to do so.

They rode the elevator up to Ralph's apartment. It was a dingy, motel-like thing with shelves lined with sketchpads and bronze beakers. Ca'zehro walked around it, lifting, tipping, and touching things.

'All of this is what you did to get here?'

'More or less,' Ralph said.

'For your – what do you call it again?'

'Particle transference.'

Ca'zehro nodded, studying one of Ralph's unfinished atom smashers.

'It all seems pointless now that I'm here though,' Ralph said.

Ca'zehro placed the cube down and turned to Ralph, four legs tapping the metal floor sequentially.

'Do not forget what I have already told you, Ralph Ridley: Everything you thought and solved, including your golden ratio equation, was necessary.'

Ralph bowed his head. Everything he'd thought and solved was only half of it. The other half contained everyone he'd lost along the way.

'Why do we never go to the other discs?' Ralph asked.

'Unnecessary. Wherever you are is only what you make it. You don't have to be here nor there. You only have to be.'

'But what if I don't want to *be* anymore?'

Ca'zehro tilted his head like a confused puppy. 'But here you have everything you've ever wanted. Do you not realise you do not need to seek or question anymore?'

Ralph sat cross-legged on the floor, elbows pressed into his knees, hands cupping his head.

'I know it makes sense to stay,' he said. 'I know I don't have to worry about rotating myself out of any dimension here.' He met Ca'zehro's eyes. 'But life's not normal on the Stack. I'd rather live with distorted time than live without it.'

They strolled through a subsurface auditorium the size of twelve churches. Bipedal creatures wearing robes filled the place. Bronze pillars reached to an unseeable ceiling. Rooms lined the perimeter, each home to a dentist-like chair, a wall of electronics, and a metal circle the size of a phone booth. Some were hollow, inactive. Others were washed with millions of colours and lights churning away.

Ralph didn't react to this timelapse. He was used to them now. His four-legged friend still glanced at him though.

'I know I was always meant to come here,' Ralph said. 'But coming here hasn't solved anything. I'm still no closer to finding out who or what messed with my life. Or even what I'm supposed to do about it.'

Ca'zehro nodded. 'It does seem you are here at the wrong time. I'm not sure how this has happened.'

They exited the auditorium and came to an area with the dark maelstrom hovering ahead, like a sun setting on a horizon.

'Come with me,' Ralph said.

Ca'zehro smiled. 'My journey is over, Ralph Ridley. My place is here.'

'But why?'

Ca'zehro's smile persisted. 'Because I am not confused about where I am or what I am supposed to do.'

'But I don't want to keep going alone. I've done that enough.'

Ca'zehro placed a hand on Ralph's shoulder. 'If you have done that enough, then you are equipped to do it longer.'

Ralph searched his mind for a way to entice Ca'zehro. After travelling through the void, the last thing he wanted to do was leave the first friendly face he'd encountered, even if it did mean he'd one day lose him as well.

'But don't you want more?' Ralph asked. 'Don't you want to do more?'

Ca'zehro contemplated for a moment, shook his head. 'More has already been. More is now. More is on its way.'

Ralph studied the lilac fog with its sparkling, silver stars peeking through. 'Where am I supposed to go though? Will the bubble aura return when I leave?'

'As I said when I first met you, Ralph Ridley, your silver nodes imply you are from a later period. It is intriguing you were able to make it here when you do not know simple things like that.'

Ralph looked at the nodes pulsing on his arms, tuned to the beat of the Stack. 'Then I am supposed to leave. Even if it feels like I only just arrived.'

'You were never supposed to stay,' Ca'zehro said. 'I know that now. You still lack fragmentation. But are you sure you are ready to return to the flow of time?'

Now it was Ralph's turn to smile. 'I've never been blessed with time,

Ca'zehro, why would I care if I moved in and out of it?'

For the first time since arriving, Ca'zehro didn't know how to respond.

Ralph looked at the splinter sparrow on his shoulder. 'Guess it's time for you to go, little buddy.'

Ca'zehro stepped forward, offering the golden bird one of his fingers to nibble on.

'The splinter sparrow is yours now, Ralph Ridley,' Ca'zehro said.

'I can't take your bird.'

'It is a gift. As I said, I no longer need it.'

Ralph copied Ca'zehro, offering a finger for the tiny pebble of a bird to nibble on.

'Thank you, Ca'zehro.'

'Remember,' Ca'zehro said, 'here will always be here.'

Ralph opened his mouth to respond, but the Stack collapsed, sending him back into the unknown.

He looked for the discs. But they were gone. He looked for Ca'zehro. But he was gone as well. He waited for the blue bubble aura to activate. But it never did. It never had to. Instead, the splinter sparrow chirped once and ignited, surrounding him with a sphere of golden warmth and shine.

'Now what?' Ralph asked it.

The bird chirped again, sending a beam directly into the silent, violent dark maelstrom.

'I'm supposed to go in there?'

The beam amplified.

'Well,' Ralph said, sprinkling some obsidiary dust under his tongue, 'here goes nothing.'

14
The Orbs

RALPH reformed inside the maelstrom and was immediately torn apart.

Fragmenting, he released energy, he released light. The feeling resembled transference. But unlike the familiar technique, his awareness remained. He could still think. He could still see. He could still feel the splinter sparrow on his shoulder, shining its sonar shine, guiding him, helping him, keeping him safe inside this new oblivion.

As he shot through the maelstrom with relentless speed, he was reminded of an underground sewer network. Alongside narrow, suffocating tunnels laced with faded greens and pearly, curling stripes, a smog hung in the air, old and putrid. The path twisted and curved erratically, ramping up and ramping down. Without the Stack's protective effects keeping him calm any longer, his mind dove and wound with it, catapulting him through waves of dread and uncertainty, stimulating confronting memories in disarray.

He saw the day Stephanie had pinged his intercom and he'd denied her coming up. He saw the day his book was published and felt ashamed about how most of the information was outdated. He saw glimpses of the hundreds of nights he'd spent alone, researching, writing, shuffling equations, staring at the computer, hoping, waiting, praying for a breakthrough so his life finally made sense.

He wanted to go deeper into the tunnel, into the moments from a life long ago. But his mind wouldn't allow him. It stayed attuned to reality, telling him it was all fabricated by the gloomy, plasmatic vortex. At the same time, it reminded him how lost he was, how broken, how much time he'd wasted trying to solve his curse, how he should've stayed with Ca'zehro.

He came to a junction. The energy of the maelstrom demanded he went one way. The sparrow lit the opposite. He didn't know what or who to trust.

He went with the maelstrom, going left. The sparrow shifted its sonar shine. He thanked it silently, glad it wanted to help, glad it didn't hold grudges.

The vortex pulled him deeper through the winding maze. It thrust him through caves and caverns, dropped him from heights that flipped his stomach, looped him like a rollercoaster.

He tried looking at his body. But there was no looking. And he had no body to look at. He'd become a figment of the vortex's imagination.

After some time, the maelstrom slowed. His body reformed. His mind levelled out. His senses returned. He was then expelled into the coldness of space.

As he tumbled through the void, he knew it was over. The end of the road had arrived. It wouldn't be long before the pressure differences, lack of oxygen, frigidity, and radiation would conclude his saga.

But then, the splinter sparrow ignited, enveloping him in its warm, protective shine.

His tumbling slowed; his trajectory shifted. He came to a halt half a metre away from four bright, white orbs made of swirling, wispy gases. Each were the size of ice-cream vans.

'*Abrat-afts-swer. Abrataat-se. Esfef-zef.*'

Their words came like a song, a wonderful combination of vibrations and frequencies. They reminded him of a dream he'd had about talking colours in space.

'I can't understand you,' Ralph said.

Their words changed, became more comprehensible, infused inside him.

'*Barakaka. Abrata-kaka.*'

'Thank you for pulling me from that maze,' Ralph said.

'*Kakakaba. Abrat-tata. Keeka-bara.*'

'Am I dead? Are you gods?'

'*Barakada tabadaka.*'

'You're here to help me?'

The orbs pulsed, brightened. Then, like cells in a petri dish, began to split.

They decreased in size with each division, becoming eight orbs, sixteen, then finally thirty-two.

Positioning themselves in rows of eight and columns of four, like a large stadium light, their luminosity grew and grew until it engulfed a two hundred metre radius of the area.

Ralph opened his arms and embraced the warm, white light, eyes closed. When he reopened them, he found himself inside an oblong prism, similar to a bus. Square, barred windows lined the walls. A row of wooden chairs faced an altar at one end. The floors were carpeted in grey silk and had a long, red rug leading to the altar. The ceiling, covered with thirty-two circular lights, hummed a frequency that shook the windows.

Not knowing what else to do, Ralph sat on a chair and looked out a nearby window.

Wherever he was, the darkness outside seemed different. No stars, nebulae, moons, or planets were visible. It was like he'd been pulled into a different section of the void.

The ceiling stirred, shuddered. Four lights then broke free, floating to the floor like dandelion seeds in the wind. They struck the carpet with a sound like distant thunder and began to inflate.

'What are you?' Ralph asked, standing. 'Where am I?'

He spoke with intensity, as though demonstrating his strength. But the four orbs didn't care. They enlarged in their own time until resembling oversized basketballs.

'*The Nazra tries to manipulate,*' one said, voice echoing inside the prism.

'*But the Nazra cannot manipulate,*' another said, voice lighter than the first.

'*The Nazra has already manipulated too much,*' a third, calmer voice said.

'*The Nazra has surpassed petty emotions,*' a fourth voice said, heavier, more insightful. '*It has been gone from its home for a long time.*'

'Yes,' the third voice said. '*But Nazra are delicate.*'

'*That is true,*' the first one agreed.

The orbs arranged themselves into a square-like structure. Their glow became hypnotising as they all sang at once: '*The more there is, the less you can see.*'

'What are you?' Ralph asked.

The orbs traded a vibration of humour. White electricity sparked between them.

'*Do you feel what is outside, Nazra?*'

Ralph approached a window. The darkness outside was no longer just dark in appearance, but in feeling, in energy.

'Yes,' he said, sensing a hollowness in his stomach. 'I feel… despair. And dread. What is it?'

The orbs seemed pleased with his answer, trading another spark between them.

'*Do you feel us?*'

Ralph thought for a moment, eyes closed. It took him almost a minute to notice the low reverberation emanating from them, which carried the distinct characteristic of humour laced with love and care.

'Yes.'

'*How can it?*'

'*This one is not like the others.*'

White tendrils laced from the orbs to his silver nodes. He drew back. Amusement spread through the capsule.

'Are you the ones who ruined my life?' Ralph asked.

'*The Nazra asks many questions.*'

'*It is what Nazra do.*'

'*It has pep, it is naïve.*'

'*But it has a lot to prove.*'

The four orbs spoke to one another like he wasn't even there.

He moved closer. As he neared them, they shrank back, split into pairs, and moved behind him to reform in their square formation.

'What do you want from me?' Ralph asked.

'*Do not raise your voice to us, Nazra. Our power supersedes anything you have ever come into contact with. You must treat us with respect.*'

'And what respect have you given me? Dragging me out of that vortex, putting me inside this capsule. I'm on a mission. I don't have time for this.'

The orbs were silent as they traded white electricity.

'Does the Nazra know where it is going?'

'Does the Nazra know what it is doing?'

'No.'

'It is naïve.'

'I'm not naïve!' Ralph said, swiping an arm at the orbs.

They performed the same manoeuvre – splitting into pairs, moving around to rearrange into the square.

'I've travelled across the cosmos,' Ralph said. 'I know what I'm doing.'

The orbs brightened as humour spread through the room once again.

'All the way out here.'

'All by yourself.'

'Lost and out of your depth.'

'But perhaps the Nazra is not so naïve.'

'What is this Nazra you keep mentioning?' Ralph said. 'I'm not a Nazra. I'm a human from Earth and my name is Ralph Ridley.'

This time, although he expected them to, they did not laugh.

'The Nazra harnesses energy without understanding it.'

'Or what it has done.'

'Or how it can solve its life.'

'You don't know the half of it,' he mumbled.

'Oh, but we do.'

Their light brightened, filling every portion of the capsule.

'Then tell me why you messed with my life,' Ralph said. 'Tell me why you put me through hell just to pull me from that vortex.'

'We did not mess with your life, Nazra!'

He gave it back to them with the same intensity: 'Then what the hell do you want with me? I'm not interested in playing games.'

He waited for the orbs to respond. When they simply hovered in arrogance, he took out the black diamond sack and sprinkled some obsidiary dust under his tongue. Turning to the nearest window, he began the transference.

He reformed inside the capsule, still hurtling through the infinite.

'This Nazra is different.'

'It harnesses energy in a strange way.'

'But Nazra never know how.'

'This one does.'

'Why are you talking like I'm not here?' Ralph shouted, fists clenched, shaking.

We are the Orbs of Bactuite.'

But the Nazra will know us as the Orbs of Scindere.'

'No. I don't know you.'

But you do, Ralph Ridley. But you do.'

We are the Orbs that divide.'

That cut the universe into pieces.'

That create and destroy.'

'So, you did mess with my life.'

We did nothing of the sort, Nazra,' they sang in unison, brightening.

'Then what do you want with me? I don't want to be stopped. I want to figure out why I was drawn to the Stack. And I want to find out who's dictating my miserable existence.'

'And you think you are going to find answers out here?'

'Why else would my planet have ejected me?'

The Orbs started communicating with one another in the distorted language they'd used when they'd first pulled him from the vortex. He took this chance to look around the room. If transference didn't work from the inside, perhaps he could find a door or hatch or escape pod…

This Nazra is more than we expected.'

But the more there is, the less you can see.'

Ralph kept silent as he moved about the capsule. He ran a hand across the walls and floors, tested the metal bars on each window.

Tell us, Nazra, what are the silver fragments in your flesh?'

Tell us, Nazra, what is inside the thing on your back?'

Tell us, Nazra, what is your purpose, how did you get here, how old are you?'

Tell us, Nazra, what is there more of when there is less you can see?'

He stopped at a window. The sparrow sent a beam out into the darkness. Its light barely reached more than a few metres. A feeling of claustrophobia came over him.

'Where am I?' he asked. 'Where are you taking me?'

He grasped two of the metal bars, shook them with all his might.

There is no escape, Nazra.'

'Shut up! I am not a Nazra. I am a human.'

The one who travels through space is not a human,' they sang.

They glowed brighter, forcing him to shield his eyes.

'Tell us, Nazra, what if we gave you answers?'

'What if we gave you what you desired?'

'What if we gave you what you wanted?'

'Do you believe your life could be limitless?'

Ralph shook his head. 'I don't want limitless. I don't want forever. How can you not see that? I am aged. I've lost everything. I don't want to be here. I never even wanted to leave Earth. I just wanted to solve my time curse.'

'But you are the one who tampers with space, with the quanta, are you not?'

Ralph's ears perked up. 'How do you know about quantum mechanics?'

'We know all because we are all.'

He stepped closer to them. This time, they did not retreat. 'If you know all, then you know why my life was messed with.'

They hovered, hummed, traded tendrils.

'Who are you?' Ralph asked, peering into their swirling gases.

'We have already told you.'

'But I don't know what the Orbs of Scindere are.'

'Its knowledge is insufficient,' the first Orb said.

'It does not reach into every layer,' the second one said.

'It is understandable,' the third said. *'It is only Nazra.'*

'But it can help us,' the fourth said. *'And we can help it.'*

'What do you want with me?'

'We are the Orbs that divide, Nazra. We allow for reality. We control the laws, the rules, the logic, the electricity. The light.'

If what they'd said was true, coming face to face with such creatures was more than puzzling, it was fantastically unfathomable.

'You are the rulers of the universe?'

'We were. But the Darkness has taken it from us. It has destroyed our lives. Just like it destroyed yours.'

'That darkness ruined my life?' Ralph asked, pointing out a window.

'The more there is, the less you can see, the less you can live, the less you can be.'

The capsule disintegrated.

15
The Renaming

RALPH shot through the vortex once again. Although the sparrow shone its beam ahead like a beacon, he sensed the Orbs were in control. They weaved him through the gloomy tunnels with unrelenting speed, flinging him around tight bends and down steep declines.

The coloured, contorted streaks of olive and pearl flashed by. The putrid smog whipped his face. His stomach lurched. His mind danced with exhilaration and disorientation.

He felt like he could've stayed on the ride for hours. But without warning, the Orbs spat him out onto a rocky surface. The splinter sparrow changed its shine just in time to soften his landing.

Getting to his feet, he studied his surroundings.

A burgundy desert with jagged rocks and faded, yellow cacti and shrubbery stretched out around him. A lake flowed nearby, bordered by stones, and riddled with dying reeds and the rare ripple. To his left, a drop into a canyon reached to shadows. Above, a dark sky swelled, menacing, roiling.

What you see above is what is tearing the universe apart,' the four Orbs sang, emerging from the lake like full moons breaching the horizon.

'What is it?' Ralph asked.

The end.'

A fork of indigo lightning split the sky, followed by a deep, distant rumbling.

The Darkness is misbehaving, Nazra. It is unstable. It is disturbing our duties. It must be stopped.'

Ralph tracked another fork. 'The Darkness is what ruined my life?' He recalled the ancient dark energy equation he'd never been able to solve. 'The Darkness rotated me out of the regular flow of time?'

The Orbs of Scindere flared.

We are the questioners, Nazra! Your kind have questioned for too long.'

'You don't understand,' Ralph said, contending with the concoction of conflicting emotions inside him. 'I've been chasing this meddler my entire life.'

'You are too young, too insufficient with knowledge to formulate anything from the answers we could offer you.'

Ralph wandered over to the lake, hands in pockets. Getting to his knees, he leaned over and studied his reflection.

The indigo flashes above provided a ghastly image of a face and body he hadn't laid eyes on in a long time. He looked like a teenager now, sixteen or seventeen years old. His face had elongated. His jaw had widened. His blonde hair had grown, thickened, darkened.

How long had he lived on the Stack? How long had he travelled through the vortex before the Orbs had pulled him?

'Judging by the body I have,' he said, standing, 'my formula tells me I'm well into my second or third century of life.'

The Orbs glowed, spreading white tendrils of electricity. The lacing sparks touched the plants and the lakebed, where the other twenty-eight Orbs sat like pearls cast to the bottom of the sea.

'Is that all?' they sang. *'Two or three centuries? What is your unit of measurement? What is your understanding of eternity?'*

A rumble overhead followed a crack of indigo lightning.

'If the Darkness is what messed with me and everything,' Ralph said, 'then I need to keep going. I need to figure out where it comes from and how to end it.'

'But where will the Nazra go? What will it do? How will it find the Darkness?'

Ralph watched the agitated sky. 'Follow it to its source, I guess. I'll figure out what to do when I get there.'

'But we have already found its source, Nazra. It is why we have come for you. We wish to mend what you did, for the suffrage you brought the universe is all your fault.'

The other twenty-eight Orbs emerged from the lake and surrounded Ralph in a circle.

'Me?' he said. 'If you are the all-knowers, then you know I'm the one whose life was ruined from day one.'

'Then tell us, Nazra, how do you stand before us?'

'What kind of question is that? You brought me here. You pulled me from my quest. And if I hadn't been cursed from the beginning, I wouldn't even be here. I would've died happily with a family after working a career, travelling, loving, enjoying life.'

The Orbs traded electricity.

'But what energy did the Nazra use to get here? The energy of the universe? Did it use the Darkness to move through it?'

'What do you mean?' Ralph asked. 'The Darkness used me.'

'Then the Nazra acted without knowledge. And in its haste, caused an energy debt so great, it destabilised reality.'

'Impossible,' Ralph said, shaking his head.

But he sensed truth in their words. Ever since Earth had ejected him, he'd known tampering with reality had its consequences. This was just another nail in the coffin.

'You are smart, Nazra. You are powerful. But you have much to learn. You have much to balance. Bypassing natural ascension has impacted everything we've worked so hard to maintain.'

Reminded of Ca'zehro's words about his early arrival on the Stack, Ralph looked at the blinking silver nodes in his arms.

'Putting these in my arms ruined reality? You can't be serious.'

The Orbs flared. *'It is not about what you think or wish, Nazra.'*

'But they were only meant to help. How was I supposed to know trying to fix my life would destabilise the energy of the universe?'

But even as he said these words, he recalled Kirby et al.'s energy debt theory and the first law of thermodynamics.

'I destroyed energy? That can't be true. That's supposed to be impossible.'

The thirty-two Orbs flared even brighter. All humour had evaporated from their demeanours. Only concern flowed in the air.

'To a Nazra, maybe. To the cosmos, not so.'

'But that presence,' Ralph said, looking at the Orbs in desperation. 'Something invaded my lab. Something told me to keep going. If you're going to blame anyone, blame them.'

'Nothing but an attempt to push you to solving matter manipulation. To grow. To

strengthen itself. To destroy everything.'

Ralph bowed his head. 'But I didn't know.'

'We are sad you feel this way.'

'Could I really have affected things that much? In the grand scheme of the cosmos, its abundance of energy—'

Their white electricity lashed out. He had no time to get out of the way before it struck his nodes, sending him to the ground with volts disabling his coordination.

'Yes, the Nazra was not the only one.'

'But the Nazra provoked it, made it consume.'

'Made it destroy.'

'The more there is, the less you can see.'

The electricity waned. Ralph sat up, pulled his legs to his chest.

'I didn't mean to,' he said. 'I only wanted to be set free.'

The Orbs of Scindere hovered closer. Their luminosity was overwhelming. Their humming, disturbing. Ralph braced for another dose of electricity. But when they spoke again, melody had returned in their tones.

'We are happy to cross paths with you, Nazra.'

'Can't you do anything about what I've done?' Ralph asked.

'The one who caused it, must destroy it,' the first Orb said.

'The one who willed it, must conclude it,' the second Orb said.

'The one who changed it, must repeal it,' the third Orb said.

'This is the only way,' the fourth Orb finished.

'Then tell me how to stop it,' Ralph said.

'It is not a matter of stopping it, Nazra. It is a matter of destroying it.'

In a snap, he was pulled from the desert and sent streaking through the vortex again.

Fragmenting into pieces, his light and energy swirled amongst the smog and the colours. More memories came to him as he travelled, ones he'd suppressed, ones he'd put under lock and key while cooped up in his penthouse and cave-lab.

He saw the Christmas Stephanie had organised that he'd left early. He saw his mum holding him at Stephanie's funeral. He heard the final vessel leaving Earth, felt Cyclops's thin, greying fur on the day she'd died on the mesa.

The sparrow's shine enhanced, pulling him back to reality. He thanked it, eyes scanning the vortex's swirling stripes.

Before long, the ride ended, liberating him from the addictive whirlpool of memories. He landed on a decagonal ice disc with nothing but darkness surrounding him. As he got his bearings, he stumbled. The ice disc tilted with the weight shift. He collapsed to the frosty surface on his hands and knees.

'Do you feel this, Nazra?'

From all fours, he scanned the abyss, teeth chattering. The darkness surrounding the ice pulsed with sinister intentions.

'Imagine you are the universe on this disc,' the Orbs sang. *'Imagine you are surrounded by a powerful energy. Imagine what one wrong foot could do. Do you understand, Nazra?'*

'But how could I have known my particle transference would cause an energy debt that would ruin everything?' He raised his voice. 'And if you knew I was doing this, why not intervene?' He squeezed his eyes shut, fingernails digging into the ice. 'And why should I even care? I never asked for my life to be ruined!'

'Your emotions are primordial. This is not what must be thought at the age you say you are.'

'What do you mean? I've never had a chance to enjoy a regular aging process. My curse has convoluted everything about me.'

'Your curse is not a curse, Nazra. It has given you life. It has given you time. It has led you here.'

'But why make me suffer for so long?'

'You already know this answer.'

'No,' Ralph said, slamming his hands to the ice repeatedly. 'I don't. I never wanted to be here. The only reason I am is because I tried to fix my life.'

'And if that is not fate, Nazra, then please tell us what is.'

Ralph spoke through gritted teeth: 'Don't tell me my life has always been predetermined.'

'You are looking at it all wrong. You chose this fate. You chose this path. By realising this, you can stop complaining and start helping.'

Ralph sighed. 'Just tell me what I'm supposed to do then. I want to go home.'

'You have all the knowledge you could ever need.' Their voices reverberated through the chasm. *'You just need to unlock it.'*

Their light and humming faded, vanished, leaving him alone in the ice abyss.

'You are different, Nazra.' Their voices came from high above. *'You would not be here if you weren't.'*

Their words were careful now, instructive. Ralph craned his head to their new location.

'If I'm supposed to destroy the Darkness,' he said, 'tell me how and let me get it over with.'

'It is not that simple.'

'If there's a way to rebalance everything and give me my life back, I'll do it.'

The Orbs were silent for a moment, trading white electricity.

'To balance everything, you must go far away, Nazra.'

'For a long time.'

'You must not progress. You must not meddle.'

'You must only exist.'

Ralph got to his feet with great care, slipping and sliding with every movement.

'Where?' he asked. 'I'll go straight away. Just tell me you can take me home to my mountain after all of this.'

'You please us, Nazra. You are the quanta entangler we yearned to meet.'

Ralph was thrust back into the vortex. Sucked through the narrow tunnels, thrown around like a toy, he didn't bother trying to focus or stabilise this time. Instead, he submitted, handing the reins to the Orbs.

When the journey was over, he was shot back out into deep space. The splinter sparrow ignited, enveloping him in its shine.

'What is your name, Nazra?'

'Ralph Ridley.'

'What is your species, Nazra?'

'Human.'

'You are the Quanta Human, Nazra, the Quanta Man, the one who harnesses the energy of the cosmos.'

'And what are your names?'

They all sang at once: *'We are the Scindereans.'*

'But what are your names?'

Four tendrils of electricity laced out from them, breaching the sparrow's shine and connecting with his nodes.

His eyes widened as new knowledge poured into him, like an information download. He learned the names of the Orbs in an instant.

One was called Repulsion. One was Attraction. One was Deterioration. One was Light.

'Thank you,' Ralph said, bowing his head, grateful for their trust with such knowledge. 'On Earth, we call you the fundamental forces in science.'

The Orbs of Science,' they all repeated, as though learning the word for the first time.

'You are not like the ones who came before you,' the Orb of Light said.

'And how long ago was that?'

It still does not understand eternity,' the Orb of Deterioration said.

'Will it ever?' the Orb of Repulsion said.

'Its journey is not complete,' the Orb of Attraction said.

'But it is time for it to go,' the Orb of Light said.

'And where am I going?' Ralph asked. 'How do I repay the debt I've created? How do I destroy the Darkness destroying everything?'

'The Quanta Man must travel to the deepest part of the universe,' the Orb of Attraction said.

'There, they will construct a blade of silk,' the Orb of Deterioration said.

'The blade of silk must be folded 999 times,' the Orb of Repulsion said.

'No more,' the Orb of Light said as it combined with the Orb of Deterioration.

'No less,' the Orb of Repulsion said as it combined with the Orb of Attraction.

'Once the Nazra has constructed the blade,' the two remaining Orbs said as they combined, *'return to us.'*

Ralph went over the details in his mind. 'A silk blade?'

The remaining Orb glowed brighter than the blip of light he'd seen after Earth had ejected him.

'The folds must be strict,' it sang. *'They must be perfect. They must be made from the silk of the worms at the Bottom of the Universe.'*

Ralph nodded. 'I understand.'

'*You must listen to us, Quanta Man. If you do not, the Darkness will grow and consume. Do you listen to us?*'

'Of course. I'll do whatever it takes.'

'*Once the blade is forged, balance will be restored.*'

'And how will I find you when I'm done?'

But the connection was severed as the Orb faded, leaving him floating alone in the silent expanse.

He took a moment to digest the information, scanning the cosmos and its variety of distant stars. He then looked at the splinter sparrow perched on his shoulder.

'Do you know the way to the Bottom of the Universe?'

It chirped once and ignited.

16
With Wings

GETTING to the Bottom of the Universe was easier than Ralph had expected. With the splinter sparrow pinpointing pockets of energy to pursue, after forty-odd transferences, a trail of celestial objects helped guide him the rest of the way.

Upon arriving, it took him a while to comprehend what he was looking at. For the most part, the Bottom of the Universe resembled a wasteland, a place where everything left over from the Big Bang came to die.

Surrounded by the void, a spanning stretch of stars, moons, planets, comets, asteroids, rocks, dust, and debris, of all sizes, shapes, and colours, floated about like blobs of wax in a lava lamp. Just looking at the immeasurable congregation made him question the validity of the Cosmological Arrow. For, if the universe was forever expanding, why were otherworldly objects and their offspring pooling here?

He reformed on the other side of some spiky asteroids. A bird's eye view of this new oasis greeted him.

Far below, two broken chunks of land, as though ripped straight from Earth, hovered beside one another. Separated by forty metres, each were the size of hockey fields. On one, pine trees surrounded a weaving stream leading to a waterfall. On the other, dirt, rocks, and the surprising existence of an A-frame wooden hut, garden, and barn.

Ralph squinted to ensure he wasn't seeing things. He bit his tongue to contain the excitement.

What was a dwelling doing at the Bottom of the Universe? Why were fresh fruit and vegetable crops growing beside it? And was that chimney really billowing a steady plume of smoke?

He couldn't transfer fast enough.

When his consciousness returned, he stood out the front of the homestead. Large enough for two bedrooms, its wood was weathered, unstained. Portions of it were made from different types of wood, as though repaired over the years. Scratches and dents covered the door and window frames. A cobblestone path led to the front gate, where a scuffed brass bell hung in waiting.

He bolted to the bell and clanged it with unbridled excitement.

'Hello!' he called. 'Is anybody home?'

His voice carried with a fading echo, as though no sound had occurred here before.

'Hello?' he said, louder, more desperate. 'Is anyone home?'

He jogged around the homestead, jumping every so often to glance over the fence.

How long had the people been here? Where were they now? Out collecting silk for their own silk sword? At the shops, the post office, the cinema?

After lapping the house twice, he came to a rest, breathless. Although he was at the Bottom of the Universe, it felt like he was at high altitude. Every step was difficult. Every breath, insufficient.

He took a moment to recover, eyes on the gentle movements of the celestial objects. Their interactions reminded him of magnetism. Similar objects knocked against one another. Opposites repelled.

Although a display of objects parading and clashing above should've been daunting, he didn't feel troubled. He didn't need to be. Not when it was clear the Bottom of the Universe's gravity worked in synchronicity with the objects, pulling and pushing them in just the right way, preventing any from ploughing into his new home.

Breath back under control, he peered over the fence. The barn to the left of the house looked straight out of a nursery rhyme book. Red and trimmed with white, it was tall enough to keep a giraffe. Through its open doors, a flickering fire painted the walls and rafters inside.

'Excuse me?' he called. 'Hello?'

He didn't know what to expect. He didn't even know if calling out at the Bottom of the Universe was wise. For all he knew, the residents were watching him, waiting for the right moment to tranquilise and turn him into a taxidermy mount.

He called out a few more times. When no answer came, no movement, no laughter, no whispering, he entered the yard.

Tiptoeing between the crops, he moved slow, staying low. Passing a caged enclosure, he glanced inside to find twelve footless, hovering chicken-like creatures. He watched them pecking at the ground for a moment, bewildered, then continued on.

At the barn, he stuck his head inside, waited, listened. He scanned the shelves lined with straw, the assortment of wooden equipment, the fire in the drum in the centre of the room.

It seemed likely people should be found inside. But the silence told him otherwise.

'Sorry for intruding,' he said, entering. 'I've been sent here on an assignment by the Orbs of Scindere. But don't worry. I won't be staying long – only 999 days. And maybe you can help speed it up by pointing me to the silkworms.'

He inspected the wooden equipment. Some of it reminded him of antique spinning wheels. Others reminded him of guillotines and piano skeletons, complete with levers, pulleys, pedals, and ropes.

Although he'd never collected or woven silk before, an inkling told him he'd be using these devices in the coming days.

He ran a hand across one of the spinning wheels. Its surface was smooth. Its craftsmanship was impeccable. Every join, flawless. Every metal hook, polished to perfection. The presence of the pink thread wrapped around it added to its pleasing aesthetics.

He strummed the thread. It vibrated warmly, shooting faint pink sparks into the air.

Who had collected this thread? Did they have more of it stored somewhere? Why did it look like they'd abandoned their work in such a hurry?

He called into the barn one last time. When only the faint crackling of the fire responded, he headed to the house.

'Honey, I'm home!' he said, opening the front door. 'Did you miss me? I'm sorry I'm late. I've been travelling through the universe, living on a stack of discs, being abducted by orbs. You know how it is.'

He explored the dwelling, checking every room, inside every cupboard, under every bed. Everywhere he looked, not a soul could be found. Not a silkworm munching on mulberry leaves either. And much like the equipment in the barn, everything in the house lay about in disarray – saucepans, cutlery, half-eaten sandwiches, pots of tea, washing piles. It was like the owners had been invaded by zombies and had to make a break for safety.

With the house recon complete, Ralph slumped onto the frayed three-seater couch in the living room. An old CRT television faced him. A pile of what looked like VHS tapes sat beside it. Scattered across the coffee table lay books sans text or titles.

It probably should've been weird to find stuff like this at the Bottom of the Universe. But the Bottom of the Universe seemed like the perfect place to find such items. What Ralph couldn't wrap his head around was who had collected them, when, where, and why.

Back outside, he searched the garden for signs of silkworms. Lifting leaves, branches, fallen foliage, he looked for the familiar white things from Earth. Unsuccessful, he then made his way to the gap between the two chunks of land, kicking up dirt and stones, splinters of wood, and fragments of rusted metal along the way.

He came to a stop at the gap, facing the other chunk. Its pine forest stood tall, green, thick, luscious. The crystal-clear stream weaving between the trees flowed unusually fast for a river with no glacier mountains feeding it. What made the sight even more unusual was its complete lack of sound.

He tracked the tumbling water over the falls to the base of the land, where it disappeared underneath to wrap back around. The sight both enchanted and disturbed him. But it did explain the river's rapid flow.

He smiled at this intriguing phenomenon, at where he was, at what his life had become. He almost couldn't believe he'd once been a kid driving a 4WD out to the Simpson Desert to tinker and experiment with all kinds of items. That life seemed like a lifetime ago, a reality ago, one that didn't even feel real anymore.

Getting to his hands and knees, he peered over the edge. Green vines intertwined between the two chunks of land. Below and through the tangled mess of thorned strands, the Darkness stared back at him, the same Darkness he'd seen outside the Orb capsule, the same destructive Darkness that'd ruined his life.

And he hated every particle of it. He wanted to pull it from its canvas, shove it inside an atom smasher and annihilate every last part of it.

The light shifted.

He looked up as a cluster of rocks passed over two distant stars, plunging the Bottom of the Universe into night. The only light illuminating the two chunks of land came from a marble moon.

'Oh no!'

The voice came from his right, feminine, distressed.

He swivelled his head around as a silhouette floated down, humanlike with wings.

'Get away from the edge, young man!' they said, landing beside him like a bird perching on a branch.

Standing four-feet-tall, the creature was a mix between a girl and an owl. She wore a full body, sleeveless, ivory gambeson with a high collar. She had long, eggplant purple hair, pale skin, and a sharp-featured face. Her eyes were a rich yellow, bordered by heavily shadowed sockets, and accentuated by thick, angular eyebrows. A dense layer of white feathers covered her hands and arms. A gold bangle wrapped both biceps.

'I am terribly sorry for being late,' she said in a complaining tone. 'I did not think you would arrive so quickly. Oh, how I feel horrible!'

Ralph was lost for words. He'd never been told someone would be waiting for him at the Bottom of the Universe. Let alone an owl-girl.

'I've just been so busy,' she said. 'Other than learning your language and customaries, I've been cooking and cleaning and collecting items to make sure the house was just right for your arrival. I must have lost track of time. But I shouldn't have.' She furrowed her eyebrows, eyes darting about like an owl's. 'I was on time last time. I'm always on time. Yes. No. Well, I made sure to…' She paused as though realising she was rambling. 'Forgive me.' She came forward, feathered hand outstretched. 'And what do they call you?'

Something told Ralph to be confused and startled. But he'd just left the Stack. He'd just lived amongst strange creatures. He'd just been sent to the Bottom of the Universe by four gaseous, luminous orbs.

He shook her hand. 'Ralph. Who are you?'

The girl leapt into the air with a backflip, stretching her wings wide. 'I am Veška, your new friend and – Wait! I almost forgot.'

She shot across the gulley into the pine forest, disappearing amongst the greenery. A moment later, she blasted back out and landed beside him.

In one hand, she held a plate of sandwiches. In the other, an orange-coloured drink in a metal cup.

'You are hungry, I assume?' she asked. 'All of you are always so hungry when you arrive.' She placed the plate on the ground, gesturing to it. 'I hope it's all right.'

Ralph stared, stunned. There were so many things to ask, think, do.

'What do you mean "all of you"?' he said. 'I saw the equipment in the barn. Someone else has come here to make a silk sword?'

She swiped a hand through the air impatiently. 'Oh, don't get me started on silk and swords. The last one wouldn't shut up about that. They stayed in that darned barn trying to make a shield to go with theirs. They never came out to play or explore or eat or anything!' She took a sandwich from the plate and bit into it with purpose. 'Quite frankly, I hated them in the end.'

Ralph's head spun. Another person making a sword? Why was he now making one? How many had made one before?

'And what happened to them?' he asked.

'Well, they took him in the end, darling. But that's not important. Eat!'

The sandwiches on the tray were made of a white bread with thick layers of meat, complemented by slices of what looked like cheese.

'It's a little like salami,' Veška said. 'It's what you people eat, right? I read it somewhere… Oh, do please try one. And tell me if you do not like it. I'm more than happy to make something else. It doesn't take too—'

'Wait,' Ralph said, stopping her. 'What do you mean they took them in the end? Who took who? When? What's going on?'

'Oh, come now. You're not really going to be this boring and ask all these questions, are you? I mean, look at where you are. You cannot be consumed by questions and goals at the Bottom of the Universe.'

'What are you talking about?' he said, shaking his hands in frustration. 'I'm not here to eat sandwiches. I'm here to make a silk sword to destroy the thing that ruined my life.'

Chewing away, Veška studied him with her shadowed, yellow eyes. 'And you will. For now, it's time to eat.'

He pressed his hands into his face, tensing his body until it hurt.

'Take a few breaths, dear,' Veška said. 'You'll be all right.'

He dropped both hands to his sides with a sigh. 'Can you at least tell me where the worms are?'

She laughed. Crumbs flew from her mouth. 'I didn't arrive yesterday, you know.'

The light shifted again. Ralph watched the cluster of rocks move away from the distant stars. When he looked back down, Veška had changed. Her hair and eyebrows had become green. Her feathers had become a glossy-black, like a raven's.

'Oh, never mind this,' she said, gesturing to herself with an air of frustration. 'It could happen again when real-night comes.'

More questions than he'd ever had about obsidiary paste came crashing into his mind.

She pointed to the plate of sandwiches. 'I'll eat them all myself if you're not careful.'

He sat, knowing it to be unwise to pass up a meal with the lifestyle he now lived.

'So,' he said, taking a sandwich, 'how long have you been here?'

She hiccoughed from eating too fast. 'In your time, about 26,000 years.'

The sandwich came to a standstill beside his open mouth.

She giggled. 'Oh, it's not that long. You'll see. Down here, there's so much to do. It goes by very fast.'

He shook his head. 'I'm not here to be a tourist.'

'That's just the naïve Ralph talking. You haven't even been here a day yet.'

It wasn't just her eccentric avian features he found interesting. It was her twitchy gestures and movements.

'Well,' he said, 'I've got to be here for 999 of them.'

She leaned forward, lowering her voice to a whisper. 'Between you and me, Mr. Ralph, you'll be here for a lot longer than that.' Her normal voice returned with another hiccough. 'Now tell me, how's the sandwich?'

'What do you mean?'

'I mean, what do you think of it?'

'No,' he said. 'What do you mean I'll be here a lot longer than that?'

She stared at the sandwich in his hand.

He took a bite into it. 'It's good,' he said, distractedly. 'What do you mean I'll—'

'Just good?' she exclaimed.

'Veška, stop. Please just tell me what's going on.'

She laughed. 'Oh, Ralph. You mightn't be as bright as the last. But surely you know you need silk to fold a sword.'

He looked at her with sarcastic incredulity.

'Which means you first need to collect the silk, silly,' she said.

'Which is why I asked you where the worms were.'

Her head tilted in sudden realisation. 'Oh. Well, yes, I know where they are. But I can't take you right now. You haven't finished your sandwich.'

He finished it with three eager bites. 'Let's go.'

She shook her head. 'I'll only show you if you promise me one thing.'

He jumped to his feet. 'Of course. Whatever.'

'Promise you'll come exploring with me after.'

Now it was Ralph's turn to laugh. 'Sure.'

'No, Ralph,' she said, sternly. 'Promise me.'

She reminded him of a nagging child, which was strange given her age of over 26,000 years.

'I promise I'll come exploring with you,' he said.

She hopped closer to him like a caique parrot. 'You really mean it?' Her voice resembled a kid requesting an ice-cream at a carnival.

Ralph looked down at her, realising it was the first time he'd spoken to anyone shorter than him in his whole life.

'Yes,' he said. 'Let's go.'

Veška shot into the air, knocking the cup over and spilling the orange juice over the remaining sandwiches. 'Sorry! I'll make you more later. Follow me!'

She dove over the edge.

17

Silk Collection

RALPH approached the gap between the two chunks of land. Below, Veška hovered amongst the intertwining vines, yellow eyes watching him, black wings flapping with elegance.

'I can't fly,' he said.

She rolled her eyes. 'Then how did you get to the Bottom of the Universe?'

His cheeks warmed.

'But never mind that,' she said. 'You don't need to fly. Gravity is whacky down here. Just step over.'

He thought about the waterfall wrapping the land, the celestial objects surrounding them…

'I thought you said to be careful near the edge?' he asked.

She withdrew a flutelike instrument from her waistband. 'Oh, that was for a different reason.'

'And what reason's that?'

'I'll tell you another time. What kind of music do you like?' She played a fruitful tune. 'I can play pretty much anything.' The tune became slow, jumpy. 'Tell me if you like anything in particular.'

She continued changing tunes as Ralph went about satisfying his scepticism.

Taking a stone from the ground, he hurled it at the darkness below. It shot towards it like normal until its inertia ran out. It then bounced along the vertical surface to a rest.

'Nice throw,' Veška said, breaking from playing the flute.

Ralph threw another stone.

132

'Oh, that one was even better!' she said, returning to the flute a moment later.

Again, the stone maintained its trajectory, lost inertia, came to a rest.

A bizarre spectacle. The logic baffled him. But coming from a planet with a gravity constant of 9.81 m/s^2 would do that to you.

He looked at the splinter sparrow perched on his shoulder. 'You ready to catch me?'

It chirped once in support.

Ralph got to his hands and knees and reversed over the edge, like climbing down a ladder.

When the toes of one foot came in contact with the cliff's surface, they slammed against it as though magnetised. The sensation destabilised his sense of direction. He took a moment to get his bearings, then brought the other foot around to stand perfectly upright on the cliff's previously-vertical surface.

'Bravo, bravo,' Veška said. 'Now, come on. Try to keep up.'

Still playing her flute, she took off, zigzagging between the vines. Ralph went after her, ducking and stepping over them, avoiding their thorns.

When they came to the edge, she continued on out into the shadowy darkness. Before it swallowed her, her green hair returned to purple, her feathers returned to white.

'Can you see me?' she asked.

'Not at all.'

'You will.'

A few seconds later, a purple aura faded in, outlining her figure.

'The worms are out there?' he asked.

'Nope.' She pointed to the surface just out of sight.

He got to his hands and knees again and peered over to where no light reached.

'Light,' he said.

The splinter sparrow ignited, sending out pulsing waves of shine, illuminating the environment.

Amongst boulders and patches of moss, a group of white worms grazed like a herd of cows. Each was the size of a train carriage. Canine teeth protruded from the bottom of their mouths. A spiky orifice above their rears expelled trails of glowing, pink string as they wriggled about.

'Okay,' Veška said. 'Time to go.'

'Wait,' Ralph said. 'I have to get some of their silk.'

'No,' she said, pointedly. 'You said we would explore as soon as I showed you where they were.'

'At least let me figure out how to collect the stuff.'

Veška's purple aura contorted as she folded her arms.

Ralph reversed over the edge and approached the nearest worm.

'Excuse me?'

Trying to communicate with gigantic silkworms might've been odd. But after living with the creatures on the Stack, normality had gone out the window.

'I'm not here to hurt you,' he said.

The worms continued grazing without the slightest interest of his arrival.

'I'm only here to collect your silk for a sword to stop the Darkness.'

Their eyes twitched at the sound of his voice. But none broke from their grazing.

'Come on!' Veška said. 'This is boring.'

'Give me a minute,' he said.

He approached the herd. The splinter sparrow's shine swept across the worms. They didn't seem to enjoy the light at all. In retaliation, they growled low, sending wafts of putrid breath in his direction.

He pinched his nose, telling the sparrow to dim. Once his eyes had adjusted to the change in light, he headed over to the closest trail of pink string.

Hand above it, he felt its warm energy. He touched it with a cautious finger. A spark laced out, lashed at his nodes, and launched him into the air.

Veška burst out laughing as he crashed to the ground several metres away. He scowled in her direction. He would've liked to say something to put her in her place, but the growling from the two worms wriggling his way snapped him to attention.

Scrambling to his feet, he sprinted for the edge. Along the way, he realised his stupidity, changed direction, and headed for the surface with the homestead instead.

He climbed over and looked back at the worms, pleased to find they'd already forgotten about him.

Veška landed beside him. 'How's your butt?'

'Why'd you make us go between the vines? We could've stepped over to the worms from here, from the top.'

'But the top is only the top to the side you think is the bottom, silly. Besides, I thought it'd be fun to go between the vines.'

He cursed under his breath.

'Gee whiz,' she said. 'You really are an uptight one.'

'I'm not here to play games, Veška. If you're going to screw around with me like this, the least you can do is tell me how to collect their silk.'

She wagged an index finger at him. 'Nuh-uh. No more work. Time to explore. You promised!'

'No! I'm not exploring. I don't have time. I need to collect their silk so I can get started on the sword.'

Her expression turned sour, then grim, then savage. 'That's what you all say.'

With a flap of her wings, she shot upwards. A few seconds later, he lost sight of her amongst the flow of celestial objects.

He buried his face into his hands. A heads up from the Orbs about Veška would've done nicely.

But he couldn't be too troubled by encountering her. She had just shown him the beasts that produced the silk, the silk that contained far more energy than he'd expected.

Now all he had to do was figure out how to collect enough of it without being eaten in the process.

✦

Time, much like on the Stack, was elusive at the Bottom of the Universe. But unlike Where Time Stood Still, a rhythm dictated it, a rhyme, a ticking and turning of each moment that allowed Ralph to be present, to think, to be, rather than living through timelapses and relying on memories.

'Could you get some sticks from the forest?' he asked.

With a quick nod, Veška took flight.

After her outburst, she'd returned a few hours later with a bowl of mashed potato and a pair of sneakers.

Ralph hadn't cared too much for her apology gifts. He hadn't come to the Bottom of the Universe to make friends. Once he'd folded the sword, he'd never see her again. For now though, he couldn't deny the benefits of having a local around.

She landed beside him with a handful of sticks. 'What are you going to do with them?'

'Learn the day-night cycle.'

'You need sticks for that?'

'It's easier to keep track of minutes with something.'

'Do all humans have trouble remembering simple things?'

'We do have watches on Earth.'

'I know. I've read about them. Why don't you have one?'

He shrugged. 'Never liked wearing them. They always got in the way of my titanium gloves.'

'Your what?'

An ache struck him as he remembered his kit and cave-lab. His thoughts moved to Cyclops next, the farm, the kids…

'Never mind.' He lay back, cupping his head with both hands. 'I'll study their general movements first. Then I'll count.'

Veška lay beside him, glancing at him a few times to mimic his posture.

Studying the celestial objects for a few days, he learned the day-night cycle. The days, for the most part, were governed by two white dwarf stars and a red supergiant. They lasted between eighteen and nineteen hours. As for the nights, other than a few brief periods of darkness caused by asteroids and debris passing over the dying stars, they were governed by a group of pale grey moons, lasting between six and seven hours.

His counting was crude. It was rough and subject to change. But knowing the Bottom of the Universe's ebb and flow gave him a schedule to commit to.

His next task was silk collection.

'Is there a trick to stop the silkworms' thread hurting me?'

Veška stopped playing her flute and laughed, reminiscing. 'Can you speak worm?'

'No. Can you?'

She looked contemplative. 'I tried learning when I first arrived. But they're awfully rude when you interrupt their grazing.'

Ralph nodded in thought. 'Maybe there's an easier way.' He took out the notepad and pen from his backpack and flicked to a new page. 'Maybe I could try trapping them.'

For the next few hours, he sketched various traps and cages. Veška watched on, *oohing* and *aahing* with each one he came up with. But the more he planned, the more he thought, the more he came to terms with how complicated trapping anything the size of a train carriage would be.

As the light faded on his fourth day at the Bottom of the Universe, Ralph and Veška ate dinner together, legs dangling over the edge between the two chunks of land. A selection of rabbit jerky from his backpack, boiled eggs from the hovering chickens, and smoothies made from a blue fruit found in the garden were splayed between them.

'So,' he said, chewing on some jerky, 'why've you been here for 26,000 years?'

'You can't seriously be asking me that,' she said with a laugh.

'Why not?'

'Because no one ever asks me that.'

He stayed silent.

Her laughter continued for a moment before she seemed to become self-conscious. 'You really want to know?'

He nodded, sipped the smoothie, wiped his blue moustache. 'Of course. I want to know a lot of things. Why you're here. Where you're from. Who else has been here.'

'Yes,' she said thoughtfully. 'I read about humans and their inquisitiveness. Well, if you must know, I came here after being banished.'

His eyes widened.

A nervous laugh escaped her. 'Oh, it's a long story. But on Zoroya, it's not normal to be able to change like I can. There are ancient stories about "the dividing deities who morph in the night." It's seen as dark magic. I personally think it's a load of hogwash. But before I did or could or wanted to do anything horrendous in one form and tried to live out the lie in the other, they banished me.'

'You've been gone from your home since you were a kid?'

'In your years, I left when I was four. As soon as my wings were strong enough.'

'And you've been here ever since?'

She shook her head in her twitchy, avian way. 'Around a thousand years after being banished, I heard about this place on one of the Docks. I've been here ever since.'

He took a boiled egg. 'So, you're older than 27,000 years then.'

'In your understanding of time, yes.'

He bit into the egg. 'How long do your people live?'

She swallowed some jerky with a birdlike tilt of her head. 'That depends on a lot of things. But Zoruvians typically live about two or three million years.'

Ralph almost choked on the yolk. 'Two or three million?'

She smiled with curiosity. 'Your whole understanding of time is very funny, Ralph.'

He chugged some smoothie to clear his throat. 'Yeah, I've heard that before.'

'Can I ask you a question now?'

'Go ahead.'

She pointed at the silver nodes in his arms. 'What are they? I've never met anyone with them before.'

He scoffed. The tampering of his body never alluded the creatures he met on his journey through the universe.

'Silver nodes,' he said. 'I use them to channel and boost my energy for particle transference.'

'What's that?'

'A technique that transforms matter and teleports things.'

Her eyes lit up. 'Can I see it?'

After finishing their meal, Ralph transferred across the gap to the pine forest. Veška flew after him, clapping and laughing.

'Really?' she said, landing with a flutter of her white wings. 'Eat some dust, close your eyes, and think about a location? That's amazing.'

'I used to need a golden rod to transfer myself. But ever since I went to the Stack, something changed. My focus or ability. Or something.'

She smiled, eyes beaming. He wasn't sure if they beamed with the same warmth and curiosity people once looked at him with, or something entirely different.

'So, why are we here?' she asked, breaking eye contact. 'You want to see what I've collected?'

'Maybe another time.' He strode across the crunching foliage to a tree.

'I figured making a trap and getting the worms inside would take too long, so I've decided to try a simpler method first.' He broke off two branches and stripped them to resemble the letter Y. 'Have you got anything we can use to collect stones?'

She disappeared into the greenery, returning with two metal buckets.

'Perfect,' he said. 'Okay, let's go.'

On the way to the barn, they filled the buckets with stones. Inside, Ralph lathered the Y-branches and rocks with obsidiary paste. He then used the metal buckets to perform particle transference.

'Incredible,' Veška said, watching the branches and stones flicker, flash, become metal, tarnished. 'I've never seen anything like it.'

He smiled. 'You can fly and change appearance. That's incredible to me.'

Her pale cheeks turned crimson.

'Now we just need some rubber,' he said.

Taking two of the sticks he'd used to count minutes, he asked the splinter sparrow to heat them. Once they were supple, he stretched them into an elastic material, then fitted them to the metal Y-branches.

With their slingshots and buckets of ammo, they spent a week practicing their accuracy. When their aim felt true and they could hit fruit in the trees from twenty metres away, they returned to the dark side of the cliffs.

'Remember, little buddy,' he said to the sparrow, 'no light. We need the element of surprise.'

The sparrow chirped in acknowledgement.

'Are you ready, Veška?'

She nodded eagerly.

He climbed over the edge and dashed for the closest grazing worm.

Tracking the beast, he learned its path, its behaviour and speed. It seemed the more moss it ate, the more string it produced. Whenever it stopped eating to move to a new patch, the pink thread from its orifice severed.

He waited for the worm to clear a moss patch. When it wriggled for another, he dashed over to its severed line.

Hand above the string, he felt its vibrant energy. Warm and powerful, it interacted with his nodes, turning them into a blinking mess.

He shook his head in frustrated realisation.

Everything he'd interacted with since leaving Earth – the bubble aura, the Stack, the Orbs – had traded energy with him in some way. He'd been a fool to not realise the thread required a similar transaction.

Once his nodes had resumed their usual, gentle pulsing, with a hesitant finger, he touched the string.

Instead of being launched from his feet this time, the string's glow merely dulled.

Relief washed over him. A severed line was a safe line.

'Nice job,' Veška said from above. 'Now, grab it and let's get the heck out of here!'

Ralph coiled the length of thread around his arm. He then found another severed line and collected that. And another.

While roaming and keeping away from the worms, he came across a cave emanating a pink glow. Peering inside, his jaw dropped in greed at the sight of three luminous, bulbous clumps of pink silk.

'Veška,' he called. 'We've struck gold.'

She swooped in to land beside him. 'Oh wow, I've never seen worm eggs before.'

'I think they're cocoons. Getting them back to the barn would save heaps of time.'

He thought about the logistics for such a mission, calculating how much obsidiary paste he'd need, determining lines of sight to make the transferences. Before he could do the rough math though, a growling came from behind, followed by a putrid stench.

He wheeled around. Veška shrieked.

'Time to go,' he said.

Veška took flight for the light. Ralph stayed put. After hanging the reels of silk thread over his neck, he removed the slingshot from his back pocket. Loading it with shaky hands, he took aim, fired.

And missed by a good five metres.

'Not bad,' Veška said, playfully, peering over the edge.

He took out another stone, aimed, fired.

This time, he managed to clip the worm's face, enraging it further, and attracting the attention of its friends.

With four worms chomping their jaws towards him, he backed away, loading and firing metal stones with as much accuracy as his anxiety allowed.

'Feel free to join in,' he said.

Veška flew above the herd and started pelting the worms with her own metal stones. While most of her shots missed as well, she managed to land a few good hits alongside his.

When the worms came too close for comfort, Ralph called on his safety net.

'A little help?' he said, and the splinter sparrow ignited.

Sending its sonar shine out, the silkworms hissed and recoiled, turning to wriggle away. Ralph used the distraction to his advantage and dashed for the edge.

Veška landed beside him a few seconds later.

'That was so much fun,' she said, hopping closer to him. 'Oh, look!'

He followed her feathered finger to an unmoving mass of white ten metres away.

'I think it's asleep,' she said.

After the worm's friends had vacated, Ralph climbed back over the edge and approached the fallen beast.

'Tone it down a bit,' he told the sparrow.

The bird dimmed its shine to a metre radius.

Up close, Ralph was in awe of the worm's size and appearance. Other than some tinges of what looked like sunburn on its face, pronotum, and prothorax, no doubt caused by the sparrow's shine, its skin was a brilliant ivory. Its rear, spiky orifice resembled a face, reminding him of the caterpillars on Earth that'd developed the same survival guise to ward off aerial predators.

The worm twitched. Veška squealed. A new wave of stench struck Ralph's face.

They both dashed for the light, giggling away.

Back at the barn with his twenty metres of thread, Ralph got acquainted with the wooden equipment. Veška delighted in teaching him all about them. She showed him how to load the spinning wheel, threading it around the bar with hooks, through the opening, around the bobbin to the wheel. She showed him how to load the loom, how to hold the thread as he fed it, what angle prevented it from catching, and how often to press the pedal.

In three days, he'd spun the collected thread into a spool the size of a carrot. In another three, while tearing close to sixty percent, he'd woven a piece of glowing silk the size of a handkerchief.

His efforts were laughable, making him realise Veška had been right. He would be at the Bottom of the Universe for a lot longer than 999 days.

18
Folding and Sealing

'CAN we go exploring now?'

They'd just spent four days building an enclosure in the barn. Made from scraps of wood and metal, it had a covering to keep a worm permanently in the dark and a trough to keep it fed.

'Once we get a worm and cocoon here,' Ralph said, 'yes.'

Veška folded her arms. 'I don't believe you.'

'C'mon. You know how close I am to fixing everything. The sooner I fold the sword, the sooner I can—'

'Leave,' she finished.

He sighed. 'I have to save the universe.'

She rolled her eyes. 'Oh, don't be so dramatic. You're not *saving* the universe.'

'That's not true. I told you what the Orbs said about how I ruined things with my transferences.'

'Yet you keep performing them.'

'Because the damage is done. But it's only a matter of time before I reset that damage.'

'Has anyone ever called you obsessed?'

When night fell, they headed to the dark side of the cliffs where the worms resided. Armed with obsidiary paste, slingshots, and plenty of ammo, they positioned themselves above the glowing cocoon cave.

Ralph turned to Veška. 'Ready?'

She took flight without responding. He tracked her purple outline into the darkness. When she was in position, he reversed over the edge and sprinted for the cave. Inside, he sprinkled a pinch of obsidiary dust under his tongue, then got to work covering one of the cocoons with the paste.

Halfway complete, a low growling came from outside. He sped up his smearing, rolling the cocoon over, covering it with the ashen paste.

'They're coming,' Veška called.

Before the worms had breached the entry, he placed a hand on the cocoon, pointed the golden rod to a spot outside the cave, imprinted the location in his mind, and began the transference.

Recompiling in the dark with the cocoon, the worms turned, sniffing out his presence.

Ralph didn't waste a moment. Placing a hand against the cocoon again, he transferred it to the topside of the chunk of land. As it decompiled, one particle at a time, he withdrew his slingshot and joined Veška in the barrage.

Firing metal-stone after metal-stone at the silkworms, they managed to deter two of the more cowardly ones. The other four didn't seem fazed by being struck though. They continued wriggling towards him with intention, their putrid stench making him feel ill.

Backing away, he fired continuously. When he became overwhelmed, he called on his trusty splinter sparrow.

'Now!'

And the bird ignited.

With an audible hiss, the worms recoiled from the shine. Ralph waited until they'd retreated a safe distance before resuming the onslaught.

For the next twenty minutes, they repeated this method, firing stones at the worms, using the sparrow's shine to deter them when necessary. Eventually, they managed to knock one unconscious. Once its friends had returned to grazing, Ralph dashed over to it, covered it with obsidiary paste, and transferred it, the cocoon, and himself to the barn.

Veška returned a few minutes later, carrying two buckets of moss.

'You can leave them there,' he said, pointing at the trough.

She threw the buckets to the ground. The moss spilled everywhere. Before he could say anything, she shot back outside.

He shook his head, watching her disappear into the surrounding flow. While her helpfulness had been priceless so far, her childish tendencies, tendencies Piri and Jamaki had never exhibited, continued to get in the way.

He headed back inside. Running a hand over the cocoon, he located a loose end of thread. Combining it with the one dangling from the unconscious worm's orifice, he fed them through the spinning wheel.

Over the next few days, while the worm slept, he collected moss. While awake and munching away, he pedalled the spinning wheel and loom, weaving the pink thread into sheets of glowing fabric.

Veška came and went during this time. Sometimes, she sulked in the barn's rafters. Other times, she played her flute in the garden.

He did his best to ignore her whenever she was around. He'd made it clear from the start he wasn't here to play games. If she didn't want to help, he didn't want to talk to her.

In a matter of weeks, the worm had settled into its new home. It seemed more than happy in its enclosure, making him wonder if it liked being lazy and domesticated, like many animals on Earth, or if the act of extracting its silk was equivalent to milking a cow.

In either case, it didn't matter. His efforts had been rewarded with a constant supply of thread. And once he'd woven a few hundred metres of the stuff, it was time to begin the folding.

✦

One hundred days into the folding of the silk sword, an ice moon breached the Bottom of the Universe's firmament.

In a matter of hours, the two chunks of land were blanketed in white. The river slowed as ice sheets formed on its surface. Puffs of snow whipped about in erratic fashion, falling in accordance with the strange gravity.

Ralph was out collecting moss when the temperature dropped. Hurrying to finish filling the buckets, he jogged back to the barn with the splinter sparrow's shine keeping him warm and dry.

Upon entering, he found green-haired, black-feathered Veška perched at one end of a wooden table laden with food.

'I thought you'd be hungry after all your weaving and folding,' she said with timidity.

It'd been a month since he'd seen her. Their last dispute had caused the latest rift, a dispute much like all other disputes: She wanted to do things. He wanted to work. Both were stubborn.

He placed the buckets of frozen moss beside the fire drum to thaw.

'I'm not hungry.'

'But,' she said, 'I made all this delicious food.'

Plates of fruit, boiled eggs, and bread covered the table. Candles and metal cups with a dark juice filled in the gaps.

'You know how important this is to me,' he said, sitting at the loom. 'I can't stop. Not when I'm so close to finishing something I've been pursuing my whole life.'

She flew over to him with a flap of her wings.

He focused on feeding and weaving the thread. With every centimetre he produced, he added to the length of pink silk leading to the beginnings of his sword.

Veška waddled over to the sword on the box by the snoring worm and peered at it. 'I've never seen one like this.'

Before he'd started folding the blade, he'd imagined the one he wanted. But the act of actually forging it had proven difficult. He remembered typical blades from stories and movies. He knew their edges, their curves, their points and hilts. But without any guidance or images to go off, memories were all he had.

'It's called a scimitar,' he said, pressing the loom's pedal rhythmically. 'I'm not sure if it's what the Orbs want. But these types of swords were once typical in certain cultures on my planet.'

'Earth,' she said, turning to him.

His pedalling flow slowed as he looked into her eyes. The shadow bordering them gave her an appearance of deception and mystery. Her nature was nothing of the sort. Everything she'd done since he'd arrived had shown him her true colours.

He resumed the pedalling. 'That's right.'

But could he blame her? Being banished from regular life, forced to fend for herself since she was a child…

'Could you tell me more about your planet?' she asked, hopping towards him.

Memories of Stephanie asking him questions while he worked floated into his consciousness. He saw her pinging his intercom, calling him every other day. His mind turned to Piri and Jamaki next as they tended to the farm, made food for him…

'Let me do this fold,' he said, 'and I'll tell you about it at dinner.'

Her wings fluttered as she seemed to lose clarity on what she was doing. She waddled one way, then the next, turned and hurried over to the banquet she'd prepared.

He watched her hop onto a chair, feeling an emptiness inside him.

She was, in so many ways, just like him: a lost, lonely child.

Fresh sheet of silk woven, he moved over to the sword. Positioning it beside the fold he'd made yesterday, he wrapped the sheet around the subtle curve of the blade and pressed down.

The splinter sparrow ignited, sending a narrow beam of heat into it, compressing the silk, sealing it.

With the folding complete for another day, he joined Veška for dinner.

✦

Two hundred days into the folding, they headed out into the carnage surrounding the Bottom of the Universe. Using transferences and the splinter sparrow, he followed her as she weaved between the objects.

They passed clusters of rocks and ice, small and large moons. She glanced over her shoulder every few minutes, smiling in sheer satisfaction. He couldn't help but return his own smile whenever she did.

Some of the areas she took him to baffled him. Some rattled him. Others made him speechless, like the areas where items pooled.

'But how?' he asked.

'Everything has to go somewhere, silly.'

Amongst the collection, he found pendants and crystals with their own distortion fields. He found items resembling toys, vials filled with different liquids, Platonic solids made from plasma. Of the items he could carry, he loaded them into his backpack. The rest that piqued his interest were covered with obsidiary paste to transfer at a later date.

'These spots are where you found the books about Earth?'

She nodded. 'I have an entire library on that asteroid over there.' She pointed to a large, crystalline rock. 'It's how I learn about the tourists that come here and those sent by the Orbs.'

'When did they tell you I was coming?'

'They came two days before you arrived to let me know.'

'And you learned my language in two days?'

She chuckled. 'Of course. Zoruvians don't have limiting capacities like your brains do. It's one reason why we are natural navigators and explorers. Once we learn or see something important, we remember it forever.'

He wondered if such a skill had led to a lack of emotional development in the thousands of years she'd been alive.

'Come on,' she said. 'I want to show you the sound planets.'

They continued on through the immeasurable congregation. The more Ralph studied each object they passed, the more he became struck by the overall harmonious movement of the entire spectacle. Although he'd associated the general motion to a lava lamp when he'd first arrived, it was clear there was more to it than that. It was almost like every object was consciously aware of one another, like a network of living creatures, like the mycelian networks of Earth.

Veška led him to an area with twenty planetoids. Pastel in colour, each exuded a different sound. Some thrummed low and grim. Others sung high-pitched and screechy. But none were obnoxious or damaging to his ears like loud music. Their sounds resonated inside him, vibrating his bones, connecting to his silver nodes.

Passing a cloudy, fuchsia planetoid, its frequency came captivating, flickering his nodes. Passing a taupe one, a sluggish sensation swelled around him, dimming them, transporting him back in time to the day his erratic transferences had resulted in him leaving the Solar System.

Would being attuned to objects and their frequencies have helped back then? Maybe being calmer, more aware could've helped him map out where he'd been ejected to. And maybe that way he could've found Earth.

Earth.

What a distant memory. And what a distant desire he had to return there.

Of course, he still missed his home. He still missed the mountain and the Adelaideans. He still missed his routine of planning in the shade by day and experimenting by night. But it was hard being sentimental while flying amongst celestial objects with a Zoruvian at the Bottom of the Universe, a few short hours after making a fold on a silk sword that would finally give him his life back.

They passed a pale-green planetoid next. It emanated an assimilating, prevailing frequency, causing him to shudder. They then exited the pastel moon zone into an area with pockets of dense, colourful gas lit by a nearby neutron star.

'Look how pretty this place is,' Veška said, white wings flapping with an ethereal flow.

Ralph smiled, tracking his eyes from her to the collection of glowing gases reminiscent of fairy lights.

'Can we go check out those mirror blobs next?' he asked, pointing into the distance.

She smiled and took off. He went after her.

✦

After making the three hundredth fold, they headed out to the marble moon for dinner.

From their perch, they gazed at the two chunks of land below. With the snow still covering their surfaces, along with the waning light of the white dwarf stars and red supergiant, everything had taken on a glossy appearance.

'Look how cute the house looks covered in all that powder,' Veška said.

Ralph nodded. 'Reminds me of Christmas movies.'

'Oh, I would love to watch one of those.' She hopped twice in excitement, moving closer to him so their skin touched.

'Me too. Maybe one day one will show up here.'

They were silent for a moment, taking in the scenery, pretending they weren't sitting so close to one another. He was ashamed to admit it, but the moment made him question why he was even bothering to fold a sword.

He shook the thought away. To waver this close to the halfway mark of the clearest deadline he'd ever had was unjustified, stupid.

He bit into the sandwich.

'Why does it all pool here anyway?' he asked. 'I get that it's the Bottom of the Universe. But what does that even mean?'

'I used to wonder the same thing. But it's not really the bottom of the universe. It's more like a well, so to speak.'

He thought for a moment, shook his head. 'I still don't get it.'

'You know how everything is moving away from what you call the Big Bang?'

149

He nodded, placing the sandwich down and taking a blue muffin.

'Well,' she continued, 'as everything moves away from that initial spark, this place pulls everything used and unwanted backwards.'

He offered some of the muffin to the sparrow.

'Does that mean the darkness below is the edge of the universe? Is that why you told me to be careful when I first arrived?'

'Not exactly,' she said. 'Ever since the energy ratio was disrupted, the Darkness has been encroaching more and more. This is why we can see it so close.'

He bowed his head in disgust. 'And it's all my fault.'

She put a feathery hand on his, smiling. 'Have you always been so dramatic? You're not the only one who has tampered with reality.'

'That's not true. There might've been others who disrupted the balance, but I am the one who destroyed it.'

'That may be so. But now that you know what caused the problem, you must feel a little more relaxed?'

Ralph almost laughed. 'I won't feel relaxed until the Darkness is destroyed.'

'I don't know how you stay focused on one thing for so long.' She glanced around with avian twitchiness. 'Although, when I think about it, I still haven't solved why this place keeps moving. And I do tend to think about that quite often.'

His ears perked up. 'The Bottom of the Universe is moving?'

'Oh, yes. It's moved quite a bit since I arrived.'

Ralph flung his backpack off and took out the coordinates device.

'What's that?' Veška asked, leaning closer.

'A coordinates device.' He booted it up. 'It tells you your location in the universe. Supposedly.'

'Really? I just use stars.'

The letters, numbers, and symbols on the LCD screens scrolled, split, locked into place. Although the top row told him he was even further from Earth than last time, the bottom one looked more peculiar and meaningless than ever.

~898TAU / ~14.2Gly / ~4.3Gpc | 02h 43.40m 08.21s + -48° 52' 1.37'
TF-2.5±19(21.18^5)-20a15b[4^{18}(9.14b11)-25(15c21)18]-13.9(12^{15})-OF

He handed the device to her. 'You take a look.'

She studied the screens. 'Hmm. Some of it seems familiar. But without anything to compare it to, I doubt I can make much sense of it. We should fly out to the nearest star to get another reading.'

Ralph fiddled with the buttons on the side. Pressing one changed the code to the one that'd loaded when he'd last used it. 'That's the location of the Stack.' He pressed the button again. 'And that's somewhere in my solar system.'

'Oh, wow. I could go to these places using these codes.' She scrolled back to the Bottom of the Universe's readout. 'This would take some time to understand. But I think it's possible.'

She made to hand the device back, but he shook his head.

'You keep it.'

Her eyes lit up. 'Are you sure?'

'It was never useful to me. Maybe when I leave, you can go visit the Stack and meet Ca'zehro.'

She placed the device on the marble moon's surface, shoulders hunching. 'You're really going to leave?'

He sighed, realising he was again doing what he'd done on Earth.

He had the food, the tasks, the companionship, the freedom, and he hadn't even built a new atom smasher yet. With the variety of objects surrounding the Bottom of the Universe, what other secrets could be found? What other aberrant particles could be extracted? What other equations and theories could be studied and solved?

'You know I can't deviate from the task set by the Orbs of Scindere.'

They were silent again, watching the celestial flow, the lands below.

'But maybe,' he said, 'after I destroy the Darkness, I could come back and we could travel the universe. Or something.'

Her posture straightened. She hopped up and down. 'Really?'

'Why not? I'm not sure what'll happen once I use the sword, or even how I'll get my life back, but—'

She leant forward and planted her lips against his. He froze as his mind swirled and his cheeks warmed.

They stayed connected for almost ten seconds, unmoving. They then broke away. She grabbed the coordinates device and started fiddling with it. He took another muffin and bit into it.

After ten minutes of only the dull hum of celestial objects filling the ambience, the sparrow chirped hesitantly, as though reminding Ralph about his mission.

They laughed.

'You're right,' he said, offering a finger for it to nibble on. 'We should head back.'

✦

Four hundred days into the folding of the silk sword, Ralph was becoming bored, braindead, restless.

In the old days, when he'd focused on something, he'd only ever spent a few months before moving on to a new task or having a breakthrough. But with only one task to complete each day, his patience was being tested like never before. It was like he'd become some sort of karate kid, forced to do what his sensei told him just to please them.

He knew what he was doing was supposed to be hard. The fate of the universe relied upon it. But he was torn between his goal of solving his dilemma and enjoying his newfound freedom and friend.

✦

Six hundred days into the folding of the silk sword, the day-night cycle changed with the arrival of new objects.

Ralph was excited about this. It broke routine. It added new variables around moss collection. It altered the worm's sleep schedule.

In other words, it added spice to his otherwise boring existence. It also gave him a nice excuse to have some time off.

As he familiarised himself with the new schedule, he gardened, cleaned the house and barn, and explored every corner of the Bottom of the Universe with Veška.

She showed him her item collection in the pine forest. She showed him her library on the crystalline asteroids. She took him to places he'd never been, like the edge of the congregation, where moons covered with remnants of ancient cities floated.

'Are you upset for being banished?' he asked as they left a moon with crumbling pillars and hexagonal pyramids.

Out of nowhere, she burst into tears, falling to the ground and curling her wings around her face.

He crouched beside her, placing a hand on her shoulder. 'Sorry. I didn't mean to—'

She spread her white wings wide with a grin. 'Oh, my goodness, look at your face!' She took flight, backflipping four times before hovering above a crater. 'Why would I be upset? They banished *me*. I had no say in the matter. Besides, look where I am, look who I'm with. I have everything I could ever want down here.'

They met each other's eyes. The tinkling pulses coming from the pyramids were the only noises for quite some time.

'C'mon,' he said, preparing a transfer, 'let's keep going.'

Without a sole focus on the folding, the days began to fly. And with each one that passed, the more reluctant Ralph grew towards his work.

Of course, he never strayed too far from it. He still extracted the worm's thread. He still topped up its trough. But other than simple chores like these, he started doing the one thing he hadn't done since being born.

He started living.

With the ice moon melting, warm rain fell across the chunks of land, turning the Bottom of the Universe into a beautiful haven. The stream flowed powerfully once again. The silent waterfall tumbled and sloshed. Green grass sprouted on the dirt surrounding the homestead.

Life was great.

But three months after abandoning the folding, as Ralph climbed into bed one evening, body sore from another day of exploring and looting with Veška, a reverberating, melodic voice shook the house.

'You have forsaken us, Nazra!'

19
The Return

RALPH blinked once and found himself back at the canyon. Flashes of indigo lightning forked across the dark, roiling sky. The energy from it was as absorptive and oppressive as he remembered. Yet it did not swallow any light. Everything in the area remained perfectly lit – the burgundy rocks, the dying trees, the thirty-two Orbs surrounding him.

'You have forsaken us.'

Their words came haunting, powerful, binding. Their gaseous glows were so bright, he felt like he was in an interrogation room.

'You have forsaken me!' he said, voice breaking. 'Why was I even put up to this? Why was it me who'd been cursed from the start? I don't want to be here. I don't want to be folding a stupid silk sword. What the hell am I supposed to do with it anyway, throw it at the Darkness?'

The Orbs waited for him to finish his outburst. But what an outburst it was. It felt good to shout. It felt good to let out words he hadn't realised had been swimming around in his mind.

'Is that all, Nazra, Quanta Man, Thing Who Has Spent His Entire Existence Pursuing a Cure to His Curse, Yet Allowed a Zoruvian to Distract Him?'

Ralph inhaled two deep breaths. 'Veška didn't distract me. She just showed me what I've been missing out on. And now that I've met someone who won't die like everyone else in my life—'

The Orbs brightened. The four familiar ones then came forward, inflating to the size of oversized basketballs.

'Do not forget,' the Orb of Light said, *'it was you who tampered with reality.'*

'And you were given an option to redeem yourself,' the Orb of Attraction said.

'And out of all the beings in the universe, we gave you the chance to help,' the Orb

of Repulsion said.

'*And help us you did,*' the Orb of Deterioration said. '*Until now.*'

A rumbling stirred in the restless sky.

'I don't care,' Ralph said. 'I don't want to be a prisoner any longer. You could've intervened at any moment before I caused the energy debt. You allowed this.'

The Orbs flared. '*Do you not see your task has not yet been completed?*'

Ralph folded his arms. 'Maybe I'm not up to the task.'

Indigo lightning tore the sky.

'*You forget, Nazra,*' the Orbs sang, '*we are fighting the same fight. We want the same things. If you do not realise this, if you do not complete your part of the plan, you will condemn the universe to suffer for eternity.*'

'I've already suffered for centuries, why should I care?'

'*You are not at liberty to not care until your destiny has been fulfilled!*'

He turned away from them. 'I didn't choose to be cursed.'

'*Yet you still have not done enough.*'

Ralph scoffed. 'What a stupid thing to say. I've dedicated my life to breaking free from the shackles of time, to figure out what's wrong with me. I've sacrificed everything and everyone.'

'*But you still have not earned the right to know what you must.*'

'I don't care. The blade's been started. There's more than enough silk at the barn. Find someone else to finish it. Or, better yet, finish it yourselves.'

The Orbs flared. Ralph sensed no care or humour in their auras.

'*If you wish to be like this, Nazra, we will mark you for all the universe to know. You will not be able to go anywhere without feeling the effects of your lack of compliance. You will not be able to enjoy anything without remembering your failures.*'

Ralph opened his mouth to respond, but another white flash engulfed him, transporting him to the barn. He took a moment to get his bearings, scanning the room.

It was a scene straight out of a nightmare.

Not only was the worm he'd kept and fed for two years dead and shrivelled, but the silk sheets and sword were ripped to shreds.

Ralph lifted the remains of the cold, dim sword. 'What have you done?'

'*Do not blame us,*' the Orbs sang. '*Time ticked. Entropy took over. It is the way of the universe.'*

He shook his head, mouth dry. 'No. You did this. You're the Orbs of Scindere. You ruined my work to prove a point. Just like you ruined my life by allowing me to leave Earth.'

Humour spread through the barn.

'No, Nazra, you did this. This is how the universe works. This is how time works. You did things and things did things to you. And now you understand what it means to not listen to the ones who know the way.'

Ralph let the silk fall between his fingers.

'By sitting at the Bottom of the Universe, you were seduced by delusions, by things you believed mattered.'

He felt like crying. He felt like screaming. He felt like running home to Earth where things made sense.

But that was never going to happen. Those days were over, a distant memory, a moment in time, a time when he should've been more present, more grateful, more attentive.

'You were destined for greatness, Quanta Man. It was you who was supposed to destroy the Darkness. If only you could abandon your greed and archaic understanding of time.'

He bowed his head. He'd failed. He might've been filled with knowledge that'd allowed him to traverse the universe. But he was still stuck. Still lost. Still no closer to rotating himself out of hell.

'Your ego caused you to deny the path you were meant to walk.'

Ralph slumped at the loom. 'How was I supposed to know?'

'You were blessed with time, Quanta Man. You were given the chance to balance it all, make things right, allow the universe to flourish once again.'

'All that time I wasted. All that work, gone.'

He lifted a shredded silk sheet from the ground. Its lack of glow and heat made him miserable. The slashes across the worm's corpse reminded him of the scratches on the A-frame house.

'Who did this?' he asked.

'A giranticore,' the Orbs sang. *'A harbinger of harmony. A crawling, winged beast from below. And it would've destroyed more if we had not intervened.'*

The Orbs traded white electricity.

'Do you understand the cost of your greed and tampering?'

Ralph nodded, eyes on the ground.

The energy. The balance. The debt he'd caused. It'd been his fault the Darkness had begun to consume all. If he'd never tried fixing his life, if he'd taken his curse on the chin, living out a life on Earth, travelling to Proxim with the others, he never would've even been here.

'*You are at a crossroads, Nazra. You must choose what you will do next.*'

The choice was an illusion.

'You already know my choice.'

The Orbs hovered closer. '*And what choice is that?*'

He looked from them to the destruction in the barn. In a low voice, he said, 'I want to finish the sword.'

Although the Orbs possessed no eyes, he could feel them peering into his soul.

'*Why?*' they asked, moving closer.

He took a moment to consider what he would say. 'I don't know.'

The Orbs backed away, began to fade.

'Wait,' he said, stepping forward. 'Because I want my life back. Because I want to live like a normal human. I want to explore. I want to love. I want to know why I've been screwed with. And if that means I have to stay down here for another 999 days, then so be it.'

The luminosity of the Orbs returned. Their aura changed from one of disappointment to satisfaction.

'*Do not betray us again, Nazra.*'

They began to merge.

'*We are relying on you. We will be watching.*'

The four Orbs became one.

'*Finish what you have started. Prove you are the redeemer we perceived you to be. Prove you believe in us as we believe in you.*'

They faded from view.

He watched the last of their swirling, luminous gases dissipate, then wandered over to the fire in the centre of the barn.

He'd been an idiot. He'd had no right to go against them, falling victim to human instincts. He mightn't have been the first to mess with reality, he mightn't have been the only one messing with it, but he'd been the one to ruin it. How could he have ever let Veška, a creature he'd only just met, someone he'd one day never see again, distract him from his mission?

He shook his head, despondent, disheartened.

The Orbs were right. And of course they were. Their attraction, repulsion, deterioration, and light allowed for the fluctuating fields of reality, for the same energy he'd used to tamper with the universe. He'd been a fool for not listening to them. They'd shown him things he'd never seen. They'd told him things he'd never known. They'd explained exactly how he could fix his life.

'What happened, Ralph?'

Veška's timid voice came from the rafters. She dropped to land beside him.

'Where did you go?' she asked. 'I came to check on you in the morning and saw your bed empty.'

'Leave me alone,' he said, eyes on the licking flames in the drum.

'What do you mean? I didn't—'

He wheeled around. 'Why didn't you tell me about the giranticore?'

She shrank back. 'I… I've only ever seen it a few times. I don't know much about it, only that it lives under the lands and dislikes noise.'

'Liar! You wanted this to happen.'

She shook her head rapidly, desperately. 'Why would I want that?'

'Because you don't want me to leave.' He cursed under his breath. 'It's so obvious now. I should've known you'd try something like this.'

'I didn't try anything,' she said, voice shaking. 'Of course, I would love for you to stay. But—'

'See! Your greed ruined everything I've been working on my entire life.'

He scanned the room. The giranticore hadn't just torn the silk to shreds but had also damaged the weaving equipment.

A feathery hand touched his arm. He ripped it away.

'Leave me alone,' he said.

Her eyes widened with fear. 'But Ralph, I thought we were friends.'

'What? We've never been friends. I've been cursed my whole life and have never had the time nor luxury for friends.' He turned back to the fire. 'Just go away.'

'But I don't want to. I like being around you.'

'Go away!' he yelled. 'I want to be alone. This is how it's supposed to be.'

'But Ralph—'

'Get the hell away from me!' he barked, breath uncontrolled.

She stayed for a moment, trembling, staring. Then, with a waddle to the front door and a great flap of her white wings, she was gone.

✦

Four hundred and fifty-five days into phase two of the folding of his silk sword, Ralph had fallen into a strict, purposeful groove. He didn't sulk. He didn't explore. He barely left the homestead.

His mornings consisted of gathering fresh moss for the worm. He'd spin the length it spooled. He'd weave it into a sheet of silk in the loom. He'd then break for breakfast.

His afternoons involved gardening, drinking tea, and revising equations. He'd also taken to filling empty books in the house with his methods for particle transference and silk collection. If he happened to fail the Orbs again, he hoped whoever came next would have an easier time than him.

His evenings were all about the fold. Like a prayer before supper, a morning run before work, a chapter before bed, it was the most ritualistic, religious thing he'd ever done in his life.

He'd head to the barn as the light faded. He'd lay the fresh length of silk on the table. After removing any creases and dirt, he'd position it perfectly, perform the fold for the day, then head straight to bed.

It was a simple, boring, orderly routine. But it got the job done.

Sometimes, he glimpsed Veška flying between the celestial objects as he collected moss. But he never called to her. And she never approached him.

It was better that way.

When the final folding day rolled around, Ralph spent an unnecessary amount of time cleaning the barn and house. He knew it was more important to finish the sword. But he feared losing his simple existence at the Bottom of the Universe.

But he couldn't prolong the inevitable.

As the day waned on the nine hundred and ninety-ninth day, after the worm had finished its meal, he kited the creature outside.

'You're free to go, buddy,' he said, patting its slimy flesh.

The worm stayed put, chewing cud, staring.

'Please.'

He patted the worm again, prompting it to wriggle away. But leaving Ralph seemed like the last thing it wanted to do.

'Have it your way then.'

After covering it in obsidiary paste, he transferred it home to the dark side of the cliffs. On his return, he found Veška perched atop the barn's door, face solemn, wings folded.

'Hi,' she said.

'You shouldn't be here.' He headed for the entrance. 'You're just going to make it harder for yourself.'

She dropped from her perch and landed in front of him. 'I made something for you.'

He sighed. 'Why?'

'Because I wanted to. You gave me the coordinates device, after all.'

He stepped around her and entered the barn. 'I didn't give you that so you'd have to repay me.'

She hopped after him. 'What do you mean? I've read all about humans and their transactional relationships.'

He headed over to his sword. As he busied himself positioning the last portion of silk, she hopped onto the loom beside him.

'But I didn't make you something because of that,' she said. 'I wanted to make it. And I think you will really like it. And if you do, maybe you could stay a few days to enjoy it.'

He doublechecked the silk sheet's position, dusted it, removed its creases. 'You know that's not possible.'

She hopped onto the box with the sword, leaning forward to inspect the curved blade like a budgie would inspect a mirror.

'It's beautiful, Ralph,' she said. 'I'm proud of you.'

Staring into her eyes opened a vortex inside his chest, much like the one that'd opened on the morning he'd found Cyclops's stiff body on the mesa.

He didn't want to lose another person. He didn't want to abandon another routine he'd adjusted to.

'What if,' he said, 'we go see what you made before I head back to the Orbs?'

Her wings fluttered. She trotted this way and that, took flight, landed.

'That would be lovely. And I must say, Ralph, I never meant to annoy you, I only tried to—'

He leant forward.

And with that, their second kiss, longer than before.

A warmness swirled through him this time, a giddiness. But it didn't last long.

In a matter of seconds, the familiar coldness returned. His stomach sank. His throat tightened. Like a black hole consuming all light, guilt swallowed the moment as he remembered his curse, his reality, what he still had to do.

He broke away with a gasp. 'I'm sorry.'

Eyes still closed, she spoke in a whisper. 'What? Why?'

He paced, searching for words, trying to make sense of the conflict in his mind, heart, and soul.

'A lot has been riding on this moment, Veška. A lot of years. A lot of pain. A lot of…' He stopped pacing. 'I know it mightn't seem long to you, but I've spent my whole life getting to this point. And in all this time, after everything I've been through, I'm finally on the brink of the next stage.'

She hopped from the box to him. Her eyes were glassy. 'Then finish it, Ralph. Finish the fight. Fix your life.'

He stared at her, a million thoughts churning away. Then, with a nod to himself, to her, to the moment, he approached the sword.

The end. This was it.

Folding the last sheet of pink silk over the blade, he pressed down firmly. The splinter sparrow chirped and ignited, sending a beam of heat into it, sealing it, compressing it. Completing it.

He stepped back, lifting the scimitar sword by the hilt. It glowed and glistened in his grip.

He smiled. A moment more momentous than anything he'd ever experienced or achieved. And instead of being congratulated by lambs bleating in the distance, he was congratulated by the knowledge of how far he'd come.

Holding the sword was everything. Every breakthrough. Every punishment. Every loss and sacrifice. Every night he'd spent alone. Every person he'd pushed away.

He lifted it high. Veška eyed it and him, smiling. He smiled back.

Heavier than expected, he brought it back down. Its energy thrummed with a power greater than the unspun silk.

He was impressed, excited. But he didn't have long to enjoy the moment.

Before he could say anything, a familiar white blanket of light swallowed him, pulling him from his home at the Bottom of the Universe.

20
Wrongful Worship

BACK in the Orb capsule, Ralph rocketed through the disorientating darkness inciting nothing but despair. The familiar lack of stars, planets, moons, and nebulae outside provided a feeling similar to what he believed being buried alive would be like. The only difference was the presence of the indigo lightning from the canyon, which coursed through the darkness, illuminating ghastly balls of gas.

'The sword is complete,' he said to the thirty-two glowing dots on the ceiling. 'It's time to end the Darkness's reign.'

White electricity coursed between the dots. Some of it leapt out and struck his nodes, the chairs, the altar.

Ralph raised his voice. 'You pulled me from the barn just to be silent? I've sacrificed my life to forge this weapon, and now you will not speak?'

But they *were* speaking. He could sense it. He could feel the energy passing between them.

'I've done what you required,' he said. 'Now let me finish this.'

The Orbs brightened. Four of them then floated down, inflating to oversized basketballs.

The sword, Quanta Man,' they sang. *'You must offer it to us.'*

Ralph turned the glowing silk sword over in his hand.

Do not worry. You have done well. You will be rewarded. But to complete the task, you must offer it to us.'

'And what will happen next?'

A flare of light told him they did not like the question.

'I did all that work, and now you're—'

It does not need to make sense, Nazra! You have played your part. We will take it from here.'

He shook his head. 'Am I not the one who must defeat the Darkness? "The one who changed it, must repeal it." I was the one who destabilised the universe.'

The Orbs of Scindere moved closer to him. No matter how long Ralph had been alive, the luminous spheres had a knack for making him feel like a toddler again.

'If you could finish this fight,' Ralph said, 'why make me spend all that time collecting, weaving, and folding?'

The Orbs flared.

'And still, here you are, contemplating the primitive notion of time. Why must you cling to such an archaic concept, Nazra? Why must you refuse to understand eternity?'

This was the most outrage the Orbs had expressed since they'd pulled him from the vortex.

'It does not matter how long you performed your task,' the Orb of Light said. *'It does not matter what you think is right.'*

'We did not make you do anything,' the Orb of Repulsion said.

'You accepted your fate,' the Orb of Deterioration said.

'You said yes,' the Orb of Attraction said. *'You wanted to help.'*

And they were right. And of course they were. They were the all-knowers of the universe. They'd been here since the beginning, giving the universe its fundamental laws. They were the causes for every effect. Ralph, a mere human, a Nazra, a cursed boy who'd tampered with reality, didn't have a right to say anything.

But still, something didn't sit right with him. Call it intuition, scepticism, or his human inquisitiveness Veška had talked about, something told him to be wary.

'You are the all-knowers,' Ralph said.

'Yes, Quanta Man.'

'You divide reality.'

'Yes. Now, place the blade on the altar. It is time for the end to begin.'

Ralph held the sword above the altar. A pink mist fell from it like snow as the altar began to extract its energy, decompiling it.

Ralph ripped the sword away. 'Wait. Please, one question and one question only.'

The Orbs traded thin strands of electricity.

'*Ask, Nazra, or forever hold your peace.*'

'Why didn't you fold the sword yourselves?'

'*Silly Nazra. Out here further than your kind has ever been. Yet still so feeble and ignorant in the mind.*'

A wave of hot anger washed through him. 'You used me? You put me through all of that when you could've just done it yourselves?'

'*No, Nazra. You played your part.*'

They moved closer.

'*In this dimension.*'

Ralph's eyes widened as his stick figure theory from college came to him. 'You're from a different dimension?'

They hovered and hummed half a metre away. Their silence told him everything. And he felt stupid for not having known it already. The way they could appear and disappear, teleporting him to any location without obsidiary paste, had shown him they wielded a power he'd never even considered existed.

'You can't interact with objects in the third dimension?' he asked.

White electricity struck him, wavered his vision, altered his breathing.

'*We can interact with it enough,*' they sang.

'Then which dimension are you from?'

They struck him again. '*You have asked enough questions, Nazra. Now it is time to submit.*'

Ralph could've laughed. 'I've been at the Bottom of the Universe for years. I think it's safe to say I have submitted to you. What I still don't understand is why you didn't tell me about the Darkness before it showed up in my lab, before I tampered with it.'

Their lack of information and communication felt equivalent to a lie. Their silence was like a form of deceit, a betrayal, an irritating refusal to provide the truth.

'You allowed for my life to be ruined,' he said. 'And for what, a blade you won't even let me use?'

'*Why does it matter what your life has been like?*' the Orb of Repulsion said. '*So many Nazra dedicate their lives to activities — hobbies, jobs, sports, relationships — that are all the same in the end: meaningless.*'

'*But we cannot blame the Nazra,*' the Orb of Attraction said. '*We cannot judge. They have always been caught in this cycle. We may be the forces causing all,*' *but we cannot alter the effects.'*

'That is right,' the Orb of Deterioration said. *The Nazra, the never-happy, never-fed creatures who do anything to put themselves through grief and misery, find pleasure in the struggle. Harmony? Happiness? Utopia? These are pursuits reserved for the fools of their kind.'*

'But do not worry,' the Orb of Light said. *For the end is upon us. The Nazra may be caught in its cycle, but the end is here, and it is because of this one the conclusion is possible.'*

Ralph didn't know how to feel about any of this. He'd been used. He'd been lied to. He'd been betrayed. But the Orbs were right. The end had arrived. And this was all he'd ever wanted.

'You can't blame humans,' he said, as though sticking up for humanity. 'For every task we put our minds to, we try, we seek, we struggle. But in the end, we overcome, we adapt. A long time ago, a girl told me why: because our souls desire to learn and be free.'

'Yes,' the Orbs sang. *But do you think your species is the only one that learns and grows? The Nazra fail more than they succeed. Why else do you think they have been caught in the same cycle of seeking power, prompting wars, while offering convenience and protection as a way for their people to accept slavery?'*

'Our systems have flaws,' Ralph said. 'But they give us structure. They allow for creativity and exploration. It's why I'm here. It's how we sent spaceships to Alpha Centauri.'

'Ah, yes,' the Orbs sang in amusement. *The escape onboard the Seven Ships to Centauri. If only you saw what became of them, Nazra.'*

Ralph tried to disregard their comment, but the possibilities for the fate of all those onboard the Ships hurt him.

You may believe the Nazra are successful, but your species is held back by things you have termed virtues — patience, kindness, pity, faith, charity. These virtues are distractions, excuses, used by those who only wish to feed their ego.'

'Is that why you didn't help me when I still lived on Earth? You wanted to punish my species?'

We do not teach lessons, Nazra. We only provide formulas for evolution. We only divide to unify.'

'Yet I forged the blade. You couldn't do that. And that means more than anything you could ever say or do to me.'

The Orbs traded their signature laughter. But their condescension didn't hurt this time. Ralph's mind had cleared with the knowledge he possessed a power in this dimension they did not wield.

'Meaning!' the Orb of Light said. '*Another concept created by the Nazra. There is no point to meaning. Everything is without reason. There is no good. There is no bad. There is only balance.*'

'*We should know,*' the Orb of Deterioration said. '*Nothing the Nazra ever pursued or created has lasted. It has all wasted away with the test of time.*'

What could Ralph say to their words? What could he do? Humans weren't perfect. They didn't know everything. But the eternal striving pushed them along. It was why he'd gone from college to a cave to the cosmos.

He raised the silk blade, pointing it at the four Orbs. 'If you want this sword, then take it from my dead body. I'll no longer be treated like an idiot.'

The Orbs flashed, enlarged. Their energy grew. Their luminosity became blinding, engulfing the capsule.

'*Do not threaten us, Nazra. We have given you life. Who else could say they were part of the cure for the primordial Darkness?*'

Ralph lowered the blade.

'Yes, Nazra,' the Orb of Light said. '*That is better.*'

'*Do what is right,*' the Orb of Repulsion said.

'*It is time to end this phase,*' the Orb of Attraction said.

'*For the end allows for a beginning,*' the Orb of Deterioration said.

'But if you are the forces that cause all,' Ralph said, 'if I took you out of the equation, we could stop everything. We could fix everything. It'd be like annihilating quarks in an atom smasher.'

He had barely finished his sentence when a shroud of darkness billowed into the capsule. It came through the four vacant spots in the ceiling with a sneering snigger, like a pack of hyenas. The Orbs tried to fight the shroud, to brighten, but their light could not defeat its devourment.

'*See what you have done?*' they sang with a fading cry.

Ralph called on the splinter sparrow. But it was mute. Its eyes were shut, its beak clasped. It was unconscious. It was dead. It was no longer observant to what was happening.

He studied the sword in his hand. The blade still glowed pink, shining through the shroud.

'You have made things a lot easier by coming here,' Ralph said, raising the sword.

A nip came at his heels. Several nips. Like a bite from a piranha, each one came painful, aggressive.

He swung the sword at the Darkness. His blade slipped from his grip. But when he glanced down at it, he still held it.

He shook his head. His sense of reality was collapsing inside this untimely arrival of the Darkness.

He scanned the ceiling. The Orbs were trapped. Dying.

'Release them!' Ralph shouted. 'They've done nothing wrong.'

The shroud's voice came conniving: 'You came all this way to fall victim to the imbeciles known as the Scindereans?'

Their words were inconceivable, like a hybrid language, a combination of strange noises, tones, and inflections. How Ralph managed to decipher their words made no sense. It also worried him.

'Believing in false gods is what, three thousand years?' the shroud shrieked, slamming into him, biting his flesh with squealing delight.

Ralph swung the blade about, twisting and turning, slashing.

'Release the Orbs of Scindere!' he yelled.

The shroud ripped the sword from his grip. He made to snatch it back, but they lifted it higher.

'Wrongful worship is a crime of the universe!' the Darkness shrieked. 'Sitting too.'

'And this one sat for a long time,' another voice came.

'And for what?' another one said. 'This silk monstrosity?'

The voices came in intervals as the shroud sparked with thousands of embers, like lava lightning bolts.

'What has the Nazra created?' a voice asked.

'Something powerful,' said another.

'Something sturdy,' said another.

'But what is it capable of?'

'Give it back, demons,' Ralph said. 'You don't deserve to hold such a weapon.'

Their laughter was severe. 'You were used, Nazra. The Scindereans are false gods.'

The shroud formed a cube in front of him. It contorted and struggled as though fighting entropy. The cube then shifted, morphing rapidly between various shapes – pyramids, stars, skulls, spheres.

'Show yourselves, you cowards,' Ralph said. 'Show me what dedicated its life to destroying mine.'

'You cannot command us,' the shroud shrieked. 'We are the gods of every particle you have ever interacted with.'

The charcoal mist enlarged, thickened. The Orbs and the capsule became clouded by the billions of tiny, dark particles.

'You were led astray by the Orbs,' the shroud shrieked. 'The Nazra may not be bright, but they know when they've been betrayed.'

The mist surrounded Ralph like a cloak.

'So, this is it,' he said. 'The end.'

'Wrongful worship cannot go unpunished!' the shroud shrieked.

'Then get it over with. I don't care anymore.'

'We are the Particle Gods!'

'Yeah,' Ralph said, deflating. 'I've heard it all before. And I don't care.'

The embers inside the mist enhanced to a sinister mix of oranges and reds.

'You are spiteful, Nazra,' the shroud said.

Ralph made another grab at the sword, failed. 'What am I here for if you have such control over everything?'

The demons of Darkness were silent for a moment, swirling around him.

'If my senses dictate reality,' Ralph said, 'let me remove everything from existence. Let me end it all.'

'You are smart for a Nazra,' the shroud said. 'We wish for you to take the blade.'

Ralph rolled his eyes. 'And how will I use it, O Great Gods, O Ridiculous Creatures Hellbent on Ruining Everything? How may I serve another band of idiots?'

Their laughter was mischievous.

'The Nazra knows how to play this game,' a voice said.

'It has done this before?' another asked.

'Maybe it knows how things go,' another one replied.

'And how do things go?' Ralph asked. 'Don't give me more *time* baloney. I've had enough of that since I left Earth.'

'But stopping the Orbs is what we do best, dirty Nazra. It is all part of the game.'

'*The game?*' Ralph asked, spittle flying from his mouth. 'You ruined my life for a game? Why me? Why not pull someone else from the flow of time?'

'Oh, don't be silly. You know the answer.'

'No, I don't. You took it all from me. I never even had a chance.'

Their sneers spread and swelled inside the capsule as more tiny, dark demons arrived.

'So young,' they shrieked, 'so naïve! Do not forget, Nazra, you used us to get here.'

'And I never would have if you hadn't screwed with me from the start.'

The Darkness may have rotated him out of the natural flow of time. It may have destroyed his life. But if it was a group of particles, it would die like one too.

Taking out the black diamond sack from his backpack, he filled his palm with obsidiary dust.

'Do not be a fool, Nazra,' the shroud said. 'We are the dividers, the causes and the effects. You cannot escape us.'

He hurled the dust at the shroud. It struck, silencing the voices. A ripple of energy then spread through the capsule, igniting the embers like fireworks. As they sparked and exploded, the shroud distorted and shuddered, shrieking in anger and glee.

Ralph raised his hands, concentrating on sending as much energy into it as he could.

The tingles spread. His silver nodes surged. Electricity leapt from them, illuminating every Darkness particle with an eerie glow.

The shroud froze, twitched in confusion. It then tore apart, exposing a gap, a window, a portal, swirling cobalt and ashen.

Ralph didn't know exactly what he'd done, but he knew it was time to leave.

Part III: Through Space

'Every living being is an engine geared to the
wheelwork of the universe.'

Nikola Tesla

21

Into the Darkness

THE tiny pebble of a bird came alive on Ralph's shoulder with a startled chirp.

'Get us out of here!' he said to it.

The bird ignited, filling the Orb capsule with its sonar shine, fighting back the darkness that was the Particle Gods. In response, they shrieked in fear and delight, clashing and annihilating, sparking and exploding, as though playing a game without consequences.

And he hated them for it. But he knew their charade couldn't last forever. Their power would wane. Their tyranny would end. They'd be swallowed up by the beast that was the universe. It didn't matter if they claimed to be the ultimate manipulators. Reality didn't like prolonged dominance or congregation of any particle.

Ralph knew this firsthand.

With the gap in the shroud still exposed, he made a break for the closest window. He leapt along the way, snatching his silk blade hovering amidst the darkness. Using the butt of its vibrant, pink hilt, combined with the splinter sparrow's powerful beam, he shattered the glass.

In an instant, the chairs, the altar, and the dark particles were sucked outside in one howling sweep. He went with it all, tumbling and flipping through the void until the sparrow stabilised him with its protective shine.

From afar, he watched the shroud pour out of the ruined capsule like a demon leaving a carcass. It dispersed in several directions. One of its trails, thicker than the others, stretched away from the capsule with rapidity, heading towards a new horror approaching, one blanketing and devouring all light in its path.

'We have to leave,' Ralph said.

The bird chirped, sending a rotating beam of light out into the cosmos like a lighthouse.

As he waited for it to find an escape route, his eyes remained glued to the approaching dark cloud. It moved through the vacuum of space with questionable ease, defying every law of physics he'd ever known.

He couldn't believe it. After everything the Darkness had put him through, here it was, arriving en masse to enact revenge on him for meddling with reality.

The sparrow trilled. Its shine narrowed to a thin beam, pointing directly into the approaching, malignant shroud.

'You've got to be kidding me,' he said.

The sparrow stayed silent.

Ralph didn't know what to think. Or do. Something didn't seem right about ploughing directly into the Darkness. But he couldn't recall a time the sparrow had led him wrong.

'I hope you know what you're doing.'

Sprinkling some obsidiary dust under his tongue, he began the transference.

He reformed inside the shroud and was immediately overwhelmed by its heavy, rowdy energy. Like a turbulent tornado of rippling vibrations, the dark particles attacked his body, stinging his skin, seeping through his pores and interacting with every bone and muscle.

His nervous system shut down in response, taking his motor control and eyesight with it. But before he lost all coherence, with the tingles still spreading, he began another transference.

When he reformed, the sparrow kicked on brighter. Its intense shine reminded him of Ca'zehro's words about the bird's protective capabilities, making him wonder what else it'd been filtering throughout his journey.

He turned on the spot, taking in the scenery.

The chaotic, charcoal-coloured particles whipped past like millions of angry bees. They laughed and sneered as they went about their war, their destruction and consumption. Their frivolity made him feel worse for initiating whatever they were planning, for killing the Orbs, and for creating the energy debt in the first place.

A wind swept through with blistering velocity, throwing up his hair, flickering the sparrow's glow, altering the flow of the dark particles.

Ralph didn't know if he interpreted the situation correctly, but it seemed they'd lost interest in him.

He scanned the shroud. It shifted, twitched. The particles then moved further away from him, hollowing out to form a tunnel, like an enormous pneumatic tube. The splinter sparrow capitalised on this new vista, scanning its radar beam, pinpointing his next location to transfer to.

Ralph didn't bother questioning the bird this time. He transferred straight to the beam's terminus in the distance.

Reforming, he tracked the beam to his next destination and transferred again. And again, over and over, decompiling and recompiling, deeper and deeper through the Darkness's tunnel.

The further he travelled, the more he became attuned with its varying frequencies and oscillating energies. In a way, it felt like particle transference's middle phase, where he could see things, sense things, but everything bordered on the margin, like a flash of imagination, like the split-second before sleep.

Gaining this insight changed his perspective, and he ceased transference to test a hypothesis.

He waited for a few minutes, floating inside the Darkness's tunnel until his obsidiary dust dose dwindled. When the tingles had faded, when he felt like himself again, he let go of his reliance on the quark's energy and focused on the power of the shroud.

It worked just like he'd hoped.

As though pitting the Darkness's energy against his own, the tension built, like pulling a slingshot back until it could go no further. Its resistance then collapsed, and he propelled through the tunnel in the opposite direction the dark particles were heading.

He shot through with a speed like no other. But unlike the vortex after the Stack, the speed was not chaotic nor erratic. It felt smooth, calm. It didn't shoot him around tight bends or down stomach-flipping drops. It kept him rocketing along with purpose, momentum.

Eventually, the winding tunnel opened out to a cavern the size of three aircraft hangars. Clusters of dark particles had taken refuge here, forming conical cylinders, similar to stalagmites and stalactites. Dripping with a viscous, black liquid, they gathered in groups beside several cave entrances riddling the cavern walls.

With the splinter sparrow still guiding the way, he waited for it to direct him.

Its beam scanned the cavern, the clusters, the entrances. When it chose his path with a chirp, Ralph focused on the cave and was immediately sucked into it.

He shot through it for less than thirty seconds before an amber light blared back at him, like a train hurtling through a tunnel. Before it collided with him though, he was spat back out into the void.

The sparrow switched its scanning, guiding beam to its enveloping shine, slowing his inertia, giving him a chance to breathe, think, look. And when he did look, he found that the light was not a train, but an eruptive mixture of hydrogen and helium, a star, one larger than any he'd ever seen. Its light dispersed through the area, illuminating rocks, debris, and a planet the size of thirty Earths.

His mouth fell open at the sight of the super planet. Even from hundreds of kilometres away, its biome of greens, blues, browns, and whites could be seen.

The sight took him home in an instant. But it didn't give him any warm or fuzzy feelings. And how could it? The frequency the planet exuded was one of suffocation and dominance, as though it wanted nothing more than his demise.

He spun around to the tunnel he'd been spat from. The shroud still swirled away, swelling as more and more dark particles joined it. He tracked their trail to the super planet, where a cloud of darkness hovered above a sector like a storm or parasitic spirit, one the size of Africa.

Whatever and wherever this planet was, it was clear the Darkness either originated from it or used it as a rendezvous point.

He scanned the void, looking for something familiar. But unfamiliar constellations were all that greeted him. The stars even seemed closer than they had back home in the Solar System, brighter, redder. In one portion, not too far away, three spiral galaxies spun. In another, what looked like remnants of a hypernova dispersed. In another, dense pockets of luminous gases twisted and blasted colourful beams in all directions.

Whatever sector of the universe he found himself in, the volatility implied it was young.

He turned back to the super planet, spotting its three moons. Spaced evenly apart, each varied in dull colours and frequencies. The rose-coloured one emanated something like hope. The teal moon exuded spitefulness. The viridian one, thoughtfulness.

They all gave him the creeps.

He transferred closer to the super planet, reforming inside a pocket of angry particles a few kilometres from its atmosphere. Whipping and striking him like the buzzing ones had when he'd first left Earth, the lacerations and pain were joined by shrieks and sniggers.

He transferred again, recompiling on the other side of the pocket.

From his new vantage point, he gained a magnificent view of the super planet. Its vast, sapphire sea was specked with silver. Untouched by metropolitans and pollution, the land, riddled with emerald and sepia trees, rocks, and mountains, spread further than his eyes could see.

What tribes inhabited this super planet? What temples had been built? What ancient myths had been told around campfires?

Or was the Fermi Paradox at play here? Was the possibility for finding intelligent life this deep in the universe out of the question?

The sparrow sent a fresh beam towards the planet's surface. Its terminus lay between a mountain range and the sapphire sea.

Ralph began the transference.

He reformed inside a dark, wrathful cloud, as though it was upset about his unsolicited arrival.

He transferred again, reforming on the other side, where he was met with a view of the terrain fast approaching.

He tried spinning around and transferring back into space. But the super planet's gravity had taken hold.

He tried transferring parallel to the ground, aiming for the sea. But something had severed his ability to transfer.

This was it? The end? After everything, he would plough into the dirt of an alien planet and die?

The wind of his rapid descent rushed past.

'Little help?' he asked the sparrow.

It twitched and chirped, batting its tiny, golden wings as its glow faded.

'What do you mean you can't do anything?'

It responded with another chirp, low, regretful, fearful.

The ground grew closer.

Ralph spread his arms, trying to mimic a skydiver slowing his descent. But it was futile.

And of course it was. He had just entered the Darkness's domain, its home world. He should've known better.

He blasted through the clouds. Dread consumed his mind as the ground filled his view.

Not knowing what else to do, he said a silent prayer to the universe, to whatever entity or entities were listening.

He imagined the message being sent out like a radio signal, reaching all those he'd lost along the way, telling them he'd be seeing them soon.

The ground drew closer and closer, until it became too close to think, do, or say anything further.

He then slammed into it with such uncompromising force, he pulverised every bone and organ in his body.

And everything went dark.

22
Planet Enqn

RALPH was nudged awake by two stout, pudgy children wearing tan, hessian robes. Their heads were globular, like bobblehead figurines, and large like car wheels. Their arms extended past their knees. They had kind faces and ovular eyes washed with nuanced shifts in colours.

'Where am I?' Ralph asked, voice hoarse. 'Who are you?'

They exchanged a glance, then returned to gazing at him.

He tried sitting up, but his body was numb, immobile. 'What've you done to me?'

They traded another glance.

'What is this place?' he asked, eyes darting about.

He was in a room the size of a barber shop. The walls and ceiling were built from a chestnut wood. A table beside his bed was strewn with folds of cloth, glass vials, and irregular bottles filled with various coloured liquids. On one side of the room, a small fire smouldered. On another, more beds.

'Is this a lab?' he asked. 'What are you doing with me? I swear I will—'

The penny dropped. His eyes widened as a memory of him crashing to the surface of an alien planet arose. The children shrunk back as though sensing his sudden desire for unhinged hysteria.

His backpack. His dusts. The sparrow.

He tried turning his head. The pain laced. But his peripherals gave him enough of a view to see the splinter sparrow no longer rested on his shoulder.

'What did you do with my bird?' he asked with urgency.

He tried sitting up again, failed. He tried moving his arms, but they were glued in place. He felt trapped as though strapped into a bed in an asylum or about to be scanned inside a machine for the next ten hours, just like when he was four years old.

The female bobblehead touched his shoulder and pointed at the rafters. He followed her finger to a marred portion of the ceiling, where the shiny, tiny, golden splinter sparrow glowed.

Relief washed over him.

'And my backpack?' he asked.

'Bukh-pukh,' the girl repeated.

'Yes. Where is it?'

She looked at her partner and traded noises similar to the various phonemes of Earth. The boy then crouched and dragged Ralph's backpack out from under the bed.

More relief washed over Ralph.

Whoever these bobblehead children were, they weren't here to cause him harm.

The boy proceeded to take each item out of the backpack, showing them to Ralph – the golden rod, the sacks of dust, the container of jerky he still hadn't finished, the various trinkets he'd collected with Veška, Jamaki's cerulean cicada. The boy then returned it all into the backpack, zipped it up, and slid it back under the bed.

Standing to his full height, he looked at Ralph with sad interest, like he wanted to ask or tell Ralph something.

Ralph studied his ovular eyes laced with dusty beige, wishing he could ask all the questions bubbling away in his mind.

The female bobblehead moved over to the table of potions. She measured a few different powders and solutions, mixing them in a small vial. She dispensed a drop of a violet oil into it, a scarlet one, then diluted the solution with a liquid Ralph hoped was water. After holding it above the fire for a few seconds to boil, she brought it to him with a cloth held at its base.

'What is it?' Ralph asked.

'Feex,' she said, her accent odd, her inflection heavy on the *x*.

'Feex?'

She nodded.

'Fix?'

She nodded again.

He knew what it could mean to drink a hot liquid from a stranger. But he was safe. The splinter sparrow was safe. His belongings were safe.

What could possibly go wrong?

Besides, for all he knew, he was already dead. Who could survive such a plummet to a planet anyway?

The girl elevated his head with a gentle hand and poured the warm solution down his throat. Ralph offered no resistance.

As the liquid travelled down his oesophagus, his vision swayed, dipped, fuzzed.

'Is this another Earth?' he asked.

'Earth,' the two bobbleheads repeated.

'Yes,' Ralph said, clearing his throat. 'Is it like Earth? You guys don't seem too different from me.'

He spoke slowly and at a normal volume, knowing the inverse of either wouldn't aid them in effective communication. But their frowning, confused gazes gave him no impression they knew what he'd said.

The girl tried her phoneme-sounding speech, lavender eyes peering into his. Ralph did his best to understand, focusing on the intonations, vibrations, and articulations of each sound. He couldn't tell if he interpreted her dialect correctly, but he managed to extract a few morsels of coherence.

One thing she told him was how grateful they were for his arrival. Another thing was that their knowledge about Earth had come from tales told by their Elders.

True or not, he didn't mind. Them knowing Earth was good enough.

'My sword,' he said, clenching his fists, pleased to find the numbness subsiding. 'Where is it?'

The two bobbleheads caught the movement of his hands and smiled. He smiled too. He then made gestures with his hands to indicate the size and shape of the silk scimitar sword.

The boy made swishing sounds, swinging his arms like he held a tennis racquet.

'Yes,' Ralph said. 'Where is it?'

The boy stopped swinging, made a snapping sound, folded his hands together.

Ralph's heart sank. 'Broken? How?'

But he knew the answer. He'd been holding it when he'd entered the super planet's atmosphere. He'd been holding it when he'd slammed into the terrain.

Another bobblehead entered the hut. He seemed older than the two tending to Ralph.

The three of them exchanged pleasantries, speaking rapidly about something that sounded important. The two males then exited. The female bobblehead returned to Ralph and crouched by his bed.

With his strength returning, he pushed himself into a sitting position. The entire room came into view, illuminated by the daylight pouring in through the open entrance.

It was indeed a makeshift hospital. Twenty empty beds filled the room. Each had white, tattered sheets. The potions on the table looked to be made from green and purple plants filling the baskets beside it.

'What did you give me?' Ralph asked.

She took his hand and spoke her strange sounds. He closed his eyes and tried to make sense of them.

While he couldn't understand everything, he pulled a few intentions and meanings from each phrase.

One thing she told him was that she was leaving to join the others to give thanks to their chieftain. Another thing was that she would return later with a bowl of musharacha.

Ralph nodded, mouth salivating. Whatever musharacha was, how she said it gave him the impression it was very tasty.

She watched him silently, allowing him time to talk. But he didn't know what to say. He wanted his sword, but he didn't know what he wanted it for. He wanted to leave, but he didn't know how or why or even where to go.

He studied her features. Her eyes were gentle, curious. Her hair was thick, braided, long. Her skin, flawless, a perfect mix of various shades and pigments.

Why had these people developed such large heads? he wondered. Had it been for a beneficial reason or pure happenstance?

'Where are we?' he asked. 'Proxim?'

She didn't seem to understand.

'Proxim,' he said. 'Or near to it?'

'Prox-sim,' she repeated.

He nodded. 'My people were heading to that planet. It's in the Alpha Centauri system.'

She pointed at the ground and sounded two syllables: *en* and *ken*.

'En-ken?' he said.

Her eyes widened. She repeated the syllables several times, as though trying to refine how he heard and said it. By the eighth, he could differentiate the *k* sound, which seemed more akin to the *q* in *queen*. He tried again.

'En-qen?'

She smiled, repeating the word a few more times.

The subtleties in the pronunciation were almost too difficult for him to notice. But he kept trying, changing how he moved his tongue and mouth, altering every tone possible in each syllable, consonant, and vowel. Eventually, he landed on a sound she understood.

'En-qn.'

She smiled, ovular eyes widening. Leaning forward, she touched her forehead to his, smiled, stood, then exited the wooden hut.

As soon as Ralph was alone, the splinter sparrow hopped from the rafters and glided down to land on his shoulder. He laughed as it pecked his ear and neck.

'What happened?' he said. 'Your shine was overridden by the Darkness?'

It chirped once and ignited, blanketing him in its warm, comforting glow, helping to soothe his sore bones.

He lay back, staring at the ceiling, hands tucked behind his head. The familiar sounds of life outside swelled into the hospital hut – laughter, chatter, the calling of animals. After a while, a calming, respectful chant replaced the commotion. Led by an older combination of voices, a mixture of gratitude and acceptance saturated the air, rising and falling in a wavering harmony.

Whoever their chieftain was, Ralph thought, they had to be special.

As the chanting continued, he drifted off to sleep. The sounds, along with the medicine concoction the girl had given him, did wonders for his bruised, broken body. The low frequency of the chanting came fulfilling and nourishing, reminding him of the Stack's beat.

As he danced between wakefulness and dreamland, he visualised his journey to Enqn.

He saw himself leaving the mountain's mesa, flying into the clouds, exiting the atmosphere. He passed satellites, the Moon, Mars, Jupiter, Saturn, Uranus, Neptune, Pluto, Sedna. He arrived amongst a cluster of new stars being born inside the orange nebula. He flew on and on, into the void, through the void, past the Stack, over the Bottom of the Universe, until coming to a dark shroud that didn't hesitate to suck him in, thrusting him through its narrow tunnels, speaking to him.

'We are glad you came all this way.'

Ralph didn't know how to feel about the Darkness's kind words.

'We did all we could so you would set off into the cosmos one day.'

How it said this last sentence put Ralph's mind into limbo.

'We hope we helped.'

Its tone was pleasant, like that of a kindergarten teacher's. But concealed behind it, within it, was something Ralph didn't want to think about, something he knew deep down: the Darkness had only given him enough time to solve things for one reason.

To kill him.

He snapped his eyes open with a desperate gasp of air. His dream shattered.

The air in the hut had become cold. The daylight had been swallowed by the arrival of a mist, a sinister mist, one that'd crept in while he'd slept.

Although the chanting outside continued, no more gratitude or acceptance laced it. It'd become hesitant, submissive, terrified. It seemed to thank the chieftain without truly contemplating what the price for thanking it was.

Ralph cursed under his breath. He should've known the dark particles would track him down to finish the job.

23

The Darkness That Owns All

WITH the dark particles filling the hospital hut, Ralph swung his numb legs to the floor. It felt like he'd been bedridden for weeks. And maybe he had.

Using the rafters of the low ceiling for support, he headed to the doorway. The dark mist retreated with every step as the splinter sparrow's sonar shine fought it back.

He prepared himself for their sneering and biting in retaliation. But it never came. The hyenalike particles that'd invaded the Orb capsule weren't here. It was a different kind of darkness, one that only wanted one thing: to consume everything, like a jackal would consume carrion.

Hands pressed against the door jambs, he waited for the sparrow's shine to illuminate outside. When it had, stumpy, wooden buildings came into view, along with an uneven cobblestoned street filled with kneeling bobbleheads facing a courtyard, where an onyx flame as high as a flagpole licked the air.

The sparrow's shine continued pulsing in intervals. The Darkness shrank back with each one, flooding back in to clamp its authority down on the population in between.

Ralph tracked the mist to the shroud in the sky, where it spread like a thick layer of pollution.

The bobblehead chanting amplified. Each head wobbled side-to-side. The Darkness seemed to relish in the sight and the sound, the submissiveness, growing larger, darker.

The longer Ralph watched the ritual taking place, the slower his brain ticked, the heavier his body became. The natural rhythm of his heart faltered. His lungs tightened. His stomach contorted.

He knew paranoia and fatigue could fabricate such sensations. But it didn't matter. The experience was real enough.

He stumbled backwards, fingernails scratching at his throat.

'Help,' he said.

The tiny pebble of a bird kicked on harder, sending a stronger wave of shine through the street. It fought the Darkness back, opening a clearing that broke several bobbleheads from their chanting and head wobbling.

As the sparrow's shine spread, more bobbleheads awoke. Shaking their heads, they looked around in dazed confusion.

The sparrow sensed success and kicked on harder, brighter, combatting the Darkness, breaking more and more bobbleheads from their hypnotised state.

The Darkness grew enraged by the sparrow's audacity. It howled and wailed like a toddler having a tantrum. It spun through the street, kicking up dirt and stones, shaking buildings. Sounds of horses whinnying in the distance joined the pandemonium.

Ralph called out an apology to the bobbleheads. But those who had broken from their trance didn't seem to care. They all just looked relieved to be free from the Darkness's grasp.

But it wasn't done yet. The more the sparrow's shine spread, the more the Darkness intensified. It lashed out like a vicious ghoul, throwing wood and dirt, scattering and toppling the screaming bobbleheads.

Ralph bolted back to the hospital bed and dove under the sheets.

'Stop,' he told the sparrow in desperation. 'It's going to destroy their village.'

The sparrow chirped and dimmed.

From under the sheets, Ralph listened to the Darkness stirring through the streets.

Bobbleheads shouted over the destruction taking place. Hatches were battened. Whistles and clicks rounded up livestock. Babies cried. Metal crashed. Wood slammed to the ground and splintered.

After an hour of the violent shroud wreaking havoc, a strong sucking sound signalled its end. Everything stopped, quietened, brightened.

With bated breath, Ralph didn't dare move for more than ten minutes.

When he did, he tiptoed to the doorway and peered out at the devastation that was all his fault.

Bobbleheads lay scattered about. Some unconscious. Some bleeding. Others were already underway with the cleanup. One tending to the injured noticed Ralph leering at the hospital's entrance.

Ralph braced for her yelling and swearing. But nothing of the sort occurred. Instead, her face lit up, kind and bright, with an expression similar to recognition. Stranger still, he felt like he recognised her too. In fact, the more he scanned the other bobbleheads, the more he felt an overwhelming connection with each of them.

What was this place? Where was this place? Who were these people?

He scanned the royal blue sky and the passing puffs of white cloud. The amber sun, the star of whatever system he was in, beamed with a perfect autumn heat.

While this super planet could've been the furthest planet from Earth in the entire observable universe, this humble village and its inhabitants took him back to a time he'd read about, a time before skyscrapers had shadowed overcrowded cities.

One of the bobbleheads approached Ralph. Then another. And another. Soon, more than forty bobbleheads surrounded him. He towered over all of them – the young, the old, the female, the male. Most wore tan, hessian robes, like the ones who'd helped him in the hospital. The rest wore various shades of ecru.

As they studied him, they muttered words and sounds to one another. Some stayed mute. Others tested their communication capabilities.

Closing his eyes, he did his best to understand them. Although he couldn't articulate every word they uttered, he inferred quite a bit by focusing on their inflections, associating the sounds with vibrations from his own language.

While it seemed many bobbleheads were glad for his arrival, others were hesitant.

'I'm sorry about the sparrow's shine,' he said, pointing at the glowing bird on his shoulder. He gestured around the village, at its homes and businesses, at the fifteen-metre perimeter wall. 'Your village is beautiful.'

The bobbleheads delighted at the sound of his voice. With bulging, ovular eyes focused on his mouth and throat, their heads swayed.

'Thank you for providing me with solace on Enqn,' he said.

They smiled and whispered to one another at the mention of their planet's name. A stir then swept through the crowd, silencing and parting them.

A woman wearing a pure white robe approached.

This bobblehead seemed ancient. Her hair was grey. Her skin was not as flawless as the others, but her eyes were wiser. Two colourful, beaded necklaces hung around her neck. When she was close enough to Ralph, she took his hands and closed her eyes. He closed his.

'This is Enqn?' he asked.

At first, her answer came stuttering, unsure. But then her words came lucid like an energy transaction, similar to when the Orbs had revealed their names.

'Yes,' she said, her frequency aligning with his. 'Or Vypri. It is difficult to explain.'

'Am I close to Proxim?'

'Proxim? No. That place is not here. That place is not of here. That place is nowhere.'

Ralph didn't like her answer. But the fact she'd struggled with her phrasing didn't give him any reason to believe she knew what she'd said.

'The Darkness,' he said, 'it's angry. It'll return if we don't do something to keep it at bay.'

'Yes,' she said.

He waited for her to say more. 'It needs to die.'

'No,' she said.

'You don't understand. After what I did with my sparrow's shine, it'll come back stronger to hurt your people.'

She squeezed his hands with something like condescension. 'The Darkness is ours.'

Communicating with the Elder reminded him of communicating with a beta version of a translator bot. While she had the foundation of his language, she lacked the ability to utilise tones and meaning. She also seemed to misunderstand the severity of the situation and what it meant that he'd landed on their planet.

'The Darkness is killing you all,' he said. 'It's controlling you. I saw what it did to your people during the ritual. It was sucking their life essence, using it to fuel itself.'

The woman remained silent. She squeezed his hands again. This time, it was in a loving way, as though she was either telling him she didn't like what he'd said or simply didn't understand him.

Ralph waited for her to speak next.

'You will stay with us,' she said. 'We will enjoy your company.'

✦

After one of the longest sleeps Ralph had ever had, he awoke in the hospital hut fresh and healed. The heat in the room was comforting, dry, reminding him of the midday sun in the Simpson Desert.

A swarm of bobbleheads had gathered by the entrance. They sprang to their feet and wobbled their heads as he exited. He smiled, preparing to communicate with any who came forward. But none seemed interested in talking. Instead, two took his hands and hurried him to an outdoor mess hall, where they served him grains and a delicious, chewy yoghurt in a wooden bowl.

Breakfast over, they took him on a tour. They showed him the residential district filled with cramped and stacked wooden homes. They showed him the farmland with its crops and six-legged steeds. They took him to the general store, a church, a café, up a ladder to the perimeter wall.

Circling the village, they stopped occasionally to point out noteworthy buildings and cenotaphs. On the southern side, they pointed to the forest and mountain range he'd seen when entering the atmosphere. They made noises and frowned as they did, as though warning him of the dangers beyond their walls.

The tour ended at the blacksmith's workshop, where he was reunited with his pink silk sword.

A bobblehead in a leather apron approached him, carrying the blade horizontally in both hands.

'Thank you,' Ralph said.

The blacksmith shook his head, releasing his grip on the sword. As he did, it came apart in Ralph's hands in two perfect pieces.

Broken, just like the bobblehead nurse had said.

The blacksmith showed him around his shop, pointing at the anvil, the furnace, his wall of tools. Muttering and shaking his head, he told

Ralph how he'd tried everything to fix the sword, but found its power too great.

'That's okay,' Ralph said. 'My splinter sparrow can help. Watch.'

The bobbleheads gathered as he placed the broken blade on the ground. He took some time to position it correctly, aligning the two portions with precision.

'Whenever you're ready,' he said to the sparrow.

But the chirp the bird made informed him something he hadn't considered: forging and fixing his blade of silk could only be done at the Bottom of the Universe.

Before leaving the workshop, Ralph offered to carry the ore in from the cart outside. Pleased with the offer, the blacksmith didn't delay in getting the furnace going, showing Ralph how to load the ore inside it.

While he worked, the blacksmith made a leather sheath for him to keep his curved blade. When he was done, the bobblehead strapped it around Ralph's waist, and gestured for them to touch foreheads.

Tour concluded, many of the bobbleheads said their goodbyes and headed off to complete chores and spend time with their families. The rest stayed behind like groupies, happy to sightsee with Ralph.

As he strolled the cobblestoned streets, bobbleheads who hadn't met him approached. They took his hands and touched their foreheads to his, treating him with a respect and fondness he'd never experienced.

Standing at least a foot shorter than Ralph, the bobbleheads never shied away from asking for his help. And he accepted each request willingly, happy to help them carry, fix, build, and shift anything they needed.

Doing something physical after travelling through the void felt great. Doing something not related to solving his curse felt even better.

Ralph's first full, conscious day on Enqn went by rapidly. During it, he repaired fences and water troughs destroyed by the Darkness. He fixed roofs and walls. He fed and groomed steeds. And as the sun dipped behind the distant mountains, he strolled the village alone, planning locations for electromagnetic coils, the same ones he'd used to power his cave-lab.

During the walk, he paused to take in the sights, sounds, and smells from the perimeter wall.

Faint, flashing stars filled the sky washed with purples and blues. The three colourful moons loomed nearby, each presenting as waning crescents. A dull, rhythmic thumping of wood being chopped in the forest dominated the ambience. Buzzing insects and the odd mammalian screech joined it.

Facing the forest, he studied the rocky mountain range beyond. Its snowcapped peaks were concealed by a fog, reminding him of the Brisbane smog. But as his eyes adjusted, he realised it was not fog nor smog, but the Darkness.

A shiver ran down his spine at seeing it so close to the bobblehead village. It doubled his incentive to install the coils and light the place. It also made him eager to figure out how to end its existence.

In the evening, the bobbleheads took their places in the courtyard and streets surrounding the fire. Ralph sat with them, watching as they lapsed into their chanting and head swaying, prepared to signal the sparrow at the first sign of the shroud.

After an hour though, the Darkness was nowhere to be seen. After two hours, still nowhere. Although it still hung low over the mountains, it stayed away.

Ralph took that as a good sign. But the bobbleheads grew worried and uneasy.

To quell the murmurs spreading, three Elders in pure-white robes took the stage. One was the woman with the beaded necklaces.

The oldest of the trio, the one with a long, white beard, stepped forward first. He held his hands up until the crowd quietened. He then spoke with calm reassurance.

Ralph couldn't infer everything the man said. But by focusing on his gestures and tonal shifts, he understood the Elder wanted their people to be mindful of not clinging to creature comforts during times of change.

Ralph prepared himself to be called on when the Elder had finished to explain his unannounced arrival, why he'd ruined their ritual, and what kind of magic his bird possessed. But when White Beard was done, he simply stepped back and gestured to the female Elder, who came forward with a wide smile, making eye contact with everyone, including Ralph. She then began guiding everyone through several songs.

Ralph stayed cross-legged, holding the hands of the bobbleheads on either side of him as they sang. He couldn't singalong or even wobble his head like they could, but he closed his eyes and embraced the melody, content with the warm vibrations spreading through the crowd.

When the songs were over, the Elders took turns telling stories. They told stories about Enqn, the village, the worlds beyond. They told tales of times gone by and times still to come.

It was hard to decipher their stories. But sometimes Ralph took away more than a few words:

'Once upon a time, a lady went below.

She was strong, she was feisty, but she had nothing to show.

Everyone in the village thought her crazy for this.

But on her return, she ceased to exist.'

The stories the Elders told were undoubtedly different to how he interpreted them. But he tried not to overcomplicate things, even when some of them reminded him of people from his past.

As the long days on Enqn blended, Ralph settled into life in the village. It was a simple life, fulfilling, one he'd longed for.

In the day, he farmed, collected water, and mined in the quarry under the village. In the evenings, he sat around the fire, listening to the stories told by the Elders.

Whenever he wasn't with the bobbleheads, he'd attempt to transfer into the atmosphere. He felt ashamed for wanting to leave a place filled with people who only wanted to help and love him. But with a broken sword and only one place to go to fix it, he was at a loss about what he was supposed to do next.

24
Tales from Enqn

ON Ralph's ninth day living with the bobbleheads, they moved him into his own home.

Situated close to the village centre, it was a wooden, boxlike building with a tall doorframe and high ceiling. With his days filled with helping the bobbleheads, not a day went by where he wouldn't return home to find his front porch loaded with fruit, vegetable, and meat baskets.

He was glad they both loved and found him useful. It felt good being helpful, wanted, needed. On Earth, with his small size and weak limbs and grip, he'd never been capable of helping anyone. Now equipped with a teenaged body that towered over the bobbleheads, he was the go-to.

No matter how much they relied on him and treated him like royalty though, he never let it go to his head. He made sure to maintain a healthy understanding of who he was, where he was, where he'd been, and most importantly, what still lay ahead.

After a fortnight without the Darkness rituals infecting the bobbleheads, they began to change. After a month, their brains ran faster, the fog on their eyes cleared, their energy levels heightened.

Ralph would've loved to call it a day, said his goodbyes, and moved on to the next planet to save. But he knew the Darkness keeping its distance was temporal, and he wouldn't leave until he saved the kind, globular-headed folks from its incessant grasp.

In the meantime, he took to life on Enqn. He spent his days helping who he could. In the evenings, he huddled around the fire with the others, singing, drinking, eating, and listening to the tales told by the Elders.

The Crimson Crystal

Once upon a time, there lived a group of miners. They had muscles as large as their heads, pickaxes as large as the moons, and moustaches for all to see.

The miners loved collecting and exploring. They spent their lives travelling the stars, searching for precious stones and precious crystals.

One day, they came across a stone capable of transporting them through space. Using this portal, they travelled to distant galaxies they'd only ever dreamed of. There, they mined the resources, consumed the delicacies, and moved on.

In time, with so many stones and crystals filling their pockets, they built sanctuaries across the cosmos. Some of these locations became civilisations. Others became junkyards.

When the miners came across people while travelling, they always made sure to tell them how big the cosmos was and how silly it was to stay in one place.

Sometimes, the mere arrival of the miners woke people up to such a fact. Other times, people resisted, clinging to their ways of life, lacking the buoyancy for the inevitable seas of change.

With many years of travelling the cosmos, the miners grew confident with their knowledge and their wealth. But they met their match when they came across Canis, the three-headed beast guarding the crimson crystals.

'Hello,' the miners said, entering Canis's dark cave.

The beast awoke with a rumbling roar, snapping its teeth, flexing its claws.

'Who goes there and what does it want?' Canis asked.

'We are miners seeking the crystal you guard. Please step aside.'

Canis roared, hoping to frighten the miners. But frighten the miners he did not. They'd travelled too long and too far. They'd seen too many things and knew too much.

'Tell us,' the miners said, 'why do you guard this crystal?'

Canis was unsure how to reply. 'I have always guarded this crystal,' he said. 'My parents guarded it, their parents, their parents, and so on, forever and ever.'

'But you do not need to do what your parents did,' the miners said. 'There is much to explore, much to do. Believe us, we have seen a lot.'

Canis's six ears twitched at the information. 'And what do you mean by "explore"? And what do you mean by "do"? I have roamed this cave for many years. There is nothing here that interests me.'

The miners told Canis about the cosmos, about the planets they'd been to and the rocks they'd mined.

'But I cannot leave,' Canis said.

'But you cannot stay,' the miners insisted.

'But here is all I know.'

'Then you owe it to yourself and your family to go.'

'But family,' Canis said, 'is all I have.'

The creature's love for its family stirred something inside the miners.

'If I do not need to stay,' Canis said, 'then perhaps you do not need to mine.'

'But we know nothing else,' the miners said.

Canis sensed conflict within the miners, for he'd learned what conflict was with their arrival.

After some contemplation, Canis decided to step aside. The miners thanked Canis, then harvested enough crimson crystal to fill their pockets and sacks.

'Thank you,' Canis said, following the miners to the cave's entrance.

'And thank you,' the miners said, activating their stone portal.

The miners bowed in gratitude and respect, for they

got what they wanted. And Canis bowed in gratitude and respect, for he got what he needed.

Once Canis took flight, the miners watched the three-headed beast disappear into the night.

Although they'd completed a noble deed, they felt empty.

The way the creature had been proud of its family had warmed their hearts, stirring memories and responsibilities from their old life.

With this ache, the miners searched the cosmos for a planet to call home.

Finding one large enough, they named it Enqn, and scattered their precious stones and precious crystals across the land.

But with Canis's crimson crystal, they planted it deep in its depths, knowing that by doing so, they would honour the gentle beast that'd once dedicated its life to never leaving the crystal's side.

The young Elder stepped down from the podium after his tale of the crimson crystal. The bobbleheads did not clap, nor cheer, nor sing in response. Instead, they hummed a warm energy, a pondering energy laced with thoughts, before food and drink were brought out.

Ralph fell asleep that night with a smile on his face, eager for more stories, eager for more strings of meaning and significance he couldn't quite understand.

The next evening, after a day of building electromagnetic coils, the female Elder approached him on his way to the town square.

'This is all temporary,' she said, holding his hands. 'You know this. I can see it in your eyes.'

'But what's wrong with that?' he asked. 'Your people haven't been free for a long time. The Darkness owned them. Trust me, I know how it feels to be controlled by it.'

She nodded, but something in the back of his mind told him she disagreed.

'Your unrest is obvious,' she said. 'I know you have had experience with the Darkness, but even you know what it means when you do nothing.'

He thought about what'd happened when he'd avoided his sister, when he'd sat too long at the Bottom of the Universe and the giranticore had torn his work to shreds.

'But I don't know what to do,' he said. 'My sword was meant to destroy the Darkness. But I have no idea how to fix it. I don't even know what I'd do if it was fixed. And with the Orbs dead…'

Veška came to mind. He saw her sulking in the rafters, playing her flute, trying to get his attention. He wished she was here. With her knowledge of the universe and the coordinates device in her possession, she would've been able to help.

'You will know what to do when the time is right,' the female Elder said, squeezing his hands.

After story time, bowls of musharacha were handed around. Ralph ate his with the girl who'd tended to him in the hospital, grinning away.

The evening then proceeded like always. They danced and sang and huddled together until the amber sun rose. And on the next evening, White Beard took the podium to tell an oddly familiar tale.

The Giant Who Fell from the Sky

The giant fell from the sky with a crash that woke the world. The giant was tall and moved about the land awkwardly and cautiously.

Strong and equipped with a knack for solving things, the giant knew many things the world did not.

The world was grateful for the giant's arrival, changing heights of roofs and doorways to cater for it, welding large forks and knives for it to use.

But no matter how kind the world was to the giant, the giant could not let go of its memories, grudges, or pain.

As the years passed, the world grew tired of the giant and decided to keep it in a cage for all the other worlds to see. But little did the worlds know, the giant could not be contained in a cage.

Not when it wielded magic.

With a puff of smoke and a crack that drew the attention of the worlds, the giant escaped its prison and returned home.

When the worlds inspected the cage, they found grains of dust on the floor.

They attempted to discover what the dust could do, testing it, playing with it, using it in cooking, shaping it into monuments. But no matter what the worlds did, they could not solve the giant's magic.

One day, the giant returned with its family and war broke out.

The war lasted for six hundred and sixteen years.

Worlds were destroyed. Giants were slain. The energy of the universe was disturbed.

The giant felt terrible for the loss of lives. To end the chaos, it offered itself to the worlds.

'We did everything for you,' the worlds said. 'Yet you only brought misery.'

'I only wanted to help,' the giant said.

'But you brought war.'

'If you understood the magic—'

'We never asked for magic,' the worlds said.

'Only because you do not want to understand it.'

The worlds were silent as the giant spoke.

'The magic I wield comes from the same source that made everything, including you. It is a part of me as much as it is a part of you.'

The worlds heard truth in the giant's words, they heard resolve. But they did not want to understand.

They cast the giant from their worlds into the next, where it was forced to move on, hoping the next world would accept its magic.

As the Elder stepped down, some of the bobbleheads were already standing. Ralph remained seated, needing time to process the story.

Food and drink were brought out, passed around. The bobbleheads ate and drank, sang and danced.

With everyone distracted by the festivities, Ralph approached the Elder who'd told the tale of the giant.

'You're afraid of my magic?' he asked.

The Elder smiled, combing his long, white beard in thought. 'Why would I be? Your magic brought you here.'

Since arriving, Ralph had made sure to never perform particle transference in public. Of course, he'd used it to build the electromagnetic coils to light the village. But other than that, alongside a few attempts to leave the atmosphere, he'd kept the magic secret.

'I'm not here to take over Enqn. I only came to stop the Darkness. I didn't even mean to crash on your planet.'

A bobblehead approached and handed him and the Elder a brew. The Elder downed his in one gulp.

'Tomorrow,' he said, 'you will tell your story.'

The next evening, Ralph stepped up to the podium. Nervous for the first time since the Particle Gods had nipped at his heels, he surveyed the sea of swaying, globular heads.

'I entered the universe on a planet called Earth,' he said.

Earth was repeated by the entire village.

'I was birthed inside a bright, sterile room with no shadows, like a solar spectacle from times gone by.'

Solar spectacle spread through the crowd.

'As the years passed, I became aware I was not like the others. While they aged and greyed, I stayed crawling around in nappies.'

Nappies.

Ralph told them about his life, detailing his curse and the Arrows of Time. He told them about all the equations and theories that'd consumed him, all the research, all the wasted focus on time machines. He told them about his sister, how he'd never been there for her, how she'd passed away when he'd travelled to Sydney for the symposium. He told them about his mum abandoning them, their absent father, Earth's evacuation.

'As the ice age drew near, people left on spaceships for Proxima Centauri b, a planet forty trillion kilometres from Earth.'

Kilometres.

'Watching the last transport vessel leave was one of the hardest things I've ever done. Being completely alone with a curse like mine had always been a fear. But this moment marked the beginning of a new phase, one where I solved things I'd never dreamed of solving.'

He went on to explain the day the presence had invaded his cave-lab. He explained particle transference and how stumbling across Kirby et al.'s energy debt theory had changed everything. He told them about the day Earth ejected him, what it was like living outside of time on the Stack, what it was like living at the Bottom of the Universe, who he'd met on his journey, how long it'd taken him to fold the silk sword.

The bobbleheads listened intently, heads swaying, eyes closed, repeating keywords. When he came to the point in the story where he theorised how he'd destroy the Darkness, the Elders hurried him off the stage, signalling for the food and drinks to be brought out.

'You must never speak of a story that has not occurred,' the youngest Elder said.

'I didn't know how else to end it,' Ralph said.

'That is the question of your existence.'

'I don't know what that means.'

The three Elders stepped forward, took his hands, closed their eyes. Ralph closed his.

'The Tale of the Silk Sword must be completed,' White Beard said.

'You must leave,' the younger one said. 'You must track down the Darkness, destroy it, revitalise the land.'

The female Elder spoke last. 'It is the only way we can be sure you are not here to take our planet.'

Ralph opened his eyes. 'I thought you didn't want me to do anything about the Darkness. Now you want me to kill it?'

The Elders smiled, eyes still shut.

'With or without Darkness,' the female one said, 'we adjust, we learn. We believe you fell from the sky for a reason.'

'Yes,' Ralph said. 'To free you.'

'No.' She opened her eyes. 'To redeem the universe.'

Ralph looked south, where the shroud still hung low over the mountains.

'Then I must travel beyond the forest,' he said.

'Yes.'

He turned back to the Elders. 'I'll need help.'

'Then help will be given.'

25
Journeying South

NOT many bobbleheads ever left the village. Those who did, required approval from the Elders. Even then, many only ever went fifty metres beyond the walls to chop wood or mine ore.

So, when it came to pursuing the shroud south to its origin, it took a total of four months to prepare a convoy of capable, worthy travellers.

From weapons and ammo to cavalry and campsites, everything had to be planned. Wagons had to be built. Bobbleheads had to be taught how to fight. Steeds had to be trained. Food, medical supplies, and creatures for protection had to be readied.

On the day of departure, an energy of zeal and determination swelled within the walls. While many bobbleheads were enthralled by the quest Ralph was taking their boldest on, some still maintained uncertainty and unrest for the death of the Darkness.

'Why think can slay, Giant Who Fell?'

The words came tangled. But the frequencies allowed Ralph to extract their essence.

He pulled on the reins of Spartan, his six-legged mare, and turned to the bobblehead, drawing the ears of those nearby.

'Let me ask you,' Ralph said, 'have you ever lit a flame inside a cave?'

The dubious, curious bunch of bobbleheads traded glances, mumbled sounds, wobbled their globular heads.

'Darkness may be all-encompassing,' he continued. 'It may seem impossible to defeat. But it's timid when it faces light. It flees, much like the shroud did when my sparrow, as small as a splinter, spread its shine on my first day on Enqn.'

He wasn't sure they'd caught every word, intention, or meaning behind his words. While communication had improved significantly in the past two months, there were always a few who missed the gist of what he said.

'I know what you're like when the Darkness doesn't define, confine, and consume you,' Ralph said. 'You tell stories. You enjoy one another's company. You laugh, dance, eat, drink, sleep restfully. If I destroy the Darkness, it will not only save your lives, but the universe's as well.'

With the group quiet, contemplative, he continued on for the western gates.

Arriving in the town square, cheers welcomed him. It seemed the entire village had gathered for their departure. Some bobbleheads had climbed on roofs for a better view. Others stood on the perimeter wall. The rest filled the cobblestoned streets, crowding the stage, waving, smiling, wobbling their enormous heads.

Ralph rode Spartan towards Tchmil, his right-hand man and translator.

'How are you feeling, Lieutenant?' Ralph asked.

Tchmil was one of the oldest bobbleheads in the village. Woodcutter by trade, he was married and fathered fourteen children. Dedicating much of his spare time to woodcarving, he aspired to one day advance to Elderhood. As an expert marksman, he'd been invaluable in the lead-up to their journey, spending countless hours training the others to shoot arrows, even teaching Ralph the basics of sword fighting.

'I am ready,' Tchmil said, nodding with conviction.

Ralph returned the gesture, then turned to the convoy.

Twenty-five bobbleheads were accompanying him south. Each had been selected by the Elders. Each would ride their own six-legged steed. Each would carry a bow, a quill, and a club. Each were free to head home at any point along the way.

Ralph nodded at the cavalry as the crowd settled and the Elders filed onto the stage. White Beard stepped forward first.

'We are gathered today,' he said, 'to see off the convoy of the one who wields the Blade of Deception.'

Cheers erupted. Heads wobbled.

'These brave twenty-six,' White Beard continued, 'will travel beyond the village walls to hunt down and slay the beast controlling our lives.'

More cheering. More clapping. Some murmurs.

White Beard stepped back, gesturing for the Elder woman to come forward. She did so, waiting for the noise to die down before speaking.

'We hope us all being here offers great luck on your journey, Giant from the Sky,' she said. 'May you and your convoy bring balance to Enqn. And your life.'

As the celebrations broke loose again, chills shot down Ralph's spine. He took it all in, making eye contact with the Elders, reminding himself that the journey, the quest, his purpose, the conclusion to his time curse, was no longer just about him, but all people and creatures across the cosmos.

Trotting Spartan to the gate, he performed a headcount of the cavalry. Tchmil had organised everyone into their respective positions. As he passed each of them, he bowed his head in acknowledgement. They returned the gesture, hope radiating in their eyes, adding fuel to his desire to destroy the Darkness, while also burdening him with the weight of their fates and reliance on what he planned to do.

After the six wagons were strapped to those who would draw them, Ralph signalled to the gatekeepers. The gates creaked open as he shouted over the noise of the celebrations.

'We will destroy the Darkness! We will release the universe from its control!'

The Elders translated his words. The cheering amplified.

'Believe me when I say this,' Ralph said over the cacophony of excitement. 'We will all live, breathe, and thrive once again.'

Not a single soul was not invested in the moment. Every eye was on him and the cavalry.

It was like they were leaving for war. And perhaps they were.

Ralph looked at the Elders. They watched their people, soft smiles touching the corners of their mouths. He caught the female Elder's attention, nodded once, then turned Spartan to face the open gate.

'Let us move quick,' he said to the cavalry. 'Let us stick together.'

Tchmil translated his words. A battle cry came.

Ralph kicked Spartan into gear and the splinter sparrow ignited, sending waves of sonar shine into the forest ahead.

The convoy took off in a thundering gallop. Woodcutters on the edge of the forest stopped work to watch them beeline past, wide-eyed, silent.

As the gates closed behind them and the foliage thickened, the cheering faded. It wasn't long before the ambience became nothing but the sounds of clomping feet and the screeching of wagon wheels.

Tchmil rode up beside Ralph while the path was still wide enough. He pointed at the four prdakuh creatures they'd brought for protection. Lean, muscular, with wicked sets of teeth, they galloped alongside the convoy like a pack of panthers.

'Now?' Tchmil asked.

Ralph tracked the sparrow's shine to where the path narrowed, thirty metres ahead. He nodded once and Tchmil whistled in an eccentric way.

The prdakuh broke away to stagger themselves in a column formation around the convoy. Tchmil then dropped to the back of the pack as they transitioned to a single file.

The path through the forest was cramped and made of dirt and crushed greenery. The deeper they rode through it, the greener and denser it became, indicating just how long it'd been since anyone had ventured so far from the village – if ever.

Unlike the pine forest at the Bottom of the Universe, Enqn's forest was full of life. Squawking birds and buzzing insects filled the air. Scurrying, furry mammals with beady eyes were spotted at every turn.

Ralph might've been leading the convoy to their death, but he couldn't help enjoying the moment as they galloped through the forest, spotting alien creatures reminiscent of possums and squirrels with different claw sizes, eye counts, and fur colours.

What ruined the beauty, naturality, and enjoyment of it all though was the shroud's presence, which tainted the forest like a virus, curling up every branch, skirting every fungus, suffocating everything without remorse.

As the light dwindled on their first day, they stopped at their planned campsite. Stationing oil-fuelled lampposts on the perimeter, they parked the wagons close together and lit fires to mimic a village.

Once organised, Ralph assigned the first patrol for the evening, basing who he selected on fatigue levels. He then climbed into his bunkbed.

He didn't sleep for more than an hour that night. With three bobbleheads snoring away in the wagon with him, coupled with the heat and the light from the fires breaching its thin walls, his mind stayed active and alert well into the morning.

When he exited the wagon the next day, the others told him they'd slept the same. They also informed him about the disappearance of the four prdakuh.

'What do you mean they're gone?' Ralph asked Tchmil.

'I am sorry, sir,' he said. 'But no one know what happen. They might have travel far from camp and lose our scent. Maybe run off in fear. Or maybe perish and soil ate them.'

With the death of their protectors, unease infiltrated the cavalry. Ralph delayed the convoy setting off so he could speak to each bobblehead individually.

After listening to their concerns, he reconciled their grievances with a short speech to the group.

'This is exactly what the Darkness wants,' he said. 'It wants us afraid. It wants us cut off from comforts. It's done this to me my entire life. But that just means it fears what we can do.'

The convoy was silent as Tchmil translated Ralph's words.

'I've travelled across the cosmos to be here,' Ralph continued. 'I didn't fall from your sky for no reason. The Darkness put me through hell. But it never knew I'd come here to destroy it. And after losing so much, I'm not going to stop until I finish this fight.'

He waited for Tchmil to translate his words.

'But please understand,' Ralph said, 'none of you need to be here. You're all free to return home to your families. No questions. No judgment.'

After Tchmil translated, all eyes fixed on Ralph with a new resolve. He waited for any to come forward. When all remained silent, he nodded once.

'Thank you for believing in me,' he said. 'And thank you for sticking with me.'

The second and third days were much the same. They rode through the forest with vigilance. They set up tight camps. They patrolled with flaming clubs and bows at the ready.

On the fourth day, the Darkness ramped up its attack. As it blanketed more of the world around them, it began messing with the bobbleheads, contaminating their minds, inciting delusions and hallucinations during the day, and nightmares that kept them tossing, turning, and yowling at night.

Ralph was lucky. He suffered none of these effects. It seemed the splinter sparrow's shine stopped the Darkness invading his mind.

On the sixth day, ghostly, translucent creatures joined the convoy. Resembling hyenas, complete with mischievous grins and agile legs, they stayed on the outer edge, moving like wisps of smoke carried by the wind. Although the flames on the wagons and the splinter sparrow kept them at bay, their presence was enough to keep the bobbleheads wary.

As the days progressed, the shadow creatures closed in. A cloudy, opaque appearance replaced their translucence. No matter how bright the sparrow shone, no matter how many fires they lit, the creatures handled it. It was as though they were made of a substance that was a direct inverse to light, swallowing the photons to power themselves.

On the tenth day, when the convoy finally made it out of the forest to an open clearing, similar to a safari plain, the shadow creatures dissipated. While the shroud remained, spreading across the land like an early morning fog, it did so thinly, providing much needed breathing room and a clear view of its origin, their destination: a volcano rising into the sky like a barbed, obsidian spire.

With the shroud's origin confirmed, the convoy picked up their pace.

They travelled through the plain for four days and four nights. On the fifth day, they reached the eastern coastline, where they followed the sapphire sea south.

As they drew closer to the volcano, the more the bobbleheads suffered. Many became bedridden, forced to rest inside the wagons as they rode. They groaned and spasmed as the Darkness infested their minds like bacteria, polluting every particle, wreaking havoc on their energy levels, and making Ralph question why they'd set off on the journey in the first place.

26
Creatures of the Night

THE helicopter touched down in the front yard. Its blades cut the air with a whipping thud, quivering the surrounding bushes and trees. Emboldened by a chimney smoke diffusing across the farmland, the afternoon sun said its goodbye with a golden light.

Ralph opened the door as Stephanie crossed the lawn.

'Can you at least power that thing down?' she asked, pulling her silver hair into a tight bun.

He signalled to the pilot, then turned back to her. 'Are you still coming?'

She gestured at her boots and overalls caked with dry mud. 'I was just about to sit down for tea. Why didn't you call ahead?'

He scanned the surrounding meadows, the cattle grazing, the rusted tractor. 'Didn't think I had to. You always come to my interviews.'

A gentle frown formed on her wrinkled face. 'That's not true. I haven't come with you for decades.'

Uninterested in another argument, he turned to the pilot.

'Why don't you stay for tea though?' Stephanie asked.

He turned back to deny her request, finding her engulfed by the chimney smoke. Through the haze, her sunken eyes stared at him in distress.

'You left me, Ralphie,' she said, voice tinlike, monotone. 'You left me for your science and your fame and your little girlfriend at the Bottom of the Universe.'

She came forward with jittery, flawed movements, pale hands reaching.

207

He closed the door with a frantic press of the button. Spinning a finger in the air, the pilot fired up the aircraft. Seconds before they took flight, Stephanie latched onto the side.

'You left me,' she said, voice muffled by the glass.

The hatred in her eyes made him regret stopping at her farm.

The helicopter rose, banked, sending Stephanie tumbling to the ground. As she struck the grass, thunder clapped, and she vanished from sight. A moment later, blaring klaxons kicked on as a vigorous rain battered the aircraft.

The pilot did his best to flee the farm. But near the edge, a lightning fork struck the helicopter, frying its instruments, and sending it spiralling towards the ground.

'You left me!'

Her words echoed through the sky. Each syllable synchronised with the pursuing, rumbling storm.

'But I'm coming for you, little Ralphie. And I won't abandon you like you abandoned me.'

The storm whipped. The helicopter shook. Ralph squeezed the edges of the baby seat, heart pounding.

The ground was fast approaching. The grass on it withered, died. The surface turned black and dusty as a rift opened on its surface, exposing a bubbling pool of churning fire. A man with a charred skull knelt amongst the flames, holding a katana, staring at Ralph.

The helicopter entered the rift. Its tail clipped the edge on the way.

Thrown from his baby seat, a flash of white light blinded Ralph as—

'Sir?'

Tchmil was leaning over him, concern riddled upon his aging complexion.

Ralph took a moment to become present, smelling the shroud's decay, listening to the steeds whinnying.

'Yeah,' he said, standing. 'Sorry.'

Tchmil shook his head, telling him not to worry. 'Another nightmare?'

Ralph nodded, gathering his backpack from the bunk he'd fallen from.

'Are you okay?' Tchmil asked.

The image of older Stephanie flashed into Ralph's mind. He'd never had the luxury of seeing her age. He didn't know how to feel about what the Darkness had concocted. On the one hand, there was beauty in seeing what could've become of his sister if her life hadn't been taken. On the other, seeing her had reawakened a great sadness and anger for what his curse had delivered.

'Yes,' Ralph said. 'Are you?'

Tchmil bowed his head. 'I miss my children.'

Ralph placed a hand on his shoulder. 'We don't have much longer to go. Once we reach the volcano, I'll go on alone. The rest of you will return home.'

Tchmil shook his head. 'We here because of what Darkness did to our lives. But we only here because of what it did to yours. And I not rest until I see it dead.'

Ralph squeezed Tchmil's shoulder in gratitude. He then exited the wagon.

The onshore wind blew strong. Flinging foam across the sapphire sea, it stained the sand with the shroud's filth, like ash cast by a bushfire.

He glanced at Enqn's sun, the star they called Blysz. Despite nearing its zenith, its heat came cold and weak, filtered by the shroud, while also telling him how long the Darkness's nightmare had consumed him.

A bobblehead holding a cup of broth approached Ralph. Taking it with a nod, he headed over to Spartan.

It wasn't the first nightmare he'd been hit with as they closed in on the spire. But it was the most violent.

Typically, the Darkness delighted in concocting general phantasms: never-ending hallways, descents into chasms, leathery creatures with bloodstained antlers chasing him through mazes. Sometimes, it reminded him of past errors: Christmases he hadn't bothered celebrating, birthdays he'd refrained from attending, nights alone at home. Other times, it highlighted scenes from his life: scouring research papers, staring at equations, praying to the gods who'd forgotten about him, praying he'd make a breakthrough someday.

Compared to the bobbleheads though, his nightmares paled. Along with the ones they suffered, delusions dominated their minds, causing many to wander about murmuring, sobbing, crawling around like babies. Whenever those effected were found, most would snap from their psychosis, apologise, and resume their patrol. More often than not though, they'd collapse in twitching fits, before being bedridden for hours, mumbling and dealing with erratic fevers.

'What is plan?' Tchmil asked, riding his steed over to him.

Ralph checked his backpack, confirmed his obsidiary dust and broken sword still sat inside, then threw it on. 'We have to redesign our vehicles before leaving.'

Tchmil took a moment to sort through his knowledge of Ralph's language. 'You wish to change wagons?'

'We have to keep the Darkness further away. It's becoming too much. If the splinter sparrow can no longer protect me, who knows what it'll do when we're closer to the volcano.'

Tchmil nodded. 'I agree.'

For the rest of the morning, they revamped the wagons. They fitted oil lamps on each corner. They constructed metal containers to keep mini bonfires on the roofs. They equipped the steeds with holders to carry flaming torches as they rode.

With the modifications complete, the next two days of travel went smoother. While delusions still plagued the bobbleheads, while nightmares still impaired everyone's sleep, the shroud's effects dampened.

Their journey then became like clockwork again. They rode, they made camp, they ate, they slept. But twenty-five days after leaving the safety of the village, everything changed when the convoy suffered their first loss.

Ralph had just finished a final lap of the camp when the pack of shadow creatures returned. From trailing wisps of translucent hyenas, they'd taken the form of wolves.

With the Darkness's constant indulgence upon his mind, he initially believed he was seeing things. But when they howled and snapped their jaws, he sprang into action, grabbing the flaming torch from Spartan and calling to the bobbleheads.

'Get behind me!'

The cavalry gathered in a tight formation, putting the sapphire sea to their backs. Ralph called on the sparrow to help. But no matter how bright it shone, its power was no match for the five servants the Darkness had sent.

'What do you want?' Ralph asked.

The leader of the shadow pack stalked forward like it was tracking prey in the middle of the night. A shade darker than the other four, its eyes gleamed crimson. Coming to a standstill, it stared at Ralph, arched its neck, and howled at the sky.

'What do you want?' Ralph asked, demanded.

'Sir!' Tchmil said. 'They not want talk. They will have our heads if we not attack.'

'But how do we kill shadows? Our fires are doing nothing. My sparrow's shine is doing nothing.'

'Light,' Tchmil said, igniting the tip of an arrow, 'is all we have.'

Other bobbleheads copied him. Bringing their bows to the ready, they took aim, just like Tchmil had taught them, and waited for Ralph's command.

'No,' Ralph said, shaking his head. 'This will do nothing but—'

Tchmil loosed an arrow. The others followed suit.

The shadow wolves retreated as the flaming arrows struck the sand where they'd stood. As Tchmil kicked his steed into gear and took off, the wolves split up. Four headed north. The alpha headed south.

Ralph mounted Spartan. 'Stay with Tchmil,' he said to the others. 'I will take care of the leader.'

He took off down the beach, galloping after the shadow wolf.

The creature dashed across the sand with nimble agility, bounding over driftwood and rocks, moving unnaturally. Sometimes it didn't bother leaping over objects, choosing instead to move right through them. Other times, it slowed to make sure it got around them.

When it came to the sand dunes, it scurried up the steep incline without missing a beat, moving in fluttering wisps.

Ralph dismounted Spartan at the base of the dune and ran after the shadow wolf. When he reached the peak, he found it cornered where the sand met the rocky mountain range.

'There's no use running,' he said, flaming torch raised.

The shadow wolf bared its teeth, snarled.

'Take me to your source,' Ralph said. 'I will end this today.'

Crimson eyes flaring, the wolf came forward, flickering like an object decompiling. After transitioning through several different four-legged creatures Ralph had never seen, it stopped on a dingo. But it was no ordinary dingo. It was the dingo he'd once known as Cyclops.

'No,' Ralph said.

Shadow Cyclops launched at him. Ralph swiped the flaming torch through the air. The creature avoided the flame, decompiling particles in the right places, before landing and refilling the gaps. Turning its head, it looked at Ralph with one peering, crimson eye.

'Stop,' Ralph said. 'I know you're not real.'

The shadow dingo pounced again. This time, Ralph didn't bother fighting. He let it pass through him. As it did, a bitter cold iced his blood, synthesising a sequence of images in his mind.

He relived the day he'd rescued Cyclops from the pecking beak of the demon rooster. He saw the nights she'd laid curled up in her bed, worn out from a day on the farm. He saw her stiff as a board after the trip to Adelaide…

Shadow Cyclops leapt again, leaving a trail of toxic, wispy darkness in their wake. Ralph ignored the creature, turning to the mountaintops, where the shroud hung low.

'What do you want?' he yelled at it.

The dingo came to a halt in midair as a familiar sniggering rippled through the area.

'You've played with me long enough,' Ralph said. 'Why are you so afraid to face me?'

The shroud rippled. A tendril of darkness descended from the sky, combining with Shadow Cyclops, converting her into a swollen, cloudlike cluster.

Ralph flung his backpack off and took out the black diamond sack.

'Get away from me, you demons!' he said, pouring a handful of obsidiary dust into his hand.

The shrieking shroud enclosed on him, swallowing the environment, darkening it.

'We missed you,' the voices said. 'Why did you leave us with those disgusting Orbs?'

'You're not real,' Ralph said. 'You're just pests fabricated by the Darkness.'

Sniggering filled the air. 'Oh, you treat us so unkind, Nazra. But it doesn't matter what you believe. We are all part of it.'

Ralph withdrew the broken silk sword from his backpack. Gripping the hilt with the damaged blade in his right hand, he held his left loaded with obsidiary dust at the ready.

'Fool us once, Nazra,' the shroud shrieked, 'but never again!'

The cloud of dark particles morphed through various creatures and objects. It became a stingray, a silkworm, a coffin, an osmium cube, Earth with the Moon orbiting.

'Do your worst,' Ralph said. 'Hurt me. Kill me. Take over my body. I don't care anymore.'

After trying a dozen different configurations, it shifted from Max Bonaparte to his mum and sister, before stopping on a person he never thought he'd see again.

'You are back,' the four-legged creature said, brightly. 'What have you learned? What have you seen? Do you still seek? Do you still question?'

Shadow Ca'zehro spoke exactly like the real one, confusing Ralph just as much as hurting him.

'Shut up. You're not Ca'zehro.'

The shadowy, translucent Ca'zehro laughed, crimson eyes blazing. 'Do you still not understand, Ralph Ridley? Believe me, if you cannot learn to be, then you will suffer for eternity!'

He came for Ralph, four legs moving across the land as smooth as a spider traversing its own web.

Ralph waited until Shadow Ca'zehro was close enough, then stepped to the side and launched the dust at his face. Before it struck him though, he evaporated, reappearing on the other side of Ralph.

Ralph spun around, bringing the broken blade up as the area fell into complete darkness. The only light came from his sword and Shadow Ca'zehro's eyes.

'Your mind is breaking,' Shadow Ca'zehro said. 'The Darkness devours all. You cannot stop it.'

Ca'zehro's voice had taken on a tone Ralph didn't remember. It upset him, making him wonder if any of this would've happened if he'd stayed on the Stack.

'And that is how we want you to feel,' Shadow Ca'zehro said. 'You should feel regret. You should hate your life. A Nazra who tampered with its body is useless.'

Here he was, still reading Ralph's mind.

'Tell me, Boy Who Never Grew,' Shadow Ca'zehro said, 'how many relationships did you ruin on Earth? How many things did you avoid? How many moments did you waste? How many people will you never see again?'

'Shut up!' Ralph said.

'You met someone at the Bottom of the Universe? How interesting. Who is she? Why do you think of her at a time like this? Why did you leave her like you left your sister and me?'

'Stop!' Ralph said, squeezing the silk sword's hilt. 'You did this to me. You put me here. You ruined my life from the start.'

Shadow Ca'zehro's body flickered, split. Tiny versions birthed around him like an army of mini Ca'zehros. They distorted, becoming celestial bodies from the Bottom of the Universe, clashing like particles, before breaking apart and forming thirty-two spheres singing an ominous hum.

Ralph stepped back in disbelief.

The shadow spheres merged to form four glowing, dark orbs the size of oversized basketballs, illuminating the environment with an indigo hue.

The more there is,' the Dark Orbs sang, *'the less you can see.'*

'It can't be,' Ralph said, shaking his head.

'Do you fear us, Quanta Man?'

'There is nothing to fear.'

'Did you miss us, Quanta Man?'

'We hoped you would.'

'You're not real,' Ralph said.

'Now the Nazra is understanding.'

'How did you find me?'

The Dark Orbs traded sparks of laughter.

'You do not need to fear us.'

'Not after you tried to help us.'

'Not after you tried to free us.'

'Not after you made it all the way here.'

Ralph's throat was dry.

The Dark Orbs kicked up a swirling maelstrom of electricity and wind.

Sand whipped up from the ground as the storm pushed back the Darkness. A thin strand of dark lightning laced out from the Orbs and struck Ralph's torso, shattering the silver nodes embedded in his arms.

'*You do not need them anymore.*'

'*They are crutches.*'

'*They hold you back.*'

'*You* are the technology, Nazra.*'

The Dark Orbs spun around one another like a group of planets. Flickering and sparking, their absorptive, wispy gases of jet-black electricity spread through the air.

'What do you mean I don't need them?' Ralph asked.

'*There is no time to explain.*'

'*Your sword is mended.*'

'*Here come the Particle Gods.*'

'*And now, we are gone.*'

And gone they were.

The shroud returned, encircling Ralph like a monsoon. His vision faded as painful nips and bites overwhelmed him.

'Get off me,' he said, swiping the silk sword.

The Darkness retreated with every swing, shrieking in glee.

'You're not wanted on Enqn,' Ralph said.

With a snicker, the shroud slammed into his chest, knocking him to the ground, winding him. It then fled along the mountain range in a howling flurry.

As it localised above the volcano, Ralph took several deep breaths to slow his heartrate. Sheathing his sword with shaky hands, he approached the dune's edge and looked back at their camp, where a group of bobbleheads had gathered around a bloodstained, mangled body.

27

Entering the Cave

THE Darkness withdrew its presence from the land, like soldiers retreating from an ambush. Pooling above the spirelike volcano, it billowed away, allowing Blysz's rays to beam down with a new radiance and heat.

The beach became a shimmering field of glitter. The sapphire sea sparkled. The trees and shrubbery, now no longer suffocated by the shroud, wavered and wobbled in the wind once again.

Enqn's beauty had returned.

What butchered the entire spectacle though, what ruined the moment, was Tchmil's slashed, shrivelled corpse in the grave atop the dunes.

'Tchmil drop fire arrow on ground,' a bobblehead named Hyith said. 'Laughing shadows come very quick.' She sliced a hand through the air. 'Shadows pounce and…'

She made a gesture with her hands as though tearing a grapefruit in two, squelching her cheeks. She then explained how the shrieking, sniggering shroud had entered Tchmil's open wounds, devouring his life essence in a matter of minutes.

'He become like this,' she said, shaking her body, twitching and blinking her eyes rapidly. 'Then he become like this.' She froze, feet together, arms by her side, staring.

Her story reminded Ralph of the icy bitterness he'd felt when Shadow Cyclops had passed through his body, making him wonder why he hadn't suffered the same fate.

The bobbleheads took turns commemorating Tchmil. Ralph went last.

'I'm sorry for your loss,' he said, remembering the empty words the funeral director had said to him long ago. 'Tchmil was a good man – smart, helpful, patient. He wanted the best for his people. But please understand, his death was not in vain.'

Out of habit, Ralph waited for Tchmil to translate. Feeling somewhat foolish, he continued.

'For more years than you can imagine, I've been pursuing the Darkness. I've lost a lot of people along the way. Some have died. Some have left me. Others I've left myself.'

A few of the bobbleheads exchanged glances, ovular eyes narrowed, concerned.

'But I promise you,' Ralph said, 'once we arrive at its lair, all the suffering it's inflicted will be over. Its malevolence will end. The universe will finally be free.'

He gestured at Hyith, who stepped forward and translated his words with plenty of stuttering, hand gestures, and sound effects. When she'd finished, the expressions on their faces told him most had not understood.

Ralph pointed at the beach, out to sea. 'See what happens when the Darkness retreats? Blysz burns brighter. Enqn flourishes. It may not feel like it, but the Darkness is afraid of us. It knows what we can do. And the sooner we get on our way, the sooner we can end it.'

The bobbleheads stared at him as he took a handful of sand and tossed it on Tchmil. He didn't care if they thought this practice was strange. It felt right to him, like a final thank you and goodbye to his right-hand man.

Gathering his sword and backpack, he set off down the dune. As he mounted Spartan at the bottom, Hyith came running after him.

'Sir?' she said, panting from the difficult descent with her stumpy legs.

Ralph waited on his six-legged steed. 'Everything okay?'

She approached him, eyes averted. Ralph waited, allowing her time to gather her thoughts and words.

'Sir,' she said, looking at him. 'We need time.'

Ralph nodded. 'None of you need to continue, Hyith. I've said this from the start. If you want to go home, I understand.'

She frowned. 'No, sir. We need to stop. We need time to think. You may have seen many death, but we have not.'

'I understand. But I'm more than capable of finishing—'

'Don't be fool,' she said.

Although her tone resembled how one might wish someone happy birthday, her words and glassy eyes snapped him back to reality.

He dismounted Spartan. Before he'd even taken one step, she leapt forward, throwing her long arms around him and sobbing into his chest.

The convoy spent two days resting and mourning by the sea. Despite the quest being so close to finishing, despite it screaming out at Ralph to continue, Hyith's words had thrown him back in time to when Stephanie was still alive, to when she'd needed her brother, before bowel cancer had taken her.

Had the Darkness taken Tchmil in the hopes of deterring him? Maybe. And maybe Old Ralph, calloused, betrayed, lonely, would've run away at such brutality. But Old Ralph wasn't in control anymore. He'd lived on the Stack. He'd been to the Bottom of the Universe. He'd seen and learned too much. New Ralph was in control now. And New Ralph knew what it meant to have people around who needed him.

On the night before they resumed their journey, he addressed the bobbleheads beside a roaring bonfire.

'I want to remind you all,' he said, 'none of you need to come tomorrow.'

The huddled bobbleheads stared. He wasn't sure if they were contemplating the offer, or if they'd even understood him. In either case, the next morning, fourteen gathered their belongings, and he sent them home in wagons covered in light.

He couldn't blame them for wanting to return home. Nothing about the journey had been simple. Moving through the Darkness was a chore in itself. Adding in the pain they suffered in their minds and bodies, and it was a testament they'd made it so far in the first place.

Once the glowing wagons had faded from sight, Ralph and the ten remaining bobbleheads turned south for the spire.

They travelled for two more days before reaching a shadowy veil separating the beach and the mountains. After ensuring the oil lamps were loaded and each steed torch burned bright, they entered.

Inside the veil, day became dusk. The environment took on an ashen, dead appearance, murky, gloomy. The air tasted stale, poisonous. If it wasn't for the sparrow's shine – as dull as it was – and their fires, Ralph doubted they'd be able to withstand the smothering energy, let alone know which way to go.

When they reached the volcano's base, they parked their steeds.

From sea-level to crater, the spire rose three hundred metres. Decaying rocks and dead trees riddled its surface. Vents and fissures gleaming crimson leaked obsidian smoke. At its peak, the Darkness billowed, seething like a hungry hurricane, flickering between creatures like the shadow wolf had. It became recognisable ones: basilisks, griffins, djinns, hydras. It became ones Ralph had no idea about. But no matter what creature it morphed into, it always reverted to one it seemed to enjoy embodying the most: a dragon.

Ralph addressed the remaining cavalry, who looked at him with stern expressions.

'Are you ready?'

The bobbleheads nodded with confidence.

They began their ascent. Ralph led the way, relying on the splinter sparrow to guide them the safest way up the steep, slippery surface.

The hike took close to four hours. Arriving at the summit, they peered into the crater at a pool of crimson lava pulsing with a power strong enough to blow back their hair and heat their skin. Wisps of darkness rose from its surface like steam. A rocky, flat area the size of a basketball court bordered it like a beach by the sea. Cracked and crumbling, thin lines of crimson branched across it like veins, leading to a cave embedded in the crater's wall.

Ralph turned to the bobbleheads. Their expressions had changed. Before the ascent, confidence had oozed from them. Now they all looked dazed, drained, defeated.

He beckoned to Hyith. She trotted over.

'You'll all stay here,' he said.

'We not leave you. We do what Tchmil wanted.'

Ralph shook his head. 'This is the end of the line for you all. I can't let you come with me.' He gestured at the others staring, mouths open. 'None of you can focus here.'

'We be fine,' she said with determination.

He shook his head again. 'Enqn is your planet, Hyith. It's your home. I'm not from here. I haven't been tainted by the Darkness's full strength for as long as you all have.'

She studied the shroud in the sky. 'This is where it born?'

'It looks that way.' He tracked his eyes across it as well. 'It feels that way.'

She shivered. 'I feel it too.'

'Then it's time you all—'

'You can't defeat it by yourself,' a bobblehead named Maija said, coming up beside them.

'But I will,' Ralph said. 'I was always meant to. It's why I fell from your sky.'

The rest of the bobbleheads joined them.

'It not right,' Hyith said. 'It not fair to go alone.'

'I've been alone for a very long time,' Ralph said. 'It's how it's supposed to be.'

A wind howled through the crater with arrogance, provocation. The sound broke any opportunity for further retaliation or refusal. Ralph took its sudden arrival as a sign of fate.

'Take cover,' he said, pointing to some nearby boulders. 'Light fires. Stay close together. I will return.'

They watched him in silence.

'And thank you for your help,' he said. 'I couldn't have made it here without you. You should all be proud of what you've achieved and how much you've grown. The confidence you have in me has given me the strength and reassurance to finish this fight.'

He made the rounds, thanking each of them personally, embracing them, trading smiles as a way to stave off tears.

Once Hyith had rounded the others up and led them to the boulders, he started his careful descent into the crater.

Nearing the crimson lava, a sensation similar to decompiling awoke within him. Fearing a sporadic transference straight into the bubbling liquid, he slowed his walk, breathing deeply, focusing on his surroundings. As he drew closer to the lava though, he realised it wasn't him coming apart, but the world around him.

Like a silent film from the past, the environment flickered and distorted with every step. Moments in time he couldn't quite comprehend flashed around him in fleeting sequences.

He glimpsed the moment the volcano had last erupted. He saw the crater covered in grass and flowers. He tracked a hot, neon river weaving across the plain and fading into the distance. He saw a thriving hamlet, a park, bobblehead children hurling a frisbee.

Noise accompanied these images: the familiar sound of traffic in the distance, helicopters in the sky, birds in trees, waves crashing on the shore.

He knew the imagery and sounds were courtesy of the Darkness. But it didn't stop them from feeling real.

Reaching the cracked, rocky surface, he headed for the cave, following the branching crimson veins.

'What are you doing here, trillions of lightyears from Earth?'

The voice entered his mind as he stepped over a spluttering vein. It was heavy, powerful. He ignored it.

'You have come to slay me? How will you achieve this? With your broken nodes? With your silk sword? With your useless splinter sparrow?'

Ralph shook his head, fighting the flow of insults the Darkness delivered.

'Turn around, Ralph Ridley. Turn around. You are out of your depth.'

He should've known the Darkness would be like this so close to its domain. Ever since entering Enqn's atmosphere, it'd been hostile. And why wouldn't it be? It didn't want him here. It wanted him dead.

'There is still time to go back. Return to the village. Return to Earth. Return to your miserable existence.'

Ralph reached the cave and unsheathed his sword. Its pink, vibrant glow combined with the splinter sparrow's shine, lighting the tunnel. He waited until the cave brightened enough, then entered.

Following the winding path down, he tread carefully, quietly. Every step he took, the Darkness retreated from the pink and gold radiating around him.

Deeper and deeper he went. Hours seemed to pass. Days.

With nothing but darkness surrounding him, he lost all perception of time. He lost all perception of his senses.

Eventually, he reached a junction where a new light greeted him. Crimson in colour, it shimmered on the glossy volcanic wall like sunlight striking dew. As he ran a hand across it, a booming voice reverberated through the underground lair.

'You should not be here!'

Ralph followed the path towards the voice, squeezing the hilt of his blade.

Rounding a corner, he emerged into a cylindrical, hollow cavern as large as a skyscraper. A ledge wrapped the perimeter. A crimson crystal obelisk, as thick as a redwood, rose to the ceiling in the centre. Coiled around it like a snake, a wispy tail of darkness led to a perched dragon as black as the night.

'You should not be here, Ralph Ridley!'

28
The Dragon

'YOU have been misled,' the Dragon of Darkness bellowed.

Perched near the apex of the crystal obelisk, the dragon glared at Ralph with crimson eyes and fiery hatred. The size of a Boeing 737, its pitch-black wings draped like a cloak. Spikes riddled its back. Its curved talons were the size of machetes. Its black, razor-sharp teeth gleamed from the combined glows of his sword, the sparrow, and the crimson obelisk.

Ralph raised his pink silk scimitar sword. 'I don't care. I've come to finish this.'

'You never should have come,' the dragon roared.

Dropping from her perch, she spread her wings like a parachute. Before Ralph could get out of the way, she crashed to the ground less than twenty metres away, shaking the cavern, loosing rocks and dust.

The dragon reminded Ralph of something from a nightmare, one the Darkness could've concocted if the journey to its lair had taken any longer. Small wisps of heat radiated from its scales, curled, dissipated. Every inch of its skin was the colour of Vantablack, a black so absorptive, it swallowed every light particle around it.

'It's your fault I'm here,' Ralph said. 'You put me inside this dilemma before I could even talk.'

The dragon lashed a lazy, playful talon at him. He hopped backwards to avoid it. But it still clipped him, slicing his cheek and sending him slamming into the rock wall.

The dragon's laughter echoed through the cavern. 'You still have not learned. You still seek. You still cry. You should not be here.'

Ralph wiped the blood from his cheek. 'Don't talk how my friends talk.'

The dragon was not only intimidating in size, but its posture implied it was battle-hardened, intelligent.

'You cannot defeat me,' she said. 'I am Kahlo, the Darkness. I am the essence of the universe, the balance. I own the day and the night. I control all.'

'I've heard that before,' Ralph said, getting to his feet. 'You may manipulate everything, but you're nothing more than another egotistical demon.'

The dragon levelled her gaze. 'Silly Nazra.'

Holding the sword like a jousting stick in both hands, Ralph charged. Kahlo stayed on the spot, smirking, almost begging him to make a fool of himself.

When Ralph reached lunging range, he leapt forward, stabbing the dragon's scaly torso with the tip of the blade. On impact, the sword crumpled, folding like paper.

The dragon bellowed more laughter.

Ralph shook the blade as though trying to wake it up. It flapped and flopped about like an oversized tea towel. His heart sank as its pink glow faded.

He couldn't believe it. Even after spending 999 days folding it, even with the sparrow sealing it at the Bottom of the Universe, even with the Dark Orbs fixing it, the blade had barely lasted five seconds against the beast that'd ruined his life.

The dragon took flight and returned to its perch. The wind of its departure sent Ralph to the ground.

'There is no use trying to destroy me,' she roared. 'You are a part of me, and I am a part of you.'

'I am nothing like you,' Ralph said.

The dragon blew a heatwave at Ralph. He dove out of the way as it struck the ground, cracking and sizzling the surface.

The dragon swooped again. The wind of her descent flattened him.

'Little help?' Ralph asked the sparrow as the gale subsided.

The bird did not respond. It did not ignite.

'You are alone,' Kahlo said. 'Just like it should be.'

The sparrow's act of defiance seemed malicious. It didn't make sense.

'You are a fool for coming here,' Kahlo said, leaping from the obelisk and landing on all fours. 'But it is okay, for I will finish you and you will finally be free.'

The Dragon of Darkness came for him, bounding across the ground.

Logic told Ralph to run. Emotions told him to run. But the sight of a colossal dragon running towards him, wings raised, froze him, stunned him, shook him to his core.

When she was close enough to attack, his brain shattered its stupefaction. He began ducking and jumping out of the way of her slashing talons, avoiding them with every ounce of energy and coordination he possessed.

His efforts, of course, were futile. Her attacks were relentless. Her reach, too great. Eventually, a talon found purchase and hurled him through the air.

He came down hard on his right shoulder, dislocating it and tearing skin from his arm and hip.

Before he could inspect the wounds, Kahlo came for him again, swiping and stabbing her tail like playing a game of Whac-A-Mole. He tumbled and slid across the rocky surface to avoid it, tearing more skin, leaking more blood. A cold sweat covered him as his adrenaline surged.

Her attacks persisted, evolved, intensified. She swiped and gnashed, stabbed and stomped. But no matter how vicious or indicative they were of her ambition to deliver death, it never happened. Like a lion playing with a zebra foal, she was only toying with him.

'I know what you're doing,' Ralph said, wiping sweat from his brow.

She laughed, took flight. The wind from her wings knocked him to the ground again.

Landing atop the obelisk, she sent another heatwave at him. He tried rolling out of the way, but it struck him square in the back, igniting his backpack. Flinging it from his shoulders just in time, it burned to ashes right before his eyes.

'No,' he said.

The sacks of dust. The jerky. The golden rod. The notepad and trinkets. Jamaki's cerulean cicada.

All of it, gone.

'I hate you!' he said. He yelled at the sparrow next. 'Why are you doing this to me?'

The bird remained silent, beak clasped.

Kahlo swooped again.

Damaged arm still pinned to his side, Ralph dove out of the way in desperation. In the process, he overshot his mark, launching himself over the perimeter ledge encircling the obelisk.

As he fell towards the crimson lava below, his life flashed before him. A timeline of events came to him, starting from the moment he realised he'd been afflicted with a time curse, leading to the moment he'd prepared tea on the mesa with the Adelaideans.

Every image flashed through his mind in rapid succession, bringing a tidal wave of emotions that painted a picture with one central theme: He'd been wrong to come to the Darkness's lair. Facing the Dragon of Darkness wasn't just stupid, it was suicide.

He hit the crimson liquid in complete silence, as though it were made of jelly. As his inertia slowed, a beat pulsated through him like the beat of the Stack, passing from his feet to his head, tingling his skin, sensitising his teeth and bones.

He looked about for the beat's source, knowing it could only be coming from one place.

Another pulse spread through the liquid, through him, heating his flesh, cooling his insides.

His right shoulder throbbed, clicked, popped back into place with an uncomfortable grating sound. The gashes and slashes stinging his skin sealed.

He took a moment to realise what'd happened, then rotated his arm. It felt fine. He studied the wounds the dragon had inflicted. They were already rejuvenating. Even the holes and silver fragments left over in his arms after the Dark Orbs had shattered his nodes were mending.

He looked up, tracking Kahlo's silhouette circling the obelisk. Shocked at the clarity of his vision while submerged in the crimson liquid, grateful for the lack of need for oxygen, he swam for the obelisk. As he neared it, more pulses hit him with dense resonance. By the time he reached the crystal, his body had mended, his energy had enhanced.

Choosing to think about all of this on the way back to the village with the bobbleheads, he placed a hand against the obelisk and closed his eyes, seeking the pulsing's source. He found it deep within. It came with a sense of familiarity and protection. But alongside its promised comfort came a rigidity, as though it only offered security at the cost of tyranny.

You are the technology, Nazra.

The words the Dark Orbs had spoken came to him. He studied the scars and silver shards in his arms.

Your senses dictate reality.

The words the invader had said when it'd first arrived in his cave-lab came loud and true, giving him pause, inciting a question.

But without his silver nodes, was it possible?

You are early in your journey if you are still asking questions.

Ca'zehro's words prompted him, provoked him.

Where there is quantum theory, there is hope.

He unsheathed his silk sword. It moved through the liquid like a ribbon eel.

Returning his hand to the obelisk, he focused his energy, channelled it, waiting and hoping for the tingles to spread.

It didn't take long before they did. The sword's silk particles then began to flicker.

An enraged roar came from above, followed by a surge of heat.

Kahlo knew what he was doing. But submerged under the liquid, she couldn't do anything about it.

He continued focusing, envisioning the curved blade, the obelisk, the end of all his problems.

With every skerrick of energy he lost during the transference, the liquid replenished it. It was like a perfect energy transaction, a perfect entropy loop – no debt, no destruction, only synchronicity.

The crystal under and around his hand began to fracture. Thin, glowing pink lines forked across its surface. At the same time, streaks of crimson bled into the silk blade until it swallowed the pink entirely. The sword then began to reform, mend, harden.

When the particle transference was complete, he turned the crystal blade over in his hand. Heavier than the silk variation, and somewhat camouflaged amidst the liquid, it gleamed and thrummed with a powerful shine.

He swam for the surface. Breaching it with an instinctive, unnecessary gasp for air, the dragon roared.

'You have become the one thing you came to destroy!'

Ralph climbed onto a nearby rock.

'I know you can't kill me,' he said. 'If I was supposed to be dead by now, I would be. Which means I was always supposed to come here. And if I was always supposed to come here, then I was always supposed to kill you.'

'You do not control fate,' Kahlo said. 'You cannot stop the end. You cannot stop what is coming. By using your primitive energy extraction, you have become more a part of it than ever before.'

'I don't care,' he said. And he meant it. 'I've come here to do one thing: to stop your senseless destruction and reclaim my life.'

The dragon swooped. Ralph waited for the right moment. When she was in range, he dove to the side, swiping the crystal blade through the air, nicking one of her legs in the process. The recoil from the connection sent him slamming into the wall behind.

Kahlo roared in rage and delight, returning to her perch.

Ralph got to his feet, studying the sword. A smear of dark, pearlescent blood stained the crystal's surface.

'So,' he said, 'you are mortal, after all.'

'You will die, Nazra. You have gone too far.'

She sent another heatwave. Ralph widened his base, blade held at the ready.

As the heat approached, it boiled the air particles, creating condensation that rained to the ground. When it reached him, the blade's crimson glow absorbed the brunt of the energy. The rest struck the ground around him, charring and cracking it.

He looked up at Kahlo. Perched on the obelisk, she licked her wound.

A strange sense of pity passed through him at the sight. And it was in that moment the ancient dark energy equation finally made sense.

It seemed so obvious now. The equation never had anything to do with him overlooking something in science. Solving it had been impossible because the Darkness could not be denigrated to mere letters, numbers, or symbols. Not when it was a complicated organism. Not when it was pure life. Not when it transcended everything humans had ever thought about and solved, superseding beliefs, concepts, values, and meaning.

The dragon landed on the ground in front of him.

She wanted to destroy him. But her energy no longer contained confidence. He sensed fear in it, sadness.

'The rotation you did to me,' he said, 'your desire to destroy and control everything has led to your end.'

He wiped the pearlescent blood from his blade with a finger. Kahlo froze, eyes wide.

'Don't you dare, Nazra!'

Placing the blood on his tongue, his body surged, tingled.

The transference began.

He reformed inside the dragon's mouth, where rows of onyx-black teeth boxed him in and a toxic smell tainted the air.

The cavity shook, jerked. He fell to his side, was lifted from her tongue, floated for a second, crashed into a tooth, tumbled, twisted.

The Dragon of Darkness was throwing herself about her lair, doing whatever she could to hinder him. But he wasn't about to stop now.

Dropping to his butt, he slid down her throat into her torso. He came out in an oddly empty space, where black ribs encaged trailing organs that wrapped and climbed things he didn't have names for. In the centre, suspended by a viscous cord, the dragon's obsidian heart throbbed away.

Ralph crawled towards it, gripping her ribs to stay grounded as she continued flinging herself about.

When he was below the heart, he used its cord to stand. He then brought the tip of his crimson crystal blade against it.

The dragon's attempt at survival ceased. Its admission for defeat almost made him feel sorry for her.

'Do not do this, Ralph Ridley,' Kahlo said, her voice as clear as it had been on the outside. 'You do not realise what you are doing. This is not what is supposed to happen.'

'And that's where you're wrong,' Ralph said.

With a deep inhalation, he pierced the dragon's heart.

A bright, white light burst from the organ, illuminating her torso. A strong gust of wind followed as everything was sucked towards the light, then sent back out in a supernova-like explosion.

Ralph found himself, once again, falling. This time though, he wasn't falling towards the crimson liquid, but straight for the surrounding ledge.

His leg hit the rocky surface on the way down. His ankle ruptured. His knee twisted. His femur popped from its socket as the momentum sent him cartwheeling towards the lava.

Head spinning, he struck the surface in silence and plunged to its depths. He tried swimming up, but the liquid's thickness was too much. And with a beaten body and broken leg, he lacked the energy to try for more than a few seconds.

So, he sank, letting the inertia take hold.

He'd killed Kahlo. But what would happen now? Why did it feel like nothing had changed? And why couldn't he feel the obelisk's pulse anymore?

He touched his bruised, swollen leg, wincing in pain. His kneecap wasn't where it was supposed to be. His ankle looked deformed.

Had killing Kahlo destroyed the liquid's energy healing capabilities?

Anxiety arose with this thought. He'd gone through all of that, travelling from Earth to Enqn to the bottom of this crimson lava pool in the Darkness's lair for nothing?

But did it matter? a voice in the back of his head countered.

The Dragon of Darkness had been slayed. He'd saved the universe. He might've perished in the process, but at least it was over. At least he could finally rest.

He closed his eyes, nodding to himself, embracing the end.

He thought about the bobbleheads, wondering how they were feeling as the Darkness disappeared from their planet.

He thought about Veška, wishing he could've told her all his avoidance and folding had paid off.

He thought about Ca'zehro, wishing he could've told him he'd been right, that everything he'd learned and solved *had* been crucial for his purpose and success.

His mind turned to Earth next, to Stephanie, the Adelaideans. He wished he could've shown them all his toiling had yielded the result he'd strived for.

He thought about all his studying, all his reading and experiments, his golden ratio equation, the questions about the number 21.6, and smiled.

They'd been right. He had been the Alpha and the Omega, the first to be born with a time curse, and the one to end the tyrant who'd inflicted it.

A pulse reverberated through the liquid.

He snapped his eyes open.

Another pulse.

His ankle stung, itched, clicked, deflated. His knee lurched, popped.

Another pulse.

His heartrate climbed. His femur snapped into its socket with an unsettling jolt.

A surge of energy rippled through him.

Sheathing his crystal sword, he swum for the surface. Breaching it, he looked around for any sign of Kahlo. But she was nowhere to be seen. Not a corpse, scale, or wisp of black smoke.

He would've loved to enjoy the moment, pondering everything he could do with his newfound freedom, one greater than he'd felt after Earth had ejected him. But it was clear he'd done more than just kill the Dragon of Darkness.

He'd broken reality.

All around him, particles were popping out of existence. Colours were disappearing. Objects were decompiling. Clusters of vibrations shot about the cavern in disarray, causing rock shards to rain down.

'You have to get us out of here,' he begged the sparrow.

With an energetic chirp, it stirred, shook its feathers, ignited. Enveloping him with a shine brighter than he'd ever seen, it lifted him from the ground.

Ralph wanted to swear at it, ask it why it'd been mute during his confrontation with Kahlo. But he chose to keep the question for another time.

The sparrow took him higher and higher to the crystal obelisk's peak. It then broke through the ceiling of the cavern, emerging above the crimson lava bubbling away in the volcano's crater.

Ralph turned, spotted Hyith and the others.

Still huddled beside half a dozen fires, the bobbleheads watched Ralph descend into the crater for the cave. More peculiar than seeing himself in the past, was seeing remnants of all of them and their six-legged steeds stretching back down the beach they'd come from.

The sparrow continued to climb.

'Where are we going?' Ralph asked it.

The sparrow stopped a hundred metres above the volcano, where the morphing smog had once billowed.

With a clear, bird's eye view of the planet, Ralph took in the destruction taking place, mind reeling, realising the collapse of the Darkness wasn't just fragmenting the dragon's lair, it was fragmenting Enqn.

Like a death throe, a final act courtesy of Kahlo, everything was being stripped, one particle at a time.

29

No More Darkness

HOVERING high above Enqn, encased by the splinter sparrow's shine, Ralph watched on as everything decompiled.

From the land to the sand to the sea, nothing was spared by the Dragon of Darkness. He suspected she wanted to take him too. But he wouldn't let her win so easily.

The sparrow chirped, sweeping a beacon across the sky. He tracked it as it breached the atmosphere, entered the void, highlighted the unrest taking place beyond.

He cursed under his breath.

It wasn't just Enqn coming apart. It was the universe.

'No,' he said. 'How?'

But could he be surprised?

With the death of the Darkness, came the death of reality. It was just the kind of thing to expect. It was poetic. It made sense.

And it was all his fault.

The sparrow trilled, narrowing its beam, pinpointing a location.

'I can't leave now,' Ralph said. 'I have to help the bobbleheads.'

He turned north for the village, scanning the terrain. But any semblance of coherence to the place he'd called home for more than six months had taken on a jumbled, leaky appearance, like a messy painter's palette.

The sparrow chirped low.

He sighed. The bird was right. Leaving now could be seen as cowardly. But being annihilated wouldn't help anyone.

If he got away from ground zero though, if he escaped the collapse, he could reassess. He could collect more items, create more dust. He could figure out how to reverse what he'd done.

'Okay,' he said. 'Let's go.'

With one last look across the land, he focused on the beam's terminus and began the transference.

He recompiled in space, in an oily, smudged patch of darkness, similar to a watercolour painting.

He tried locating Enqn. But it was gone. The super planet with its friendly bobbleheads had been lost amongst the disorder of the collapsing universe.

Gone, just like everything else in his life.

'Where to next?' he asked, determined to see the bird's plan through now.

The sparrow swept its shine.

'How far do we have to go to escape the collapse?'

The sparrow remained silent as it searched for their next location. Finding it, a short chirp followed the narrowing of its beam.

Ralph began the transference.

He reformed in another patch of smeared, liquidlike darkness. He waited for the sparrow to locate their next location and transferred again. And again, without delay.

He transferred and reformed, over and over. The further he went into the void, the more lawless environments he came across. In some, he came out near distorted quasars, supernovas, comets the size of stars, planets resembling colourful, expandable balls. In others, he recompiled beside swarms of bright, dense gases flashing and pulsing as swirling storms filled with ravenous particles fled the destruction.

Ralph did his best to ignore the insanity of it all, transferring and reforming, transferring and reforming.

His mind bent with the sheer number of consecutive transfers. Distortive loops and memories seeped in as he lost grasp of reality. Timelines and various paths he could've taken manifested in his mind.

He saw himself with a family and kids, working an office job, falling asleep on the couch every evening. He watched his children grow up, one becoming a lighthouse operator, the other becoming a motocross superstar. He saw himself alone in a retirement home, eating cocktail

reptilian friend jumped into action at the sound of it, attacking the nearest home and tearing it apart. She laughed as the beast went from building to building, demolishing everything.

Ralph spotted the A-frame house nearby and ran inside. From the living room window, he watched the creature perform Veška's bidding, shredding every building apart, eating what it liked.

'A giranticore.'

Ralph was startled as the four Orbs appeared beside him.

'A harbinger of harmony.'

He turned back to the destruction. 'I guess it doesn't matter. Everything's going to collapse anyway.'

'This is not from the present, Nazra.'

'But from a time long ago.'

'When the Zoruvian first arrived.'

'Before we met you.'

'Impossible,' Ralph said, remembering the time jumps he'd been experiencing. 'She knew the giranticore all along?'

He studied the creature. It looked like a goanna combined with a corrupted ibis. It had a long, slender body covered in ragged, patchy feathers and a vicious, curved beak.

'Yes.'

Ralph cursed the universe for showing him this. 'Why didn't she—'

Catapulted back into the void, shiny shapes shot past him like shooting stars. He watched them, bracing for the next time jump, waiting. But it never came.

He shook his head. Could he trust what he'd just seen? How real had the moment been with his parents? The one with Bucky and Violette was nothing like he remembered. Could the same be said about the one with Veška?

He waited for the sparrow to pinpoint their next location, then transferred again.

But did it matter? He couldn't allow himself to dwell inside any memory or moment, no matter how lucid. The Darkness would no doubt be delighting in doing whatever it could to mess with him as it perished.

He reformed, still shaking his head.

Besides, real or not, all the experiences, interactions, and choices he'd lived through weren't anything he could change. The past was the past. He had to refocus, think about what he'd done, about what was happening, about what he had to do next. Sentimentality, nostalgia, and regret were three games he couldn't afford to play. If he couldn't figure out how to stop the collapse, what did he have left?

In the middle of a transference, a screeching whine broke him from the decompiling. A shift of frequencies swallowed him, revitalised him, brought an energy of inevitability and destiny.

The Orbs popped into existence in front of him. Their brilliant, bright white light gleamed.

He'd never been so happy to see anyone in his whole life.

'*You did it,*' the Orb of Light said.

'*The end,*' the Orb of Deterioration said.

'*The Nazra finished the job,*' the Orb of Attraction said.

'*We never thought it would,*' the Orb of Repulsion said.

They merged and split, spreading their light.

'Wait,' Ralph said. 'The Bottom of the Universe. Was it real?'

'*You do not understand time yet?*'

'*You must, Nazra.*'

'*You must.*'

'*You are here, after all.*'

He wanted to communicate with them further, ask for help. But torn from existence, the Particle Gods replaced them.

'Thank you!' they shrieked. 'The Nazra did it! She will be delighted!'

Ralph tried centring. He couldn't tell if he was still inside a transference or he'd been shoved down a hole of delusions.

An Earth the size of an exercise ball replaced the shroud a moment later. He moved closer to the blue marble, spun it on its axis like a toy globe, and located his mountain in the desert.

He peered closer at it, spotting the Adelaideans going about their chores. The cooking pot bubbled away on the mesa. Steam wafted into the air. He tracked his eyes across the surrounding land, at the shipping containers, the livestock grazing, the river flowing.

Life looked so calm, simple, normal, he wanted to dive in. He wanted to relive it. He wanted to never bother messing with matter.

Half a kilometre from the mountain, a wall of rippling white energy encircled the area. Outside the circle, the seasons changed rapidly, the rain fell, the trees grew, people drove cars and built cities.

Everything ticked normally. Inside the circle though, everything ticked slower, stranger.

Ralph didn't have time to comprehend what this meant as a creature smashed into the toy Earth, pulverising it. It was a smooth-skinned whalelike thing with the wings of a cicada. Behind it, a herd of praying mantises as big as buses scurried after it.

Ralph spun around to see more creatures of all sizes and shapes coming towards him like a stampede. One of them, a churning cloud of complex matter, latched onto him like a leech as they passed. It stung and bit him, spoke to him.

'This is not how it is supposed to end!' it said, seething.

Ralph tried swiping the cloud off him, but it tore him to shreds.

Reforming, the matter came for him again.

'We will not allow this,' it said, latching onto him and tearing him apart.

Ralph reformed again, wondering if death was not possible this far into the universe.

The matter came for him again.

'Stop!' Ralph shouted.

The cloud stopped, quivered, shattered into tiny heptagons, became white mist, then dissolved into nothingness.

Ralph stared at the spot, wondering what had just happened. But there didn't seem to be any reason in doing so. The pattern to reality was gone. The Thermodynamics Arrow had been abolished, replaced by a new Arrow.

The Arrow of Anarchy.

He transferred again, following the sparrow's shine.

He passed through a haze of aberrant particles, a patch of darkness, a field of dense blips warping and stretching, like a field of sunflowers bending in the wind. He then arrived at the end of the road: a transparent barrier, a place where transference became no longer possible, and the sparrow's beam no longer shone.

He peered through the barrier.

On the other side, particles filed in and filled the place. Colours, creatures, currents, and energies entangled with one another. Buzzing cubes, spheres, and parallel lines fought for dominance.

Staring at what lay beyond the barrier made him confused, nauseous. The frequencies it all exuded gave him the jitters, as though he was seconds away from finding out bad news.

He touched the barrier. His finger passed through it, then his hand, his arm. He tried pulling back, but it was too late. The barrier absorbed him, sucking him through the dome of reality, the firmament of the universe.

'A little help?' he asked the sparrow.

It chirped once in affirmation, then burst into thousands of tiny, golden feathers and disintegrated.

He screamed out as the bird's shiny particles were sucked into oblivion. The crimson crystal sword sheathed on his waist went next. Then his clothes. Then it was just him, floating inside a humming, holographic void.

Ahead, an unfinished circle the size of an elephant swirled. Metallic in appearance, it had scratchy, choppy aesthetics. It emanated an energy the cave-lab invader had brought all those years ago.

He moved closer to the unfinished circle.

Mutating through various states, it spun slowly. Its energy swelled towards him, all-encompassing, overwhelming. But it didn't make him ill. Nor did it enable transference. It didn't even send him into a whirlpool of memories, dread, or despair. Instead, all he felt from it was a pure, symmetrical resonance.

He looked at his hands. Sunspots, wrinkles, and white hairs covered them. His arms were the same, weathered, dry.

Relief washed over him. It was over. He'd made it to the end of the universe, a place where he no longer had to live with eternal youth, a place where he no longer had to be the Boy Who Never Grew, the cursed Nazra.

Was reaching the edge all he'd ever had to do? He could've done this years ago! Instead of worrying about time machines, dark energy equations, and particle transference, he could've spent his time building a spaceship.

But how would he have got here? How long would that have taken?

How much fuel would he have needed?

The unfinished circle rippled a new energy, welcoming him, informing him everything in existence was meeting here to become one. From quantum particles to creatures, celestial bodies, ethereal bodies, everything was making its way to the edge to merge with reality, to become part of the grandeur of it all.

30

The Unfinished Circle

RALPH'S carousel of fate was over. He'd reached the end of space, and with that, he'd reached the end of time.

The surrounding shifting, shiny, turbulent, coiling, oily darkness provided the perfect backdrop for the end. It complemented the moment, the mood, the metallic, unfinished circle hovering in the centre of it all.

He focused his attention on the gentle, persistent hum emitted by it. It reached out with a warm energy, keeping him alert and alive.

'Hello?' he said.

It fluttered as though it'd been busy tending to matters before remembering it had a guest.

'I like what you've done to the place,' its vibrative voice said. 'Thank you for slaying Kahlo. It's always the best part when everything collapses.'

Ralph was confused by its words and humour. 'What are you talking about? Better yet, how are you talking?'

The unfinished circle wobbled, sending a wave of rippling energy out, like a sonic boom. It then started shapeshifting through various creatures and objects, some Ralph had never seen.

'Let me see,' it said, contemplatively.

It became an hourglass, tall and golden, with silver sand sprinkling from its top portion.

'No, no, no,' it said. 'Too stale. Too cliché!'

It transitioned again, becoming a jumbo alarm clock, a grandfather clock, a sundial, a candle, a clepsydra. It then flickered through various personifications of deities Ralph remembered from his mythology books:

Heh, Kali, Mahakala, Janus, Chronos, the three Norns.

'No, no, no,' the transitioning creature said, reverting to the unfinished circle. 'Too obvious.'

It flickered once more, liquefied, then became a male human with long, snowy white hair tied into a ponytail. With a flowing grey robe, they carried a cane and wore a monocle.

'Is this better?' the man asked, smirking. 'Exactly what you'd expect out here, right?'

Ralph gestured around, let his arms flop to his sides, sighed. 'Nothing is better.'

The man flickered through a few other variations, adding more legs and arms and heads, then reverted. 'It never is.'

'Where am I?' Ralph asked. 'Who are you? God?'

'Not quite,' the man with the monocle said, smiling. 'But you are exactly where you think you are, Mister – sorry, *Doctor* – Ralph Ridley.'

Ralph looked down to find himself as young as a toddler again, before flickering through a hundred different combinations of himself.

'This place is outside the universe?' he asked.

The man regarded him proudly. 'From a certain point of view, yes. But that's how it always is, always was, and always will be.'

'Don't say things like that. You know how I'd feel right now. You know how confused I would be.'

The man shrugged. 'I'll admit, it might be a little unsettling here. But I doubt you are not ready to witness this. Your whole life has been one rather whacky ride.'

'You're not wrong there.'

'But you can't be too coy, Ridley. Messing with space always leads to messing with time – i.e., me.'

Ralph stared at the being, the thing, the entity. 'I'm not believing that. You're not time. You can't meet time. That's not how it works.'

The flickering, transitioning man laughed. 'Then how does it work, Boy Who Never Grew?'

'If I've learned anything on this trip through the universe, it's that time is just a concept created by humans. I've also learned to be cautious believing the creatures I meet. How can I even be sure you're not just another configuration compiled by the Darkness?'

'How could that be? You destroyed the Darkness, remember? It's why you're here. It's why I'm here too.'

Ralph furrowed his brow.

'If you do not think I am who I say I am,' the man said, 'then who do you think I am?'

'Just another idiot wanting me to waste more time and energy solving things that don't mean anything.'

The man with the monocle laughed. 'Like the Orbs who made you fold a silk sword that broke on contact? Like the Particle Gods who invaded their capsule? Like the dragon you slayed on Enqn?'

Ralph stared at him.

'I'll admit,' the man said, 'some variants of reality can be quite the nuisance. But you can't blame them. They're all just doing their jobs, including the Darkness.'

'You mean it wasn't the Darkness that ruined my life?'

'Not in the slightest.'

Ralph shook his head in frustration. 'Why should I believe you?'

The man waved a hand through the air. 'C'mon, Ridley. I expected more from you. Surely, you understand hierarchies. Surely, you understand there are creatures above those who only wish to tamper, squabble, lie, and distract.'

'I've heard this all before.'

And he had. Here he was again facing another creature wanting to manipulate him, wanting to tell him he was the most important, powerful being that'd ever existed.

'You're thinking about it all wrong, Ralphie,' the man said. 'Look where you are. Think about where you are. Think about how and why you got here. Think about what I'm doing right now.'

The more Ralph focused on the man, the more he didn't seem real. It was like his image was temporal, translucent like a ghost, undulating like an erratic ECG.

'I don't need to squabble,' the man said. 'I know my place. I know my purpose. The others, the Particle Gods, the Orbs, the Wabobians, even the glovulafisc of the Rivers all love to frolic and consume, tamper, trying to be more important than they really are. I, however, sit outside of it all, tinkering ever so slightly to alter things.'

Ralph pressed his aged hands into his face. 'You expect me to believe you're time, *the* Time?'

'That's right.'

He met the man's eyes. 'Why?'

'The question is not why, Mr. Ridley, but how.'

His soothing tone infuriated Ralph. 'Then *how* should I believe you?'

'Well,' the man said, tapping his cane on the non-existent floor. A golden, sparking sketch of a tree stump appeared. 'Tell me, how are you here?'

'If you know so much about me, you tell me.'

'Please,' the man said, sitting on the stump, 'enlighten me.'

Ralph sighed. 'Because I transferred—'

'No, no, no,' the man said, somewhat frustrated. '*How* are you here?'

Ralph took a moment. 'Because… I killed Kahlo and fled her destruction.'

The man shook his head. 'I'm not asking you *what* caused you to come here, in spite of such things being necessary, but *how* you are here, right now, in this very moment, irrespective of the time and space annihilation going on out there.'

Ralph glanced at the barrier. On the other side, a mess of swirling, clashing, detonating colours wreaked havoc with one another like a silent massacre.

He looked back at Time. 'Because I'm supposed to be here?'

The man smiled. 'Not supposed to be, Ridley, *ready* to be. That's a big difference.'

They were silent for a moment.

'Then what am I supposed to do now that I'm here?' Ralph asked.

'That's the dilemma of all dilemmas, isn't it?' Time said. 'More dilemmary than your time dilemma. But the beauty of this place is you can look at everything objectively now.'

'Look at what objectively?'

'This,' Time said, gesturing all around. 'The edge. Think about where you are, Nazra. I may have been the one who manipulated the ticking of your time, but by doing so, I allowed you enough of it to make it here, pushing you along to complete tasks and face things you never thought you could face.'

'You ruined my life.'

'No, I prepared you for this. Everything you did was necessary for being here. And as you can see out there, I have no real influence of what is happening. As soon as anything comes into existence, including you, it will always do what it always does, forever and ever, then, now, later. Everything – every person, every place, every object – cannot help but churn and turn, create and destroy. That is Nature. That is the universe we find ourselves in.'

'You took everything from me,' Ralph said. 'You started my life in hell. Why me? Why mess up my life? Why make me suffer?'

The man tapped his cane again. Another tree stump appeared. Ralph ignored it, glaring at the thing who'd put him through every experience and emotion he'd ever endured.

'You must understand, Quanta Man, you are here for the transition. Time, like it always does, must turn over. We – you, me, Time, Space – must contribute to it. We mustn't stop it. We mustn't hold onto memories, regrets, notions, emotions, or beliefs.'

Ralph balled his fists to prevent his hands from trembling. 'You couldn't tell me this is where I'd end up? You couldn't talk to me like a normal person?'

Time shrugged. 'It's all part of the event that is the universe, my friend. The diversity, destruction, and final division allows for unification. I may have the ability to tamper with the flow of time, but everything else occurs because of its own doing.'

Ralph's head spun, but he couldn't be sure it was his that was spinning. Or if it was even spinning at all.

'Think of yourself as a knife,' Time said. 'By cutting everything into pieces and severing the Darkness, the last thing binding the universe, you allowed for a beginning.'

'This is all a game to you, exactly like the Particle Gods said.'

'Yes, it is kind of like that,' Time said, nodding in thought. 'But there must be steps that push you along. You must go through enough things to learn and grow. There must be challenges to teach you who you truly are, awaken what you are on the inside. It's what everyone goes through to see it all at once.'

'To see it all at once?'

'Everyone experiences time, Ridley, but not everyone can see it. And that's where we come in.'

Ralph stood there – which wasn't really standing, nor floating, nor even existing – staring at the man, the thing, the glitching creature, the so-called rendition of Time. A new level of introspection came over him. If he thought too hard, it didn't feel like he was thinking. If he tried thinking about thinking, he couldn't even be sure it was him who was trying to think.

He wasn't in control of anything anymore.

'There is nothing to fear here,' Time said, reassuringly.

'Don't read my thoughts,' Ralph said, pointing at him with an elongating, twisting, chromatic finger.

Time smiled. 'Here, they are my thoughts too.'

Ralph might've been floating with a strange man wearing a monocle, but the thing claiming to be Time having a window into his mind took it to a whole new level.

'Think about it,' Time said. 'If I'm Time, then I see all, right? I see every moment occur at once, right? The past, the present, the future. I don't see any of it play out like you're used to experiencing in that linear, primitive sort of way.'

Ralph thought about the Stack, the timelapses. He tried imagining what it would be like seeing everything that'd ever happened, and will happen, happening all at once. He couldn't begin to comprehend such a feat. But it did make him wonder if the lucid, interactive memories he'd faced on the way to the edge of the universe were similar.

'I believe you will know in time,' Time said, continuing to read his thoughts. 'But if it makes it any easier, think of me as the combination of the Arrows of Time, the eighth one, if you will, the Arrow of Totality. I am part of every process involved in the movement of time. In other words, time ticks, but it always ticked, and it will always continue to tick, no matter what, no matter when, no matter how. I, however, stand outside it all.'

Ralph took a moment to grasp what he was being told. It was almost too surreal to think about. If true, how could he ever have thought he'd solve his time dilemma by shuffling equations, staring at time machine diagrams, or even tampering with particles?

'It's just like what Ca'zehro said,' Time said. 'Everything you worked on and solved and overcame were all necessary components of your journey.'

'This was all fate?'

'In life, nothing is wasted. Everything you do and see and think and achieve and fail is all part of shaping your character. Learning lessons leads you to becoming the person you were always meant to be, awakening dormant traits along the way. In other words, Ridley, all rivers lead to the ocean.'

'This was all planned?' Ralph asked, feeling on the verge of a mental breakdown.

'Not entirely. How you got the Orbs to help you this time was an unexpected, yet welcome, anomaly.'

Ralph remembered back to when the Dark Orbs had appeared to mend his silk sword.

'That snippet of compassion you showed them in their capsule changed everything,' Time said. 'For example, you were never supposed to go to Enqn so soon.'

Ralph remembered back to the moment the sniggering shroud had entered the capsule and he'd demanded it to leave the Orbs alone.

'But no matter how peculiar an anomaly,' Time said, 'the inevitable, cyclic collapse must occur.'

'This is what always happens?'

'Not always, little Ralphie. But the right energy ratio always leads to the same circumstance and arrangement of particles.'

Ralph thought back to Kirby et al.'s energy debt theory, where removing energy from one area prompted an influx of the opposite.

'Exactly,' Time said. 'Just like the beginning of time and space requires the right particles to pop in at the right moment, rate, and volume, the annihilation of the universe follows the same rules.'

'I made it here to die? After everything you put me through, annihilation is my fate?'

Time's face grew stern, concerned, like a parent who wanted the best for their child. 'No, Ridley. You're supposed to take over.'

31
Unification

'TAKE over?' Ralph said. 'From what?'

'From me, of course,' Time said, fluctuating between the man with the monocle and the unfinished circle. 'I know you still won't accept the concept of eternity, but you're here now, so we have to speed things up.'

'Don't say that. I'm sick of you all saying that.'

'It's the truth. You've only lived, what, a thousand years? That is a mere dash on the timeline of the fourteen-billion-year-old universe. Furthermore, it is not as though you ever lived a normal, ticking life, which indeed impacted your personality and growth, causing you to be stunted in some areas and unrivalled in others.'

Ralph hadn't stopped to wonder how long he'd lived in a very long time. He'd become so caught up in the folding of the sword, destroying the Darkness, saving the universe…

He looked at Time, lost for words. The ambience of the area took over.

Amongst the humming, soft sounds of rattling metal, shattering glass, creaking wood, whirring wind, and sounds he had no idea how to comprehend, collisions of laughter and chatter filled in the gaps. It was as though the remaining particles of the universe were trying to break through the barrier to explain their lives, all while combining and forming new planets, objects, creatures, completely unbeknownst to the curse of reality.

'But I don't have to let this happen,' Ralph said. 'You may have done this to me, but I still have a choice.'

'A choice?' Time almost laughed. 'To what, stay here? In your own

249

words, Ridley, that's not how it works. You made it here. You should be proud. Most Nazra never even do things that challenge their base level of comfort.'

'Proud?' Ralph said. 'For what? You were the one who helped me solve particle manipulation.'

Time shook his head. 'I'm not a magician. You solved that yourself. I merely manipulated the passing of time to give you enough of it to solve transference.'

Ralph recalled the wall of rippling white energy he'd seen surrounding the farm on his journey to the edge.

'Time ticked differently for you for a reason,' Time said. 'Where you lived and dwelled, time flowed unnaturally. Outside, business per usual.'

Ralph remembered the deterioration in Adelaide, the settlement folks who'd dismissed him, Cyclops aging…

'You must understand,' Time said, 'learning how to manipulate matter is not something easily achieved in any normal Earth-human lifespan. In fact, it's never been achieved in less than seven hundred years by any species before you. I suppose it could happen, but that'd be a rather large anomaly.'

Ralph walked away from Time to gather his thoughts. But there was nowhere to walk away to and no thoughts to gather. There was nothing he could ask, say, or do to make any of this comprehensible.

'With the ability to alter the flow of time,' Time said, appearing beside him, 'I gain the ability to alter the flow of particles. Thus, I cannot solve or help anyone or anything directly. I can only influence the concentration of particles popping in and out of existence in any one location.'

Ralph thought back to all the losses he'd had over the years. He thought about what he'd spent the bulk of his time doing on Earth, and how it paled in comparison to the number of years he'd travelled through the void.

'At the Bottom of the Universe,' he said, 'who left the silk weaving equipment?'

'That equipment was from the time you were there last. Well, that's not entirely accurate. You built it, you're building it, and you're going to—'

'Build it,' Ralph said.

'Precisely. Although, the term *you* is somewhat of a metaphor here as well.'

Ralph didn't like any of this.

'So,' he said, 'by leaving instructions about the collection of silk in those books, who am I helping? The next Ralph? Me?'

'More or less. You, or another way of thinking about it, the Matter Manipulators.'

'The Matter Manipulators?'

'That's right,' Time said. 'The beings always on their way to fold their weapons of deception to slay Kahlo, the Dragon of Darkness.'

'I thought seeing the other blue bubbles approaching the Stack cheapened my life… If what you're saying is true, if this is what always happens, what's stopping me from becoming something like you?'

'Now you're understanding eternity,' Time said.

'If you influenced everything so that I'd arrive here, why not speed it up? Why not help me?'

'Fate doesn't work like that. The Matter Manipulators must learn their path. Earn their stripes. One cannot just *become* a manipulator of particles. It takes time, practice. As you saw near the end of your journey, you could manipulate everything. You could even transfer without the use of nodes, rods, or dust.'

'I hate this.'

'One must truly live to reach the beyond,' Time said. 'It would be far too disrespectful to the balance if the Manipulators did not face problems and losses. All who prosper must suffer. It's how the balance works. If it wasn't, it'd be like asking a sage for guidance and receiving the logic of a drunken, belligerent man. A true sage, like a true shaman, like a true expert, has lived through countless adversities, has learned so much, has seen so much. Just like a true Matter Manipulator must lose everything to ascend.'

'All those years I lived,' Ralph said, more to himself than Time. 'All those years I suffered alone in my apartment, in the void.'

'I – and as you'll see, *you* – wouldn't want it any other way,' Time said. 'The harder the tasks, the longer you live, the better you understand yourself, the better you are to take this mantle, this role, this responsibility.'

Ralph didn't like to admit it, but Time seemed to be speaking the truth.

'That is because the most intelligent creatures find happiness where most only find disaster, Ridley,' Time said. 'Traversing labyrinths, being hard with oneself, experiencing all the ingredients and possibilities of the cosmos helps one master themselves. To creatures like you and me and all who suffer, asceticism is a necessity, an instinct. A difficult task must be seen as a privilege, an opportunity to learn and grow. You know this. And you know yourself you are different to who you were when you left Earth. You think differently. You talk differently. You walk differently. Going through everything you have gone through has taught you far more than you could've ever learned if you'd remained on Earth.'

As Time shifted back to the unfinished circle, Ralph felt a shift of his own as Time's words filled and satisfied something deep within him.

Time was right. He was nothing like the toddler who'd once written a book about his curse. He was nothing like the kid who'd moved to the desert, or the one who'd spent every waking moment ignoring everyone and everything, laser-focused on solving his time dilemma.

'Think about it, Ralph,' Time said, 'you have become what you were always supposed to become. You are here because you are supposed to be here. It's the only way for this unification to make sense.'

Everything Time said did make sense. But Ralph couldn't help clinging to the thought about fate trivialising his life.

'Please,' Time said, 'do not fret about what you went through. You must let it all go. You have all the time to do what you wish now. You can traverse it all. Expand it. Reverse it. Speed it up. Slow it down. Just like you learned to manipulate matter, now you will learn to manipulate time.'

Ralph's eyes widened. 'I will control it all?'

'In some regard, yes.'

'I can go back to see my sister?'

'Of course.'

'I can visit Ca'zehro?'

'Yes.'

'I can visit Veška and the others on Proxim?'

'Yes, and yes,' Time said.

The unfinished circle began to rotate. Ralph's body lightened, fragmented. He then found himself – or whatever was left of himself – floating in a void, the true void, surrounded by nothing but a glassy, distorted mixture of light, like the lens of a kaleidoscope.

His life flashed before him. He saw every moment, every event, every tiny bit of information in a fraction of a fraction of a fraction of a second. He saw himself being born, being buried. He saw himself travelling into space, through space, out of space.

The stringy, metallic unfinished circle approached him. Knowing there was no use fighting it, he let down his guard and submitted, surrendered, accepted.

In a flash, they became one and the circle sealed. And it felt right. True. Good, proper, beautiful.

Ralph was the circle, but the circle was also him.

He felt time ticking. He heard it, tasted it, smelled and saw it.

The divisions of everything he'd been through had been consumed, absorbed, unified. They'd all shifted into one transparent, ever-changing, looping entity.

And it was powerful.

But seeing everything all at once didn't overwhelm or frighten him. It didn't fry his central nervous system. It didn't tear him apart. Instead, it freed him. Awakened him. Made him whole.

The circle split, reformed, combined, grew. It all happened in an instant, a spiralling, cyclic continuation of an instant.

The end became the beginning. The beginning became the end.

Being here, becoming this, becoming whole, made everything make sense. He felt ridiculous for all the emotions he'd battled, for all the losses he'd faced, all the struggles he'd lived through. He'd always thought he was unlucky being cursed with eternal youth. But now he saw how important and necessary it was.

Time had provoked and allowed for this unification. All his pain and unrest appeared as a fleeting moment with this new vision. All of it, every component, every moment, every lesson, was part of the journey towards becoming the combination of space and time.

Of course, it would've been great to know this was always going to happen. It would've helped him trust the process. But like Time had said before they'd become one, it was how it was supposed to be. And if he thought about it, if he chose to look, he could see becoming one hadn't just happened, it was happening right now, and it would happen again.

'Where will you go?' Ralph heard, felt, saw himself saying.

Words came from beyond and behind reality. 'To the next.'

'Time's quest never ends.'

'Why would it?'

And Ralph smiled, shuddered, frowned. But Time did not reciprocate.

'It does not make sense to be upset,' Time said, Space said, the Unity said. 'You and this and it and I are a drop in the ocean, an ocean of time, a drop of time, a portion of it all.'

'But what will happen now?'

'That remains to be seen. But you were and are and will always be Doctor Ralph Ridley, the Quanta Man, the Nazra, the human, the Boy Who Never Grew, the Matter Manipulator, the possessor of the crown, the Unifier.'

Now Ralph could live. Now he could enjoy a life of a regular mortal, no longer possessed by grief, worry, or confusion. He could focus on being a kid and enjoy spending time with his family, his friends. He could delight in the act of something as simple as eating a sandwich on the beach, watching the wind blow a willow, travelling to new cities and countries, loving, being.

'I will cherish all experiences,' he said. 'I will not focus on the past nor the future. I will be present each and every day. I will nurse each relationship, grow it, flourish it, mend it, be with it.'

'Why, go right ahead. This dimension is yours. It contains an infinite number of epiphanies waiting to be unlocked when you are ready.'

A separation occurred, a flash, then Time returned to the primordial version of itself: a metallic, unfinished circle. It hovered and wavered for a moment. Then, it was gone.

Everything shone, stirred, and churned around Ralph, space, time, existence. Everything began happening all at once.

He was no longer a stick figure in Stick City. He'd become the city, all cities, all sticks, planets, and particles.

And they were all him too. And they were all part of the same particle that was the universe – all connected, all one, all all.

He, them, they, it, space-time took the reins with a smile and a nod, a smile and a nod that did not truly happen, but a movement that stirred the universe.

He watched on as the universe spread and spread, becoming colder, darker, weaker. Then, it began to shrink and contract, becoming hotter, denser, filled with life.

Particles began popping in and out of existence rapidly, creating, destroying, becoming. Outliers circled it all, as though waiting to be selected, as though waiting for the next cycle to commence.

Everything continued to shrink in on itself. He watched and felt it all.

It shrunk to the size of Jupiter, Enqn, Earth, the Moon, the mountain, a shipping container, a human, a Zoruvian, Cyclops, the splinter sparrow. It then became even smaller, becoming a squark, a sparticle, a technicolour particle, an axion, the smallest bit of dust one could ever imagine.

And then, as though on cue, as it always did, as it always does, as it was always going to do, it popped out of existence.

ACKNOWLEDGEMENTS

The Hunt for Time was more than thirty years in the making. This is not to say it took thirty years to write. But a lifelong love of science, space, and mythology certainly played a part in its creation. So did an almost daily, ten-year dedication to writing.

To give you a better idea of how long it took, the first notes I wrote for it are dated November 2020. One of them simply states, 'He has a sword made out of a form of silk.' Another one says, 'Time dilation element/relativity.' The actual writing began in February 2022. The final version was sent off in December 2024.

Why am I telling you this? I suppose, in part, because it's hard to write an acknowledgement for everyone and everything that has ever influenced me to write this book. Secondly, because I think a timeline like this serves as a testament to anyone out there chipping away at a goal, especially the ones people feel will never blossom.

To get a little more specific though, a few books were instrumental to this one's synthesis (and shaping): Lawrence Krauss' *A Universe from Nothing*, Carl Sagan's *Cosmos*, Stephen Hawking's *A Brief History of Time*, and Carl Jung's *Man and His Symbols*. *Hyperspace* by Michio Kaku also deserves a mention here, as I was reading it when the idea for THFT came to me.

Next, I want to thank everyone who has ever supported my work. From my first eBook (*Game Changers*) to articles and social media posts, you are all part of the journey that led to this.

Next, I want to thank the team at Hawkeye Publishing, especially Carolyn Martinez. After rejections (and silence) from other publishers for other manuscripts over the years (including this one), Carolyn was the first who took the time to read my entire story. She was also one of the first to believe in me and my writing.

Lastly, I want to thank you, The Reader. The fact you are reading this means more than words can describe in an acknowledgment section. I appreciate every single one of you for picking this book up. I love you all.

ABOUT THE AUTHOR

Hayden Perno is a coach and writer. While completing a medical and health science degree, studying subjects like neuroscience, physics, chemistry, and philosophy, he began producing weekly blogs, articles for various websites, eBooks, and YouTube videos. As the years passed, his love for reading, writing, science, philosophy, and mythology took over, leading him to dedicating more and more time to honing his fiction craft, entering short story competitions, completing a handful of other books, before writing *Ralph Ridley in The Hunt for Time*.

Book reviews can make or break a book. If you liked what you read today, please do consider posting a review on Goodreads or your favourite forum. *Ralph Ridley in the Hunt for Time* is available at hawkeyebooks.com.au and all good bookstores and libraries.

If you enjoyed *Ralph Ridley in the Hunt for Time*, you'll also enjoy:
The Ghost Train and the Scarlet Moon by Jack Roney
Moontide by Mary Greenwood
Road to Freedom by Gabrielle Davis
Welcome to Blackwood by Khaiah Thomson
The Magic of Adeline Black by Sue-Ellen Pashley
50 Ways to Die in Space by Eileen O'Hely (Graphic Novel)
Head Grenade by Troy Henderson